Greetings from the shallow end!

I hope you enjoy reading the fifth and final book of Electra Brown, *Falling Hook, Line and Sinker*.

Electra and her friends finally hafrom Barbados, Sorrel is livin mother's drive; Lucy is totally Electra has a boyfriend who adores her, boobs of the same size and a fabulous pair of ankle boots. But when Electra meets a lad so absurdly beautiful she can't resist him, hearts are shattered, lives change forever and not even Electra can summon up shallow thoughts.

I'm often asked whether these books are based on real people and real life. Although the characters are fictitious, they *are* based on people I've met, and all the mad, bad and sad happenings are taken from real-life situations. Whilst at school I used to sit and stare out of the window dreaming of *anything* but lessons, then go home and write pages and pages in my diary of who did what to whom, and (usually) why wasn't I part of it? Years later, that dreaming and those diaries are brought to life through Electra and her friends.

With love,

Helen

X

The shallows of Electra Brown's life:

www.helenbaileybooks.com

FALLING HOOK, LINE AND SINKER

Helen Bailey

Hodder
Children's
Books

A division of Hachette Children's Books

For Eliza Ross

Chapter One

'Electra! Call 999! Lucy's choking to death!'

Bella Malone slams on the brakes of her humungous silver Range Rover, causing the Maltesers I've been scoffing to fly out of their packet and ping off the grey leather upholstery. It's like sitting in the middle of a confectionery-based pinball machine, but without the crazy music and flashing lights. I'm just glad I put my seat belt on. I doubt my head would bounce around like a chocolate-covered honeycomb ball, rather end up as chopped liver smeared across the dashboard.

It was only seconds after Luce popped the Maltesers I'd chucked her that she started flapping her hands and gasping as if she was being deprived of oxygen, so it's not unreasonable that Bella thinks her daughter is dying from inappropriate inhalation of sweets. I, however, remain icily calm, not because I have excellent first aid skills and am about to spring into action and save my best friend's life, but because we went through the same possible choking-by-confectionery routine yesterday, only in my bedroom with some wine gums rather than in Bella's car with Maltesers.

Luce isn't having a seizure requiring the kiss of life, the Heimlich manoeuvre, an ambulance and several days in intensive care strapped to bleeping machines.

She's just received the latest text from Josh, who's away doing something snow-related in France with his cousins.

On New Year's Day, Lower Sixth-former, Dogs of Doom singer, guitarist and Lucy's new matching blond-haired boyfriend, Josh Caldwell, promised he'd send her a romantic text every day until presumably they either finish or he runs out of butt-clenchingly slushy stuff to write. Other than overexcited panting at inappropriate moments – the loo in Burger King, the front of the queue at the tills in Primark and so on – it's not really been a problem as we've been on Christmas hols, but we're back to school tomorrow and I can't see Mr Farrell interrupting his dissection of one of Shakespeare's great sonnets to allow Luce to hyperventilate over Josh's latest composition.

'She's not choking,' I explain, as behind us car horns start hooting aggressively. 'She's excited about her text message from luvver boy.'

'You mean I've nearly had a car up my backside for a *text*?' Bella sounds furious. 'You girls! You're all such teen drama queens.'

Hoping that Bella has her eyes on the road rather than the back seat, I poke my tongue out, just as Luce turns round.

'Read this one,' she sighs, handing her phone over her shoulder to me. 'It's sooo beautiful.'

I'm prone to barfing if I read in the car, especially in the back seat when travelling round corners at speed, and I'm sure Bella wouldn't appreciate having to make a vomit stop so soon after the emergency sweet stop.

'You read it, Luce,' I say, pushing the phone back and rummaging on the floor for Maltesers. Bella is such a Neat Freak you could lick the carpet mats without fear of picking up anything nasty, so I have no issues with extracting sweets from under the front seats and eating them. 'It's your slush.'

'Remember yesterday Josh said I reminded him of golden sunlight?' Luce gushes. 'Well, today he's said I'm like dappled moonlight on water.'

'What, wet and blotchy?' I say, wondering how long Josh can keep the solar system theme running. It's going to be challenging when he finally has to try and compare Lucy to Uranus.

'I know nothing about these texts,' Bella says sourly. 'But then Lucy tells me very little about what she's up to. I know more about your young man, Electra, than her Josh.'

'Oh?' I have a feeling Luce has been deflecting Bella boy-interrogation by talking about my love life rather than hers.

'Lucy says his mother's a doctor at the General and his father owns a computer company. They've got a *fabulous* house in Compton Avenue, I believe.'

That is *so* typical of snobby Bella, though as she's a home stylist I suppose she's only showing a professional interest in the Burnses' pile of bricks. Still, I'm seriously tempted to freak her out by pretending that Duncan and Fiona Burns made their money by dealing in illegal drugs or dodgy diamonds, but she might swerve off the road with shock and pin some innocent dog walker against a bus stop, so I decide to keep quiet and just say, 'It's early days. We haven't even been on a proper date yet.'

'But he's been texting you loads, hasn't he?' Lucy says. 'So he must be keen.'

It's true that Frazer Burns has been texting me whilst he's been in Northumberland visiting rellies for New Year. Unfortunately, whilst Josh has been sending texts to Lucy telling her he misses her and comparing her to dappled moonlight, FB has been informing me that Northumberland has five times as many sheep as people, that he's worked out the unleaded petrol consumption of his father's BMW on the trip up north *without* using the on-board computer, and is wondering whether they will achieve the same stunning statistics on the journey home today. There's been no *Wish you were here* or even a polite kiss on the end of any of them. I thought he might at least have mentioned the Christmas Day snog on the street, or the fact that he texted me later that evening reminding me I've promised to go on a proper date with him, not a hanging-around-the-shops-type date. I'm now seriously wondering whether he'd overdone it with the festive chocolate liqueurs and was a bit squiffy when we snogged. I couldn't smell booze on his breath, but then I was so gobsmacked by having my gob kissed and FB scoring 5 out of 5 on my Snogability Scale, I probably wouldn't have noticed even if he'd been gargling with whisky and smoking magic cigarettes.

Bella turns the Beast Car into Forge Road and pulls up outside Sorrel's house.

All the other drives in front of the row of modern terrace houses have neat gardens with one, maybe two cars parked on the drive. The Callenders' house, number 5, looks like a cross between an allotment and a scrap yard, with pots of sprouting potato tops and carrot fronds fighting for space with kids' bikes, a strange sundial made out of bits of metal and the enormous black ex-funeral car Yolanda, Sorrel's mother drives.

And now something new has appeared in the front garden.

An old white caravan so tiny, it looks like an egg on wheels has been laid outside the living-room window.

After Sorrel and I caught her older sister, Jasmine, with Warren Cumberbatch (a lanky louse of a lad who Sorrel fancied) at *It* on the bottom bunk in Sorrel's bedroom, Yolanda promised Sorrel her own room. But until the housing association can find a bigger house for five children, two adults, a cat, huge numbers of jam jars with sprouting seeds and a large collection of wind chimes and crystals on strings, Sorrel's bedroom is a caravan on the drive.

'What on *earth* must the neighbours think?' The Neat Freak shrieks as we walk towards it. She's probably freaked at the thought of living next door to someone who has no interest in paint charts and coordinated soft furnishings. 'It makes the place look like some sort of Third World encampment.'

The top half of the caravan door flies open and Sorrel leans out.

'Some people in the Third World would regard this as luxury, Mrs M, given the fact they sleep in sewers or on

6

rubbish tips,' she says pointedly, but with a smile.

Luce and I rush towards her as Sorrel opens the bottom door, climbs down a couple of steps and throws her arms around us. It's *so* good to have her back from her Christmas trip to Barbados where she's been visiting her dad, Desmond. She looks fantastico. Relaxed, refreshed and totally different to the girl who ran away and lived for a week on the streets and in a borrowed flat with dodgy men last December.

'Did you have a good time?' Bella asks, trying to peer into the caravan to see what decorating disasters are lurking within. 'Did everything work out? Was your father well?'

'It was wonderful, Mrs M. Thanks for everything. Did Electra's bag and all the other stuff cover the air fare?'

To pay for the ticket to Barbados, Bella sold my Bag of Beauty – a Chloé total bling bag I'd been given by The Kipper, Dad's evil ex-girlfriend – on eBay, along with some unwanted designer stuff of hers and old clothes of Lucy's and her older brothers, James and Michael.

'There's actually a little money left over,' Bella says. 'Any thoughts on what you'd like to do with it?'

I'm about to suggest a seriously slap-up meat-themed meal in town to welcome Sorrel back, when she says, 'I'd like it to go to some environmental scheme. Plant a tree or recycle a bottle or something.'

'I'll come up with some ideas,' Bella says, taking over *yet* again.

'Thanks,' Sorrel says, as we amble back towards the Beast Car. 'Oh, and Mum said she'll run the girls home after lunch.'

Bella looks as alarmed as a woman with a serious Botox-frozen forehead can manage. Clearly the thought of the Gothmobile pulling into the drive of *Foxgloves*, the Malones' executive home on a private road surrounded by other snobby neighbours, freaks her out.

'Oh, I'm more than happy to come back,' Bella says briskly, climbing in. 'I know how your mother hates using the car for unnecessary journeys. Save the planet and all that.' Clearly Bella has forgotten she drives a gas-guzzling Beast Car just to get her morning paper.

'It's fine,' Sorrel says. 'Mum's had it converted to run on pig poo.'

'Pig poo?' Bella squeaks, her blonde highlights quivering. 'That car is running on animal excrement?'

With a totally straight face, Sorrel nods. 'You'd never know. Well, not once the car's been running for a bit. Before that a really farty smell comes out of the exhaust.'

I'm in serious danger of wetting myself with laughter as Bella slams the car door and speeds away.

Giggling, the three of us go into the caravan.

Outside, the mobile bedroom might look a bit rough, but inside it's absolutely gorge.

By the window is a little table, which Sorrel's set up with her laptop, pots of pens and pencils and a burning incense stick. Either side of the table are long seats piled with brightly coloured cushions. There's a tiny kitchen area with a shiny new kettle, rows of jam jars with tea, coffee and sugar labelled on them, and, at the other end, a couple of bunk beds with red-and-white-checked duvets draped on top, the same material as the curtains at the windows.

'Oh, Sorrel, it's fab,' Luce says as we look around. 'You must be thrilled.'

Not just sewer-dwellers would love to live here. I would too. Being detached, I wouldn't have to listen to The Little Runt, aka my nine-year-old brother, Jack, whining on about Arsenal losing, or find bunny poo squished between my toes because he's brought Theo, his rabbit, into the kitchen. I could cook pizzas and chips at midnight without a parental becoming all sniffy, and leave the washing up to fester for *weeks* without stress. But best of all, it would keep me and the sproglet apart when Mum has the baby at the beginning of June. I wouldn't have to listen to it yell, or cope with nappy smells or sit and eat my tea whilst it voms up puréed beef and carrots next to me.

I'm dreading it.

However hard I try to think about gloriously shallow things, such as hot dates with FB, what I'm going to spend my Christmas money on and whether I can get away with keeping the plum nail varnish I'm wearing today when I go back to school tomorrow, the fact that my mother is going to have a baby is becoming impossible to ignore, and not just because she's devouring jars of pickled onions, getting huge before my very eyes and her boobs are no longer Mighty Mammaries but Monster Mammaries, but because Mum's boyfriend, Phil, has this really disgusting habit of going up to her every morning, putting his hand on her tummy and saying, 'How's it cooking, Ellie?' which is gross when I'm trying to force down a bowl of Shreddies or a Strawberry Pop-Tart before school.

'Can I move in when the sprog arrives?' I ask Sorrel, only half joking. 'Not for ever, just until I'm old enough to leave home without being hauled back.'

I'm fifteen in July, so I reckon I'd have to share a chemical toilet and a bunk bed for about a year and a half, which isn't bad when you consider the alternative.

'Still got pre-natal depression?' Sorrel asks, holding up a tin of hot chocolate.

I'd emailed her in Barbados to tell her about FB and me, and about Mum's Christmas lunch announcement that there wasn't just a turkey in the oven, but a baby too. At the time I was more excited about the snog than worried about the sprog, but now the novelty of the snog has worn off and the grim reality of the sproglet has set in, *I'm* the one with the baby blues.

'It was the pits when Mum and Ray had the twins and I was eleven.' Sorrel spoons brown powder into three mugs I recognize from The Bay Tree, the organic vegan café Yolanda runs. 'Of course, The Loony Lentil had to be all earthy and have a home birth so I was totally freaked when I went to the loo and saw a whole load of red slime in the bath. I thought someone had been murdered.'

'Too much info,' I say, starting to conjure up dreadful pictures of graphic gynaecological things happening in the bathroom of 14 Mortimer Road. 'Tell us all about Barbados.'

Sorrel brings the mugs of hot chocolate over to the table and slides into the seat across from me and Luce.

'It was amazing,' she says dreamily. 'From the moment I stepped off the plane I felt *totally* at home. Everyone I met was *so* cool. I'll download some photies later for you to gawp at.'

'It must have been great to spend Christmas somewhere hot,' I say. Now I've stopped gazing at the soft furnishings, I realize Sorrel's caravan is actually an igloo in disguise. I'm shivering even though underneath my coat I've got FB's soft navy jumper on, the one he gave me to wear on Christmas

Day. To be honest, after nine days in my room and on my bod, it's ponging of a rather strange mix of deodorant, dust and perfume rather than smelling of FB and his posh house, but just the feel of it reminds me of what happened between us and sends shivers down my spine, which probably isn't helping the whole body-temp situation. 'Doesn't this place have any heat?'

'I'd rather not use the heater,' Sorrel says primly. 'Not if I can help it.'

Luce and I exchange glances. Sorrel had said things were tough what with Ray, her sort-of-but-not-yet-legal stepfather losing his job at the camera shop, but I had no idea they're so broke they're risking hypothermia.

'If things are that bad, you could use the extra bag money for the heating,' Lucy suggests. 'And you might be rehoused soon.'

That would be fantastico for both of us. The Callenders would have a bigger pad, and I could have Sorrel's cast-off caravan. We don't actually have a drive on which to park it, so I'd have to live on the street, which thinking about it is even better as I'd be further away from the squitting sproglet and FB could come round at all times of the day and night without anyone knowing.

Sorrel stares at us and then giggles.

'Thanks, Luce, but it's not because of the money I'm on

heating rations. I'm just trying to do my bit to conserve energy and save the planet.'

Now it's our turn to stare at our bezzie. Despite being brought up by the sort of rampant eco-warrior who goes out and slaps *Gas Guzzler* stickers on 4x4s and people carriers, Sorrel has never shown the slightest interest in saving the planet. In fact, sometimes she walks around her house switching lights *on*, just to wind Yolanda up.

'Did I hear right?' I say. 'Did the words *save the planet* actually come out of your mouth? Have you turned from teenager into greenager?'

'Yeah,' Sorrel nods, laughing. 'Before, when Mum droned on about saving the environment I'd look at places round here and think, *Why would I want to save Eastwood Circle?*' She takes a sip of her hot chocolate. 'It's pants.'

'It is pretty ugly,' Luce agrees. 'But I like Top Shop. Oh, and Superdrug. I'd be lost without Superdrug especially when they do three-for-two deals on L'Oréal and Lil-lets—'

'What I mean,' Sorrel says, stopping Luce before she can add more items to her shopping list of cut-price toiletries, 'is that when I went to the Caribbean and saw how gorge it is, it made me realize the planet is bigger than just my usual world of concrete shopping centres and school, and that I need to do something to save it.'

'Did you get any sleep on the plane?' I ask, wondering if

an overnight flight has scrambled Sorrel's brain.

Sorrel gets up and puts her hands on her hips. I think she'd probably like to start pacing, but there's not much room to pace in a tiny caravan. You might get two strides in before you'd hit the window at the other end and have to turn round again.

'You think I'm nuts, don't you?' she demands, sounding like the old sarky non-green Sorrel we know and love. 'Can't you see, we're killing our planet with selfishness! If I told you your grandchildren may never get to see a fresh lobster because the sea is so warm they'll come out ready cooked, what would you think about that?'

Good heavens! Sorrel's already got me being a grandmother and showing my grandchildren seafood when I haven't even been on a date with FB yet! And will I still be with FB by the time I'm a grandmother? I can't seriously imagine going out with anyone other than FB *ever*, but I can't imagine being an old wrinkly either.

'Electra?' Sorrel interrupts my thoughts just as I'm wondering whether I'll look more like bony Nana Pat or buxom Grandma Stafford when I'm ancient. 'What are your thoughts on all this?'

'What are my children called?' I ask.

Mum keeps asking me whether I have any ideas about baby names as I've always banged on about how I hate my name and how being called after the self-catering apartments in Faliraki where Mum and Dad spent their honeymoon was totally inappropriate as I'm *so* not a Greek girl with my wide-as-a-satellite-dish pasty face, mousy long hair and mottled salami limbs. I've told her that as far as I'm concerned, they can call the sprog Ermintrude or Zebedee and to leave me out of name-game.

'Your children?' Sorrel asks. 'What's that got to do with anything?'

'You said my grandchildren might never get to see a lobster, so I must have children. I was just wondering what they were called.'

'Josh and I like Jemima for a girl or Jeremy for a boy,' Luce says dreamily as she fingers Josh's leather bracelet, which is wrapped twice around her slim wrist.

'Jeremy!' I say, freaked at both Lucy's choice of name and the fact that even though they've been going out for less than a month and he's been away for a week of that, her and Josh have been having discussions about naming their as-yet-to-be-conceived kids. 'You can't call a kid Jeremy!'

'It's after his father,' Luce says primly, winning the argument as clearly I can't claim that calling your son after your dead dad is a bad thing, unless of course your father was called Adolf.

'You two can be so shallow!' Sorrel gasps. 'I'm serious!

15

Our generation has to do something or there'll be nothing left in the future. It's not just Mum who says this, Joz does too.'

'Joz?' I ask. 'Who's Joz?'

Sorrel twists one of her long black braids around her finger and examines the end. 'Daphne's son.'

'And Daphne is?' I say leaning towards Sorrel. This sudden revealing of the name Joz coupled with my bezzie's sheepish expression has made me über suspicious that we haven't been told the most exciting part of Sorrel's trip, and that she's hanging back on the holiday romance goss.

'Daphne's Dad's girlfriend. I didn't know he had one until I went over there 'cause he never mentioned her, but it turns out he's been living with her for years. She runs a seashell shop, Daphne's Designs, next to Dad's art studio. Joz takes tourists out on jet ski trips to look for turtles and things. He's really into marine conservation. He told me about the ready-cooked lobster.'

I knew it! There had to be a reason why Sorrel has gone from eco-wrecker to eco-warrior in the space of two weeks, and it was so obviously testosterone-induced. It's like when I started to spout Shakespeare at every turn. I didn't really like Billy Boy's plays, but I thought it might impress a Spanish Lurve God called Javier Antonio Garcia, aka Jags. It didn't: Jags turned out to be a Sleaze Bag from Slough, and now I can't remember a single line from any of the bearded Bard's stuff, somewhat of a worry given that I'm supposed to be doing *The Taming of the Shrew* for GCSE English lit.

I narrow my eyes, turn my Snogdar on to full power and direct it straight at Sorrel.

'Have you had a festive romance with this Joz?' I ask. 'Have you been on a jet ski discussing your future offspring's lobster lunches with him and snogging in the surf?'

'You have a one-track mind,' Sorrel says, getting up and digging around in her opened suitcase, which is lying on the bottom bunk. 'There's nothing going on with me and Joz other than the fact we both feel strongly about the environment.'

'If The Jozster is really into saving the planet, shouldn't he be using a rowing boat rather than a jet ski?' I point out.

Sorrel ignores my eco-observation. 'Here, these are for you.'

She hands Luce and me each a tiny blue tissue-paper package on which someone has pencilled *L* and *E*. When I open mine, nestling inside is a beautiful pair of dangly earrings made out of a cluster of tiny pink and white shells.

'They're gorgeous, Sorrel,' Luce says as she holds hers up to her ears, each one made out of a small creamy scallop-shaped shell. 'Thanks so much.'

'They're brill,' I say, getting up to give her a hug. 'Thanks.'

'Daph gets those from the beach and makes them into earrings, but Joz says if the seas get too hot because of global warming, there'll be no shells.'

The thought of no more pretty shell earrings is gutting, I must admit, though not as gutting as for Daphne who'll no longer have any shells to sell, which is uno major problemo if you own a shell shop.

'So there was defo no hot date with Joz the Jet Skier?' I ask. 'No frolicking in the surf or snogging in the sand?'

'Have you and Freak Boy sorted out your first date yet?' Sorrel asks, clearly trying to change the subject. 'Where's it going to be? Sitting on a station platform trainspotting or is he going to really push the boat out and take you to the airport to count jumbo jets?'

Despite my insistence that FB is more Fit Boy than Freak Boy nowadays, Sorrel still thinks he's majorly weird.

'None of the above,' I say, throwing Sorrel a sarky look. 'He hasn't mentioned a date. I don't know what's going on at the mo.'

'Perhaps he's playing hard to get,' Sorrel suggests. 'Or maybe he's met some northern girl and had a holiday romance and gone off you.'

'Perhaps he had a midnight snog on New Year's Eve and one thing's led to another,' Luce adds.

'Are you two deliberately trying to do my head in?' I say, slightly more snappily than I intended. 'I'm stressed enough already!'

There's a knock on the caravan door, but no one appears until Sorrel shouts, 'Come in!' and Yolanda's head appears over the half-door.

I am *dead* impressed. Sorrel has her mum well trained. My mother has *no* idea of teenage room etiquette. She thinks that if you knock you can then come straight in; in other words, the knock is just an alert that she's about to barge in rather than a request to enter.

'Hello, girls!' Yolanda's white smile stretches across her face. She's wearing one of her trademark brightly coloured scarves around her head, her skinny dreads bursting over the top like a hairy black chrysanthemum. 'Lovely to see you.'

'Hi!' Luce and I chorus back.

'Did you have a good Christmas, Mrs C?' I ask.

'Well, we missed Sorrel, but we did our best to give everyone a good time,' Yolanda says, her face clouding over at the thought of festivities without one of her brood. 'But what I really want to know is, how is your ma, Electra? Sorrel tells me she's expecting a little one. You must be thrilled.'

'She isn't,' Luce says.

'And are you hoping for a little sister or brother?' Yolanda asks.

'She's hoping for a puppy,' Sorrel giggles, which is true.

'And all is well, she's fine?'

'She had a scan and it seems to be,' I say, remembering the blurry photo of what looked like a tadpole in a whirlpool that's stuck on the side of our fridge under a letter-B fridge magnet.

'I'd love another baby,' Yolanda sighs. 'A little girl called Saffron or a boy called Bay.'

'Mum, you cannot be serious!' Sorrel shrieks.

'Maybe I already have my hands full.' Yolanda sighs.

A dark-skinned lump of a girl with braces and specs appears at the door. It's Senna, Sorrel's nine-year-old sister. 'Lunch is ready,' she scowls, before disappearing.

'Would you girls like your lunch out here so you can carry on gossiping?' Yolanda asks. 'It's just some spicy chickpea patties and red cabbage salad.'

'Yes please, Mum!' Sorrel says, smiling. 'That would be great.'

Pre-Barbados Sorrel would have turned her nose up at what she calls fart-food, but now she looks delighted at the sound of the menu. I'm slightly worried that I won't be able to concentrate on my history assignment this afternoon for continuously raising my bum off the chair to deal with the after-effects of curried chickpeas.

'Can one of you just come and help me bring it over?' Yolanda asks.

'I'll go,' I say, just as my phone vibrates in my pocket.

I fish it out, look at the screen and open the text.

I can't get my breath. I'm flapping my arms around and I think my heart is about to explode it's beating so fast.

'Electra!' Yolanda cries. 'What's wrong? What is it?'

I wave my moby in the air, still gasping.

Sorrel grabs it.

'It's a text from FB,' she says. 'That's what's set her off.'

'Oh, no!' Luce cries. 'Has he snogged a northern girl after all?'

'Doesn't look like it,' Sorrel says. 'It says: "Back. Missed You. What about that date then?"'

Chapter Two

What a difference a year makes.

One year ago today I was waiting for the bus at the stop in Talbot Road after the Christmas holidays, off to start a new term at Flora Burke's Community School, worrying about my uneven boobs, totally stressed and sleepless after Dad dropped the bombshell that he was leaving Mum because he was having an affair with a dental hygienist, and with not even a sniff of testosterone following me around.

Now Mum's happy, I've got a lush new boyfriend, my boobs are of approximately equal (if rather meagre) size, and other than the small matter of a mewler appearing in a few months, life is so perfect I actually sprang – well, staggered – out of bed when my alarm went off at seven-thirty this morning and didn't hit the snooze button once.

After FB's text, Luce, me and Sorrel spent about an

hour deciding how quickly I should text him back and what to say.

Sorrel thought replying too quickly looked desperado, and I should leave it just in case I get to school and find he's reverted to looking like a beaky freaky alien.

Lucy thought I should text *Yes* immediately in case the Burnses stopped at a motorway service station and FB bonded with some leggy minx over a tin of boiled travel sweets and I missed my chance.

In the end I left it until teatime and just sent a message that said I was glad he was back and I'd see him at school. Friendly yet slightly mysterious. Warm yet with a slightly cool edge. Interested without being desperate.

I can't wait to see him though! I'm stressing as to whether I should go up to him first or let him come up to me, and what I should do when I actually see him. My preferred choice of greeting is to throw my arms around him and snog his face off, but this might be a bit OTT in front of the school, and potentially embarrassing if a teacher wanders by and sees us playing tonsil tennis before first reg.

Ahead of me Claudia Barnes, aka Tits Out, is leaning against the bus stop, her boobs thrust forward under a new three-quarter-length black jacket. She's hitched her green tartan kilt up so high it looks as if she's wearing nothing other than a pair of thigh-length white socks and ballet flats

23

under her coat. No wonder we call her the Queen of Sleaze.

Claudia has to know *everything* that's going on and sometimes I get fed up of her daily bus-stop interrogation, particularly when I've usually got nothing exciting to report. But today I can't wait for her to ask *What's up?* I'll tell her about Mum being preggers and then just casually toss the fact that FB and I are going out into the conversation and watch her dark eyebrows disappear into her bleached-blonde hairline with shock. Claudia 'Been There Done That' Barnes has snogged every boy in the school, even Josh Caldwell, but she's never had her over-glossed smackers near FB.

I've been at the bus stop for approximately two nanoseconds and Tits Out *still* hasn't launched into her questioning routine, but I can see she has a glowing purple hickey on the side of her neck so she must have had some festive lurve action.

'Hi, Claudia,' I say. 'Great jacket. How were the hols?'

'Pants,' she says glumly, chewing gum. 'Total pants.'

'But you obviously met someone,' I giggle, nodding at her badge of slaggery. 'A tasty vampire?'

Claudia touches her neck and winces. 'No such luck,' she moans. 'I burnt myself with my hair-straighteners.'

'You were with your dad and stepmum, weren't you?' I ask.

Claudia's family is even more complicated than mine, with both her mum and dad remarrying people who already had children, then having more sprogs with their new partners.

'Stepmonster more like,' Claudia growls. 'What a total cow. Gave *her* kids and *their* kids loads of pressies, but just gave me a big box of make-up.'

'Well, that's cool, isn't it?' At least it's an appropriate present given the amount of make-up Claudia wears, and better than the lemon-and-white knitted bobble hat my godmother in Australia sent me. Not only is it foul, but she seriously underestimated the width of my head, as it didn't fit. When I first opened it I thought it was a tea cosy, but then the note said she hoped it would keep me warm. I'd rather have had a box of slap any day. 'Make-up's OK,' I say.

'Cheap make-up from the market and the same box I gave her for Christmas last year.' Claudia sounds mega bummed. 'She re-gifted me my own pressie!'

'Wasn't that the make-up that your gran gave you the year before?' I ask.

'Totally!' Claudia shrieks. 'The wretched thing is just orbiting around the place. I'm going to have to chuck it out.'

'Give it to Nat,' I suggest. Claudia wears loads of make-up, but is almost au natural compared to her bezzie, Natalie

'Butterface' Price, so named because of the thick layer of yellow greasy slap she trowels on her face every day. 'Not as a present, just as an unwanted gift.'

'Nat's driving me nuts as well,' Claudia grumbles, clearly in a major first-day-back bad mood. 'She's got it into her head that Buff fancies the thongs off her. Won't stop gassing about him. It's Jon this and Jon that.'

'Our Buff?' I gasp, wondering what planet Butterface is on if she really thinks our lush geography teacher would so much as look in her direction, unless it was to ask her to explain sedimentary rock formation. He's total blond teacher totty, but about as likely to go out with Natalie Price as I am to go out with David Beckham, i.e. only in racy dreams about older lads.

'Yeah, *our* Buff.' Claudia rolls her eyes. 'She saw him out and about over the hols with some bloke and apparently Buff says to this bloke, *This is the lovely Natalie Price from my class.*'

'He said the word *lovely* about Nat?' I'm wondering if Buff Butler is another possible casualty of the drunk-by-chocolate-liqueur scenario.

'So she says.' Claudia pulls a face. 'And she says he gave The Look.'

'The Look?'

'The Look of Lust,' Claudia explains. 'She's already

planning her teacher-baiting outfits for our field trip.'

I keep quiet. Since last September when I learnt we would be spending three days and two nights away from school with the luscious Buff, I've been planning how I can wear an anorak and wellies suitable for paddling in rock pools in February without looking a total dork, whilst wondering if the *No Dangly Earrings in School* rule still applies when physically I won't be *in* school, even if it's during school time. And as FB is going on the geography trip too, my wardrobe planning has reached a new peak of anxiety as I want FB to see me looking gorge and appropriately dressed for every occasion, rock pool or after-hours lights-out sneaking around.

'What about you?' Claudia finally asks.

'I think I'll buy a new pair of PJs,' I say. 'And some pink wellies.'

'Not the trip.' Claudia sounds snappy. 'Your hols?'

As the 210 bus will be here any minute, I decide to lob both bits of explosive news out at once.

'Mum announced she's preggers and I'm going out with FB.'

'Frazer Burns!' Claudia gasps, brightening up at my news. 'You're seeing Razor Burns? Since when?'

'Since Christmas Day,' I say, wondering when our official going-out date starts. From the snog? From the as-yet-to-be-arranged date? And as we haven't been out yet, is he even my official boyfriend?

'He's still mega freaky but he's defo got potential,' Tits Out says as the bus approaches. 'But he's too much of a nerd for you and him to last long.'

'Crappola,' I say, miffed that Tits Out is already predicting our break-up before we've even started to go out. 'You hardly know the real FB.'

'Nah, but I know you,' Claudia says. 'I give it two months, max. Today's what, the seventh of January? By the seventh of March you and he will be curtains.'

'Electra's mum is preggers and she's seeing Frazer Burns!' Claudia announces as she scrambles to the top deck and sits next to Natalie as I sit behind, next to Sorrel. 'What about that?'

'What, Razor Burns got your mum pregnant?' Butterface turns to me, her face as gormy and blank as usual, despite the potentially freaky news that my mother has been having an affair with a fourteen-year-old schoolboy.

'No!' I say. 'Mum is pregnant and I'm going out with FB.'

'So Razor doesn't have anything to do with your mum getting up the duff?' Nat asks, as everyone groans and I slap my forehead and shriek 'NO!' again.

'Frazer is such a kid compared to Jon,' Nat sighs. 'Jon

must be about twenty-two, twenty-three.'

Claudia turns round, pulls a face and mouths, *Told you so* at me.

'Listen, Nat, Buff doesn't fancy you, I'd put all my Christmas money on it,' I say. 'Anyway, teachers aren't allowed to fancy Year 10 pupils.'

'Er . . . newsflash,' Nat snaps back. 'Teachers aren't allowed to *go out* with pupils. No law can stop them fancying one.' She gets out her make-up bag and starts adding another layer of slap. 'We can't help who we fall in love with.'

'I thought you were still in love with James Malone.' I remember Nat's tears and tantrums when Lucy's older brother at King William's School for Boys dumped her for Fritha Kennedy, a right cow from Queen Beatrice's School for Girls.

'James was *such* a kid,' Butterface sniffs. 'Practically a Zitty Bum Fluff Boy.'

'So, how was the Caribbean?' Claudia asks Sorrel. 'You're looking good.'

'Brill,' Sorrel says. 'Totally top mint.'

'I detect a holiday fling,' Claudia says suspiciously, leaning over the seat, her mascara-drenched eyelashes quivering with excitement at the prospect of juicy foreign-action. 'Go on, cough up the details. Remember, if it's

29

abroad it doesn't count so you can tell the truth. Under-the-bikini action or just over a beach wrap?' She waggles her hands towards Sorrel's boobs.

Sorrel bats them away and scowls. 'You lot are obsessed with boys and make-up and shopping,' she says. 'There's more to life, you know.'

'Like what?' Butterface says, turning round. She's totally overdone the blusher and looks like a rag doll with rosy cheeks.

'Like the environment, the impact man is having on nature, global warming, energy conservation, your carbon footprint . . .' Sorrel counts off the things she now finds more important than lads and spending money.

'Sorrel's had a conversion,' I explain. 'She's seen the light and it's a low-energy environmentally friendly light.'

Claudia giggles and Nat looks blank.

'Joz says—' Sorrel starts.

'Joz?' Claudia queries. 'Who's Joz?'

'Rides a jet ski in Barbados and tells stories about lobsters being cooked in the sea,' I grin.

'So you *did* have some lurve action,' Claudia gushes. 'Is this Joz some hunky local lad with dark rippling muscles and a defined six-pack?' She's practically drooling. I've seen the photies and it pretty much describes The Jozster astride his water bike. 'Was it sex in the sand?'

Sorrel slumps down in her seat and says nothing.

'Well, if Sorrel won't spill, how far have *you* got with Frazer Burns?' Claudia says. 'Does he actually know what to do with it?'

'Claudia!' I shriek, shocked at what she seems to be suggesting.

'His tongue,' she says coyly. 'What did you think I meant?'

By the time we get off the bus and walk through the school gates, FB is waiting for me, or at least I think he is, unless he just likes hanging around holding his twenty-four-geared mountain bike and his orange helmet for the sake of it. Sorrel walks ahead and Claudia and Nat push me towards him before heading off arm in arm in fits of giggles.

'Hi!' FB says shyly as we amble towards the bike racks where Lucy and Josh are having a blonde-on-blond snog-fest reunion. 'How are you?'

'Good,' I say. He looks even more gorge than I remembered him looking on Christmas Day and he was pretty hot then, but to still look lush in school uniform and with slightly sweaty helmet hair is quite something.

Then neither of us says anything, as if we're total strangers, which clearly as we've snogged in the street and his dad's study, we're not. And just remembering snogging him makes my face burn and throb, which probably means I look like one enormous pulsating zit on meaty legs.

I bite my lip and stare at my feet. I'm wearing my burgundy ankle boots, a Christmas present from Mum. To be honest they look well odd with school uniform, but they're so lush, I *had* to wear them.

Finally FB says, 'Did you get my texts?'

'Yeah,' I say, looking up and smiling. 'Thanks.'

'It's just, you didn't reply to them all.'

It was quite difficult to know what to say about petrol consumption so I didn't always text back, so I just say, 'It was good your dad's car didn't use much petrol.'

'Diesel,' FB corrects me. 'Diesel. That's probably why it was so economical. Some people say you can't get the acceleration from a diesel the way you can from a petrol-driven car, but Dad's Beamer goes like stink if you put your foot down, give it some gas and really floor it.'

I look straight at FB. He might look gorgeous and be a super snogger, but at this moment I could cheerfully take his bag from his shoulder, get the strap and throttle him with it. Instead of telling me he's missed me or arranging a date, we're standing by the bike racks in the biting wind, talking about diesel consumption. Josh Caldwell wouldn't sweet-talk Lucy with tales of his father's car, not just because his father's dead and therefore can't drive any longer, but because Josh is the sort of lad who writes romantic texts for his girlfriend and snogs her when he sees her. I seem to have bagged someone who gets turned on by motorized metal and fuel.

FB pushes his bike between the silver hoops and starts fiddling with his bike lock, whilst I hang around wondering what happens next, trying not to listen to the slurping noises coming from Josh and Luce, who are still eating each other's faces.

'So that's settled then?' I hear Josh say, and decide that unless he has amazing powers of ventriloquism and can snog and speak clearly at the same time, it's safe to look in their direction without feeling as if I've stumbled across a racy movie being filmed in the playground.

'Can't wait,' says Luce, looking dreamily at Josh whilst clutching his hand.

'What's up?' I say.

'We're going out on Saturday night,' Luce beams. 'To The Curry Cottage.'

'Er . . . we were going to go out, remember?' FB says. He's locked the bike to the rack, sorted out his helmet and is now hovering by my side.

'Oh? Yeah. Something like that,' I say casually. 'I vaguely remember one of us mentioning it.' Don't want him to think I've spent days obsessing over what I'm going to wear, where we're going to go, how much make-up is appropriate and whether the evening will include a major snogging session.

'Well, I've got computer club tomorrow and extended maths on Wednesday, but I thought we could go to Eastwood Circle on Thursday after school, maybe have a burger?'

He just doesn't get it, does he? I haven't spent the last ten days planning what I was going to wear on our first date if it involves loitering around a grey concrete shopping centre.

I am *so* not happy.

'I don't want a burger,' I say.

FB bites his lip and looks cute, if a bit goofy. 'KFC then?'

How am I going to explain this to Maddy, my New York-based American Wundercousin? She emailed me over the hols to say that her parents threw some mega-boring party, and whilst Uncle Hamp and Aunty Vicky were networking over champagne and canapés, Mads was doing her own networking, outside, with Clarke Loewe Clarkson III, the son of some banking bigwig. For their first date, Mads and her triple-barrelled hunk went on a horse-drawn carriage ride in Central Park, snuggled under a fake-fur blanket. No way am I going to settle for low-rent food sitting on a graffiti-covered bench in the shopping precinct as mine.

'Luce and Josh are going for a curry on Saturday night,' I say, hoping this will prompt him into realizing that even the Colonel's special spice mix smeared on a chicken drumstick isn't doing it for me. 'They're going to The Curry Cottage in town.'

'We could go for a curry,' FB says, and my heart leaps at the thought of sharing a plate of crispy poppadoms and mango chutney with him. 'Say after school on Thursday?'

Is this guy for real? Who on earth has a curry date at ten to four?

'Will a curry place be open that early?' I ask, trying to keep sarcasm out of my voice.

And failing.

'The thing is,' FB looks embarrassed, 'an evening might be difficult for me.'

'Oh?' He's never had a problem before. 'Why?'

FB starts tugging at the collar of his white shirt under his green blazer. 'I haven't told Mum and Dad about you yet. So we might have to leave a proper date until I get all that sorted. I mean, we can still hang around together, as long as I'm back for normal teatime.'

'What do you mean, *get all that sorted*?' I say.

FB shifts from one foot to another. 'Well, technically I'm still banned from seeing you after that fight with Pinhead,' he says. 'I was excluded from school, remember?'

I can hardly forget, not just the fight in the classroom, but being marched to the headmaster's study and the embarrassment of having to explain to Tosser Thomson why two boys were fighting over me.

'But that was last term!' I squeak. 'And I didn't start the fight. You decked Pinhead because he was going on about my boobs. Anyway, your dad invited me back to your house on Christmas Day, so he can't think I'm all bad.'

'He brought you back because he found you sitting in the gutter wearing a paper hat and an apron, sobbing,' FB says. 'He thought you were pregnant.'

'It was MUM who was pregnant, not me!' I screech. 'Haven't you made that clear to them?'

FB shrugs. 'Well, I tried, but . . .' His voice trails off.

'In other words, they still think I'm trouble,' I say icily. 'Well, thanks very much, Mr and Dr Burns!' We're at the door to the main school, at the bottom of the stairs below our form room. I'm going to have to get up those stairs and into room 3A Upper in the next sixty seconds if I'm not to get a late mark from The Ginger Gnome on day one of the new term.

'Don't be like that,' FB pleads. 'They'll come round – as long as you don't for a bit. In the meantime, I'll work on them.'

'Oh, forget it,' I say, taking the stairs two at a time. This

36

is hardly the romantic reunion I thought it would be and I'm annoyed that FB is being so wimpy when it comes to deceiving his parents. It's the Browns and the Burnses we're talking about here, not the Montagues and the Capulets.

'Electra!' he calls after me, but I just wave him away and stomp into the classroom.

'What's wrong?' Luce asks, as I flounce towards my desk and plonk my butt down. 'You two had a row already?'

'Apparently I'm not good enough for his parents' precious son,' I snap. 'So I have to eat chicken tikka at four o'clock in the afternoon.'

'I'd find it difficult to get out without giving an explanation of where I was going and who I was with,' FB says lamely. I hadn't noticed him lurking by my desk.

'So do what everyone does and lie!' I say through gritted teeth as Mr McKay comes in and starts to noisily shuffle papers at the front of the class. 'Tell them you're out with a bunch of friends. They'll never know the difference.'

'No, don't lie,' Lucy butts in. 'Come to The Curry Cottage with me and Josh on Saturday night. Then you can say you're going out with friends and it's the truth.'

Chapter Three

Two floors below me, the doorbell rings.

I sit up, wait for a moment in case Mum hollers up it's someone for me, and then when she doesn't, flop back on my bed, snuggle into FB's jumper, flick through his texts, even the ones about fuel consumption and mileage, and wonder if it really is possible to burst with happiness, although clearly I hope that I don't explode before Saturday night as covering up great gashes in my body might provide a challenge for even the most extensive wardrobe.

Although I am ridiculously happy about my first date with FB, I'm actually glad that Luce is going to be there to avoid potential embarrassment in case FB and me run out of things to talk about, or, after half a shandy, he turns into octopus boy, his hands roaming everywhere. Luce has also invited Josh's best friend, Naz, the one with the wonky eye who plays drums in The Dogs of Doom, and he's bringing some girl he met at a Christmas party called Trisha. I can hardly believe that not only am I going out with FB, I'm going on a triple date with sixth formers! How grown-up does that sound?

Mum was totally cool that I was going out on Saturday night but, to avoid suspicion and an embarrassing birds-and-bees talk, although I mentioned FB would be there I told her we would be in a crowd of mates and overemphasized the mates bit, rather than the dates bit.

Every afternoon after school I've come home and put on the jumper he gave me and snuggled into the soft wool. I'd wear it all the time if I could, though clearly Big Date Night requires something better than a lad's navy sweater. I need something super stylish that gives out just the right signals (casually trendy, as if I've just thrown something on and found I looked totally gorge), which is why I'm planning to go shopping on Saturday with Luce and Sorrel to spend my Christmas money and get something totally fabulosa! Then it's back to mine for some serious pre-date pampering and preening before Mum drops me and Luce at The Curry Cottage to meet the others. I did ask Sorrel if she wanted to come along, but she said she'd feel a 'freakin' gooseberry', so I've promised her I'll order an extra samosa, take it home and deliver it on Sunday.

The Little Runt hammers on my bedroom door. 'Mum

says, tea in ten!' he shouts, before scampering downstairs.

We're having spag bol and I'm starving, so I shoot off the bed, out of the door and race down two sets of stairs. But when I reach the bottom step I screech to a halt on the green Axminster as I come face-to-face, or rather toe-to-wheel, with the most horrific sight.

There, at the bottom of the stairs blocking the hallway, is a black and silver pram, the first sign – other than Mum's expanding tum and exploding boobs – that life at Mortimer Road is going to change for ever, and I'm going to have to share my space with sprog paraphernalia.

Annoyed, I kick its silver wheels and try to get past, but as I do so, I feel something pull me back.

I'm not going to let some stupid sprog buggy get between me and meat-smothered carbs, so I lunge forward, and hear a ripping sound coming from my arm.

I look down and gasp.

It's total yarn carnage.

The left sleeve of FB's jumper has caught on the pram and, as I pulled away, the wool has started to unravel. Clearly the wretched buggy has taken its revenge for me giving it a good kicking.

'YOU STUPID THING!' I yell, trying to unhook myself from the sprog carrier, but only making things worse as row by row, the jumper's sleeve gets shorter and shorter.

'NOW LOOK WHAT YOU'VE DONE!'

The Little Runt darts out of the front room as Mum comes up the stairs from the basement kitchen.

'I've told you not to speak to Jack like that!' Mum orders as we face each other over the evil pram. 'You know it upsets him.'

'I wasn't talking to The Little Scroat, I was talking to that thing!' I kick the pram again and it wobbles. 'I couldn't get past it and now look what's happened! It's assaulted me!'

I raise my left arm and another row of blue stitches comes apart in a flash.

'You know FB gave it to me,' I wail. I'm almost in tears and still shackled to the wheeled monster. 'At this rate, there'll be no jumper left!'

'Who's FB?' Jack asks.

'Her boyfriend,' Mum replies.

Jack giggles, makes slurping noises on his arm and then says, 'If it keeps coming apart, will you be starkers?'

He starts making retching noises and putting his finger in his mouth. I'd put my fist in his gob but I daren't make any sudden movements for fear of yet more sleeve vanishing before my eyes.

'As if!' I snap, which isn't quite true. I've been taking off my school shirt and putting FB's jumper on as it feels so soft next to my skin.

'Let's have a look, love,' Mum says, leaning over the pram and fiddling about, which does absolutely nothing other than irritate me. 'Maybe if you take it off it will be easier to sort out.'

There's no *way* I'm going to strip to my Miracle Air Bra in the hall with my little brother looking on, so there's only one thing for it.

'You'll have to cut me free!' I say dramatically. 'You'll have to sacrifice the sleeve.'

As Mum goes to get some scissors, I shoot evils at the pram, Jack goes back into the front room and then the front door opens and Phil walks in, still wearing his AA uniform.

'What's that?' he asks, dumping his fluorescent jacket on the end of the banister and nodding towards the sprogmobile.

It's a bit of a worry that Phil is having a baby with my mother and yet can't recognize a bit of basic infant travel kit.

'A jumper-eating pram,' I say sourly. 'What did you think it was?'

'Bad day at school?' Phil asks.

'Bad afternoon in the hall,' I mutter under my breath, as Mum appears brandishing a pair of orange-handled kitchen scissors.

'Hello, love.' Mum leans over the pram towards Phil, who's next to me, and kisses him. I'm so close I can hear lip-on-lip slurping. Disgusting at their age.

'Isn't it a bit early to be getting that sort of stuff?' Phil asks, examining the pram with me still attached to it. 'I thought we were going to wait until the second scan?'

'I know, but I saw it advertised on the noticeboard in the doctors' surgery and it was too good an opportunity to miss.' Mum snips through the last strand of blue wool and frees me. 'It's never been used. The poor woman bought it, had a scan, and then found out she was having twins and has had to buy a double buggy. Her husband has just wheeled it round. He says it folds up easily. We can put it in the front room.'

I momentarily stop freaking about FB's jumper and turn my freakery to the thought of Mum having twins. There's *no way* I'd push a double buggy round the streets. I'd *have* to move into Sorrel's caravan.

I examine the wrecked jumper. There's plenty of hairy blue string dangling from my arm, but the left cuff has vanished and the sleeve is *seriously* shorter than the supposed-to-match right one.

'It's ruined,' I cry, waving my arm around. 'Totally ruined!'

'Give it to Nana Pat and she'll reknit it in a flash,' Mum says, as Phil struggles to fold up the pram, whilst I stand clear in case it attacks and mauls my other arm as revenge for my additional wheel kicks. 'She knitted you loads of stuff when you were a baby.'

Nana Pat is Dad's mum, and although she only lives on the other side of town, since Dad left we hardly ever see her because whilst Mum has sort of forgiven Dad for having an affair, she's never forgiven Nana Pat for being in on the web of deceit and covering up for her sneaky son.

'And when am I going to see Nana Pat?' I say. I'd like to put my hands on my hips in a defiant gesture, but I'm worried this will result in more sleeve carnage. 'I can't use the jumper until then and you *know* how special it is to me.'

Phil's finally beaten the pram into fold-up submission. He drags it into the front room as Mum heads downstairs to the kitchen, closely followed by me.

'Take it over when you see her for lunch on Saturday,' Mum says. Her tone of voice implies that this bit of rellie-visiting info is something I should already know. She walks over to the stove and stirs a pot of boiling water.

'Since when has this been decided?' I demand.

Mum slaps her head and laughs. 'Sorry, love, I've got a bad case of baby brain at the moment. Pat thought it would be nice as you didn't get together over Christmas.'

In a cloud of steam, Mum drains the spaghetti over the sink into a colander, puts it in a bowl and then hands the bowl to me.

'Did you know we're going to Nana Pat's on Saturday?' I snarl at The Little Runt, snatching the bowl and banging it down on the table as he sticks a mitt in the spaghetti and pulls out a long cream strand. 'Did they tell *you*?'

'Yep,' he says, sucking the strand between his lips so that it disappears like a worm down a hole. 'Years ago.'

'Great!' I growl, furious. 'So you remember to tell Scroat Face even though he hasn't any social life to disrupt, but you don't think to tell me. Typical!'

I then do quite a lot of flouncing around the kitchen just because I feel like it, although the combination of anger, FB's woolly jumper and a hot kitchen is making me sweat like a pig, so then I start to stress that FB's jumper will now stink of BO.

'Well, I can't go,' I say, stopping the flouncing by the fridge and opening the door to cool down. 'You knew I had plans!'

'I thought they were evening plans?' Mum says. 'You said you had to be there at seven.'

'Yes, but I've stuff to do first!'

'Stuff?' Phil asks. 'What stuff?'

I give him my best *Are you stoopid or what?* look which is totally lost as he's fiddling about with a pan of mince.

'Mum, tell him!' I wail. Surely she's still young enough to remember that Big Date Night preparations take *all* day?

'She's seeing her new boyfriend,' Mum explains to Phil, and I catch her giving him a wink. 'You know, that serious-looking lad who's been round a few times.'

'*And* I'm going shopping,' I say, kicking the fridge door shut as the bleeper has started going off. 'It's all arranged!'

'Electra, if you get out of bed on Saturday morning instead of sleeping in you've got plenty of time for stuff *and* shopping,' Mum says. 'Oh, and next time you're near Eastwood, could you nip into that big DIY shop on the roundabout and pick up a bunch of paint cards for when we decorate the nursery? Yellowy colours so it doesn't matter whether the baby's a girl or a boy.'

'Nursery?' Today is going from bad to worse. 'What nursery?'

'The little study upstairs,' Phil says, handing me a bunch of cutlery to put on the table. 'We thought we'd put the cot in there. Perhaps you might like to paint some cartoon characters on the wall?'

What are these people on? Clearly neither of them have any idea of the lengthy preparations required to go out on the first proper date of my life, and think I can buy a new wardrobe, design a nursery, entertain a grandmother and then simply swing home with five minutes to spare, get dressed, lick my lips and head out looking fabulous.

'You'll just have to tell Nana Pat I had other plans. I'll go over another time.' I bang a knife and fork down at each place, but purposefully put them round the wrong way to confuse Jack. 'I'll give you the jumper to give to her.'

'I'm not going,' Mum says. 'Your dad's taking you. Even if I forgot, I thought he'd have told you.'

Dad.

I've hardly spoken to him since Christmas Day, when Mum and Phil dropped the baby bombshell. I know Dad's hurt that everything has gone so wrong for him since he left home, but *he* was the one who left. He couldn't really expect Mum to let him get his womanizing out of his system and then welcome him back with open arms, a cup of tea and a packet of chocolate Boasters. I just don't think any of us realized how quickly Mum would move on, or rather, get pregnant.

'You can't make me go!' I say, sitting down at the table. 'You can't force me against my will.'

I have visions of Mum bundling me into the car, putting the child locks on to stop me jumping out and driving off, which is what Tom Malone, Lucy's dad, had to do when her brother refused to go to the dentist to have his braces tightened.

'Electra, you *are* going to your Nana Pat's on Saturday and you *will* be the lovely granddaughter I know you can be.' Mum begins to fork slippery spaghetti on to plates.

'And that is final.'

'It's not my fault that you're a foggy preghead and forgot to tell me!' I mutter just loud enough for everyone to hear, but just low enough to pretend that I didn't mean them to.

'Electra, don't talk to your mother like that,' Phil says. 'She's got a lot on her plate at the moment and can't be expected to remember every turn of your hectic social life.'

'Er . . . hello?' I say, glaring at Phil. 'Who asked you? You don't even live here.'

'Well, he will soon.' I can tell Mum's annoyed with me. 'Phil's selling his place and moving in with us.'

'What?' With the shock of this revelation I've swiped a bunch of unravelled wool across my plate.

I like Phil, I really do. From what Tits Out tells me there are far worse step-parents than an ex-Army man with a stubbly beard and a death-head tattoo on his forearm. But the news that he's coming here full-time is too much on top of being attacked by a pram, losing half your boyfriend's jumper, being told you've got to ditch your pre-date preening plans for lunch with a wrinkly *and* finding out the study is going to be turned into a sprog den.

And does this mean Mum and Phil are going to get married soon, as if so, I absolutely *refuse* to be dressed in a shiny pastel monstrosity with ruffles.

'Did no one think to ask me what I think?' I snap,

examining the bolognese-sauce-soaked sleeve. 'Am I the last to know everything round here?'

'Yep,' The Little Runt beams, so I kick his shins under the table.

'Well, that's just typical,' I say, pushing my plate away and getting up, not just because I've gone off my grub but because Jack is about to kick me back. 'I might as well not live here. I'd be better off in a caravan!' I thought I'd throw this in, in case Mum thinks it would be a good idea too. 'No one cares what I think!'

I'm somewhere between the table and the door when Mum finally explodes.

'Electra,' she snaps. 'Phil and I have tried to include you all along. Naming the baby, decorating the nursery, anything we could think of. We wanted to involve you so you didn't feel left out but you've snubbed us at every turn.'

'Involve me?' I shriek, turning round. To be honest, right now, I'm more disappointed that Mum didn't pick up on the caravan hint than the fact I'm off to Nana Pat's. 'Involve me? I don't want to be involved with this ruddy rugrat. I don't want anything to do with it! *You're* the one who got preggers by mistake. *You're* the one who's made a mess of things, *again*. Don't look to me to babysit or choose a name or move your pram or decorate its room,' I shriek. 'Don't you understand? I *want* to be left out!'

Chapter Four

'As Mum hardly ever sees you, do you think you could drop the sulky sullen look just for a few hours?' Dad growls as we pick our way through the bikes, prams and black rubbish sacks that line the concrete walkways between the flats, one of which is Nana Pat's maisonette.

'Four hours max,' I grumble, looking at my watch. 'You've promised to get me home by five, which means we have to leave here at exactly four-twenty!'

I'm in a foul mood, not just because I've been forced to go wrinkly-visiting when I should be at home preparing for Big Date Night (after my meltdown in the kitchen there was no *way* Mum wasn't going to force me to go, even doing the whole kidnapping-in-a-car routine if necessary), but because I've spent the last forty minutes sitting in a Plunge It Plumbing Services blue and white Transit van with Jack and Dad (who owns the van and the company) whilst father and son have been having a competition to see who can fart the loudest.

Dad won, which is totally gutting as it means The Little Runt will take every opportunity to practise his bottom burps until he can eventually beat Dad's upholstery-shaking emissions.

I am not amused on *so* many levels.

Getting home at five means I've only got a pitiful hour and a half to get ready before Mum runs me to The Curry Cottage for seven. I've got to shower, wash *and* deep-condition my hair, blow-dry it, put my make-up on and decide what to wear. It's not ideal but just about do-able, although the outfit might be a problem as I never got to go shopping in the end. Sorrel had volunteered to help out at The Bay Tree as her mum was short-staffed, and Lucy couldn't meet until midday because Bella had booked her an appointment with the dental hygienist at eleven, by which time I was already sitting between two bottom-burpers on the dual carriageway.

'What's so special about this evening, anyway?' Dad asks as he stops outside a blue door and presses the bell, which chimes like Big Ben. In one hand I'm holding a rather sorry-looking bunch of white lilies bought from a petrol station, already wilting in their crackly plastic, and in the other, an orange Sainsbury's bag containing FB's butchered jumper.

'You said you were just going out with some mates.'

'I am,' I say. 'I just want to look good.'

Like FB and his parents, I've told Dad a whole group of us are going out. I don't want him interrogating me about FB and starting to stress that his little girl is going out with a boy on a date on Saturday night. Luce said that when she told her parents she was officially seeing Josh, Bella started one of her excruciatingly embarrassing sexucation talks, even though Luce tried to cut it short by assuring Bella that she wasn't going to need it for years, but her dad went abso ballistic when he found out Josh was sixteen, seventeen in June. He said it was because he remembered what he was like at Josh's age, but once he met him and realized he wasn't doing drugs behind the bus stop and promised to bring Luce home on time, he was cool about it. Bella was bowled over by the stylish bunch of blooms Josh gave her. Dad hasn't met FB, but even if he did, I can't see that he'd be cool.

There's the sound of movement in the maisonette, but before I even see Nana Pat, an overpowering whiff of citrus air freshener and stale cigarette smoke wafts from behind her door. And when it opens, I'm almost knocked out, not just by the smell but by Nana Pat flinging her spindly arms around me and smothering me in kisses. This is unfortunate, not just because she has smoker's breath and is washing my blusher off with nicotine-impregnated saliva, but because she's crushed the already weedy flowers into my chest.

''ello, Princess!' she shrieks. 'How are you, darlin'?"

'Good thanks, Nana,' I say, as she finally lets me go and starts her crushing and kissing routine with Jack.

I look down to see most of the heads of the flowers have snapped off and are lying on the doormat.

'These are for you,' I say, handing Nana the bunch of stalks as I kick the heads back out into the walkway. 'They haven't travelled very well. Sorry.'

'Ah, the lilies of death,' she says, sniffing the two flowers that have survived the chest-crushing. 'We 'ad armfuls of these at your Granddad Kevin's funeral and, of course, at your mum and dad's wedding.'

I'll pick roses next time.

'Well, don't just stand there, come in and dump your coats,' Nana orders, ushering us down the tiny hall lined with polished horse brasses, something I've always found odd as I doubt Nana Pat has ever been anywhere near a horse, unless going to the bookies to put a bet on a race counts.

'Nana, can you look at this for me, please?' I ask, holding out the carrier bag. 'It's a jumper that needs repairing. I caught the sleeve on a—'

I stop myself before I can utter the hated word *pram* as I'm not sure how much Nana Pat knows about Mum and the carpet critter.

'Bung it down there and I'll look at it after lunch,' Nana Pat says. She seems a bit overexcited, even for her. 'I've got somefink to show you!'

She pushes open the door to her front room and yells, 'Surprise!'

To say we're surprised is somewhat of an understatement. Gobsmacked might be a better word.

'What do you fink then?' Nana Pat elbows me in the ribs. 'It's been so long since the Browns was all together as a family on the actual day, I thought, blow it, it's just a date, who says it always has to be the twenty-fifth?'

It might be the twelfth of January, but Nana Pat's front room is decked out as if it's Christmas Day, complete with white tinsel tree and flashing coloured fairy lights. She's even left her Christmas cards up, which is supposed to be mega unlucky.

'Blimey, Mum!' Dad says, as Nana Pat presses a button on her CD player and Slade's 'Merry Xmas Everybody' fills the room. 'You never mentioned you were going to all this trouble. I told the kids it would be soup and a pasty from Greggs.'

'I think we should start a new tradition,' Nana Pat says,

putting a bony arm around me. 'What do you fink, Princess? As well as Christmas Day, what about we have a Brownsmas Day?'

If it means I'll get presents on Christmas Day *and* Brownsmas Day, I'm all for it.

Big Ben chimes.

'This will be your surprise guest!' Nana shrieks, ''elp yourself to cheesy twirls!' She chucks a box at me and rushes out into the hall.

'Don't tell me she's booked Santa Claus to make an appearance?' I hiss at Dad as I sit on the cream leather sofa, a packet of Parmesan cheese straws clamped between my denim-clad thighs. 'What's going on?'

'She's made a real effort,' Dad hisses back. 'Behave. And you too, Jack.'

The Little Runt has taken a cheese straw, broken it in two and shoved each half up his nose.

It's not Santa Claus, it's Uncle Richard, Dad's younger brother, who years ago went to see a play at the Edinburgh Festival and never came back. He gave up his job as a quantity surveyor and is now a crystal therapist, or something. We don't see him very often so he's a bit of a stranger to us and, according to Dad, a bit strange.

'Hello, everyone,' Uncle R says awkwardly. 'Rob, Electra, Jack. Good to see you all again.'

55

'I thought it would be lovely if we was all together,' Nana beams. 'Richard's come down especially. At my age, you don't know how many Christmases you've got left.'

Dad goes over and slaps his bro on the back, and then I politely kiss him on the cheek, though I have a feeling he'd rather I didn't as he recoils slightly. I hope that doesn't happen this evening if FB and I kiss. Maybe I've got cheesy breath? It's a fact that Parmesan cheese can smell like dried sick. I breathe into my hand and have a sniff, but the only whiff is of hand cream, not barf breath.

'You remember your Uncle Richard, don't you, Jack?' Nana Pat says.

The Little Runt just stares at him.

'He came to stay a couple of years ago and we all went to a Harvester?' I try to remind him.

'Three years ago,' Uncle Richard points out. 'I haven't seen any of you for more than three years.'

I don't blame Jack for not recognizing Uncle Richard. Last time we saw him he had short hair and looked like a normal person. Now he's got long hair scraped back into a skinny greasy ponytail, which is totally tragic as, like Dad, he's practically a coot-head on top and is going grey at the sides. *And* he's got a gold hoop earring in his left ear!

'He sends you money for Christmas and birthdays,' I hiss at Jack who's still looking blank. 'He's Dad's brother, remember?'

'Oh, the weird one,' Jack remembers, which is rich coming from a boy with a couple of flaky pastry sticks up his pecker.

'Jack thinks anyone who doesn't eat meat is strange,' I say apologetically.

Uncle Richard just smiles and looks embarrassed, and I glance at my watch. It's almost one. How long does it take to have soup and a pasty? Not three hours and twenty minutes surely, even with pud.

Whilst Nana Pat goes out for a ciggy, Dad and Uncle R have a drink and make small talk, Jack tries to unscrew the bulbs in the fairy lights and I sit on the sofa, nibble a cheese straw and mentally skim through my wardrobe whilst I decide what to wear for Big Date Night.

It might make it easier to remember what I have if things were hung up in my wardrobe rather than draped on a chair, dumped on the laminate floor, pushed into drawers or hidden amongst a pile of not-so-clean knickers, bras and pyjamas. No wonder Mum refers to my attic bedroom as The Sty in the Sky.

I decide on very dark dyed denim jeans (casual); a black and white stripy top bought last year (smart casual); my thick black patent leather belt (v. cool and hides any muffin-top rollover); the scarf I bought with Maddy when she was over (she helped choose it so it's defo dead stylish)

57

and my new burgundy patent leather ankle boots (lush). I was going to wear my biggest flashiest dangliest chandelier earrings to ensure a maximum face-lengthening look, but they weigh a tonne, and seeing Nana Pat with her long slitty earlobes reminds me that if I overdo it with the monster rocks, I'll end up with geriatric ear syndrome.

And talking of earrings . . .

'So what's with the jewellery then?' Dad asks his brother, jabbing a cheese straw at Uncle Richard's flabby lobe. 'A bit teenage, isn't it?'

Uncle R touches the gold hoop in his ear and shrugs. 'It shows that I'm creative and don't conform to normal middle-aged stereotypes.'

'It says you're a weirdo having a midlife crisis.' Dad laughs sarcastically.

'Some people have their ears pierced, others leave their wives,' Uncle R says pointedly. 'Each to his own.'

'You look like a bloody woman with that ponytail,' Dad snaps back.

Nana Pat arrives reeking of smoke, just as I think the peace-loving Uncle Richard is going to stab his older brother with a cheese straw.

'You two arguing already?' she says, sucking air between her teeth. 'It was always the same. Leave 'em for a moment and World War Three would break out.' She rolls her eyes at me and smiles. 'Hope you and Jack don't give your mum as much trouble as these two did me! How is she, by the way?'

'Fine, thank you,' I say, not wanting to go into the whole parental preggers scene before a meat pasty, though I expect I'll get the third degree on the baby news before pud.

The sound of a microwave pinging comes from the kitchen. 'Brownsmas lunch is about to be served!' Nana announces. 'Come on through.'

The tiny table in Nana's kitchen is decked out like a miniature version of ours on Christmas Day, minus Jack's dodgy modelling-clay table decorations, and I have a sudden terrible flashback to the moment at Mortimer Road when I was about to spear a sprout, and Mum dropped the baby bombshell. I can still picture my plate of vortexing veg and remember the terrible sick feeling in my stomach when I looked up to see Mum and Phil holding hands and I realized what was going on.

Nana Pat must have seen my face cloud over as I sit down.

'What is it, Princess? It's not turkey, it's boneless chook breasts from Morrisons and extra veg in a tray for young Richard.'

'It's not that,' I croak, staring at the silver crackers and swallowing hard. I can still taste the cheese so I'm sure my breath must penk of Parmesan. 'It's just the table reminds me . . .'

'Reminds you of what?' Nana sounds worried. ''ave I done somefink wrong?'

'We had a difficult Christmas Day,' Dad explains, pulling out a chair. 'It didn't exactly go according to plan.'

'I thought you were with Ellie and the kids?' Nana says, peering at the plastic tray of anaemic-looking chicken breasts. 'You end up havin' a row?'

'Mum has a baby in a bun,' Jack pipes up. 'I mean, a bun in the oven. Or maybe a baby in the oven.' He looks confused. There'll be no confusion when I pin him to a wall and remind him that in my opinion little brothers should never be seen *or* heard. 'Electra ran away.'

He's dead.

'Robert!' Nana Pat shrieks. 'Why didn't you tell me you and Ellie had another one on the way! Is you still separated? Back together? What?'

Oh dear.

I glance across at Dad, who's just sitting there looking miserable, his double chin practically on his chest, the light bouncing off his shiny bald head.

'Robert?' Nana's voice is sharp. 'What's goin' on?'

'Mum has a boyfriend called Phil Harris and they're

having a baby,' I say, trying to help Dad out. 'It's due in early June. We only found out over Christmas lunch.'

'Their stars must have been in alignment,' Uncle Richard sighs. 'It was fate.'

'It was a mistake,' I mutter under my breath.

'Was your Grandma and Granddad there when all this happened?' Nana asks me and I nod.

For a moment no one says anything, and then Nana Pat throws back her head, roars with laughter and drums on the table with both hands.

'Oh, how I'd have loved to been there to see Mrs Snobby's stuck-up nose put out of joint by *that* bit of news,' she laughs, showing practically all her yellow gnashers. 'Dorothy Stafford must have looked like she was sucking on a pound of unripe lemons whilst a hot poker was being stuck up her flabby arse!'

'Mum!' Dad snaps, banging a cracker on the table. 'That's my children's grandmother you're talking about!'

Nana Pat stabs a chicken breast with a fork and dumps the pale lump on my plate. It reminds me of the silicone pads Tits Out stuffs in her bra.

'Well, Dorothy always thought her daughter was too good for you, and that it was you who'd led her astray from her A levels. And here she is, what, fourteen, fifteen, years later, pregnant by mistake, *again*!' Nana Pat's clearly enjoying this. 'When I'm sitting here night after night on my own with just my meal from the microwave, the thought of Snotty Dotty's face will really cheer me up.'

'That's enough!' Dad's really angry now. 'I won't have Dorothy or Ellie discussed in this way.' He's gone beety red and sweat is beading on his forehead. 'Ellie's a great mother and a good person and the reason this has happened is because of *my* behaviour.'

Nana Pat's mouth opens and closes like a fish out of water.

Right,' Dad orders. 'Let's just all enjoy our first Brownsmas Day.'

Chapter Five

'Thanks for sticking up for Mum,' I say, waving out of the window at Nana and Uncle Richard, who are standing on the walkway, leaning over the balcony, waving back as we pull away from the flats on the dot of four-twenty, just as Dad promised me.

Lunch was over quickly, but then Nana Pat got out some photographs of Dad and Uncle Richard when they were kids and got all teary over Granddad Kevin drowning in a pit of wet concrete on a building site, so it seemed a bit selfish to demand to leave earlier so I could wash and condition my hair without a rush.

Dad reaches over Jack who's playing with his Nintendo DS and pats my thigh. 'Your nan didn't mean any harm, you know that, don't you? It's just . . .' He takes his hand off my leg, bangs the steering wheel and lets out a deep sigh. 'Grandma Stafford gave our family such a hard time over your mum and me getting together. Mum's never forgotten it. None of us have.'

I remember the photos of Mum and Dad's wedding.

Mum: only eighteen and in love, wearing a white meringue of a wedding dress, a mega bouquet of white lilies strategically covering the bump that was me.

Dad: young, slim and with lots of hair, beaming.

Grandma with a face like a slapped backside underneath her flying saucer of a lilac hat.

'Yeah, I know,' I say, pressing a button and closing the window. Now it's time for me to lean over and make an affectionate gesture with my hand. I pat his arm. 'You OK about Mum and the baby, Dad?' I ask, looking sideways at him over Jack, who's fallen asleep with his mouth open.

'Can't say I was delighted,' Dad says tightly, 'but there's nothing I can do about it. I had the affair and left so I'll just have to put up with the consequences. Still, Phil seems a decent enough guy, and you and Jack get on well with him, don't you?'

I don't want Dad to think we like Phil too much, so I just say, 'He's OK, for a bloke with a beard.'

'Anyway,' Dad tries to sound brighter, 'it's no good me moping over split marriages and lost girlfriends. I'm going to pull myself together and the first thing I'm going to do is get rid of this!'

He pats his stomach, which even I have to admit is getting pretty huge. In fact with his big belly and increasing man-boob issue, I'm in the embarrassing situation of having two parents who look pregnant.

'Starting from now, I'm going on a diet and I'm going to get myself a personal trainer. A leaflet came in the post at work. It's a company who come to your office or home and put you through your paces.' Dad pulls himself upright at the wheel. 'From today, you're going to see a new Rob Brown emerging.'

'Is this so you can get a new girlfriend?' I giggle, knowing what's usually on Dad's mind. 'Are you trying to buff up for some new hot totty?'

'Electra!' Dad tries to sound shocked, even though he's laughing. 'I'm doing this so I feel better about myself, but obviously if the new slimline me happens to attract some female attention . . .'

We both laugh. There was a time when I hated the thought of Dad having a relationship and I loathed his last girlfriend, but now I don't want him to be on his own like Nana Pat, eating microwaveable meals for one night after night. I want someone to think of him the way I think of FB.

At the thought of FB I reach down to touch his jumper.

The jumper!

I've left it in the hall! With it being Brownsmas Day and Uncle Weirdo turning up, not to mention Nana Pat getting overexcited about the whole sprogging scenario, I completely forgot about it!

I *have* to have FB's jumper! If it stays at Nana Pat's it will end up *stinking* of fags!

I look at my watch.

Quarter to five.

If we go back to Nana's now, grab the jumper and Dad drives speedily, we can be back for five-thirty. That gives me an hour to get ready, hardly any time, but better than leaving the jumper to marinate in nicotine.

'Dad, we have to go back!' I say urgently. 'I've left something at Nana's'

'If you want to be home by five we haven't time,' he replies.

'I've left a jumper,' I say, freaked that Dad is still driving forwards rather than backwards. 'I need it.'

'I'll pick it up tomorrow.' Dad accelerates. 'I said I'd pop over and do a few chores around the house. Richard doesn't know one end of a screwdriver from another.'

'Dad!' I'm really anxious now. 'If I don't get back until five-thirty it won't really matter, honestly, *please*!'

'So all that stuff about you *having* to be back for five wasn't really true, was it?' Dad says, as we slow down to wait in a queue of traffic at a roundabout. 'What's so special about this jumper anyway? Got a fifty-quid note tucked into the sleeve?'

'It belongs to her boyfriend,' Jack pipes up, having woken up at the most inappropriate moment.

'What boyfriend?' Dad asks, as we cross the roundabout. 'You've never mentioned anything about a boyfriend.'

'She's going for a curry with him tonight,' Jack says. 'She lurves him!'

He smacks his lips so I reach over and smack him.

'You know nothing, Scroat Face,' I say, as Jack belts me back. 'So shut up!'

'I knew you had a boyfriend and I know you kiss your mirror!' he singsongs before making more lip-smacking noises.

'Have you been spying on me again?' I shriek. ''Cause if you have, I'll murder you!'

'I'll murder you back!' Jack yells, and throws his DS at me, so naturally I lob it back.

Jack ducks and it hits Dad on the side of his face causing him to yell and yank the steering wheel.

The van hits the inside kerb with an almighty thud, bounces off it and swerves into the middle of the road.

'Stop it, you two!' Dad shouts, getting the van back under control. 'That could have caused an accident. Jack, button it. Electra, your precious jumper will have to wait.'

I am furious and sink down in the seat as Jack and I pinch each other's thighs.

'Are you going slowly just to annoy me?' I ask. Dad's normally a very fast driver, a typical White Van Man, the sort who cuts people up at junctions and gets too close to their rear bumper, even brandishing the occasional V-sign. But now we're just crawling along the dual carriageway. Clearly this is a parental attempt by Dad to demonstrate that *he's* the one in control so that I end up with no jumper and a seriously late start on the Big Date Night preparations.

'We're losing power,' Dad says as cars overtake us, flashing their lights and tooting their horns. 'Hitting the kerb must have done something.'

'Put your foot down!' I yell, remembering what FB said about his dad's Beamer. 'Give it some gas! Floor it!'

'It's no good, we can't go any further,' Dad says, as we finally limp to a stop. He puts his hazard warning lights on. 'We're crocked.'

This is all I need.

Dad jumps out and starts peering in the bonnet with a torch whilst I become almost hysterical at the prospect of not getting home until six.

I open the window. 'I'll ring Phil,' I shout, reaching for

my bag and my phone. What's the point of living with an AA man if you can't use him in an emergency and, as far as I'm concerned, the possibility of going on Big Date Night with greasy hair counts as a mega emergency.

'No you won't,' Dad says sharply, getting back in the van. 'I'll ring Spanner and get him to have a look at it.'

'Spanner?' I say. 'Who's Spanner?'

'Spanos something or other. The Greek guy who services the vans.' Dad's already on his moby. 'Hi, Spanos! It's Rob, Rob Brown from Plunge It Plumbing Services? Yep, look, mate, sorry to phone you on a Saturday but I've broken down on the dual carriageway, just near The Toby Jug pub but on the other side. Any chance of swinging by to have a look?'

I can hear fast talking on the other end of the phone.

'Cheers, mate, that's great,' Dad says. 'Appreciate it.'

'So is this Spanner guy on his way?' I ask. I'm now facing the prospect of just washing my hair, not conditioning it. If I steel myself and rinse it in cold water it should look shiny.

'He's just coming out of football and he's going to have a swift half in the pub. Should be with us in about half an hour.'

'HALF AN HOUR!' I scream. 'HALF AN HOUR!' I can see hair-washing going out the window. I'm going to turn up limp-haired. 'We don't have half an hour.' I flip open my phone. 'I'm defo ringing Phil.'

'You will not,' Dad orders, grabbing my phone off me and snapping it shut. 'I don't need anything from that mobile grease monkey.'

'Phil's an AA man!' I scream. 'And he's not in the pub with a pint of beer!'

'It's a half of lager,' Dad shouts back. 'And if you hadn't argued with Jack, none of this would have happened!'

'He started it!' I yell, digging The Little Runt in the ribs.

'I did not!' Jack yells back. 'You did!'

'SHUT UP!' Dad's voice is so loud the van rattles. 'First Christmas Day, now Brownsmas Day. Electra, why do you always have to turn *everything* into a drama?'

I'd like to answer Dad back, giving him chapter and verse on why I am hardly ever to blame for family fights, and that all I want is an easy life with a lovely boyfriend and evenly sized boobs, but I get the impression that this is the sort of question parentals don't expect answering and if I did, I might be left standing on the side of the road when the wretched van eventually gets going.

I snatch my phone from between Dad's legs and start stabbing the keys.

'I told you. Don't ring that man!' Dad orders.

'I'm not,' I snap. 'I'm texting Luce to tell her what's happened and that I'm going to be late.'

Actually, I'm texting FB to tell him what's happened.

'Now, what time are you due to meet your mates for a curry?' Dad asks.

'Seven,' I say through gritted teeth. 'Seven at The Curry Cottage.'

A text arrives from FB. `Could the timing belt have jumped?`

I've got no idea what a timing belt is, and I'm a bit miffed that he didn't at least put a kiss on the end of his text or say he was looking forward to seeing me.

'Right,' Dad says. 'In that case, I'll run you straight there.'

This is quite definitely the worst news I've heard all year, the Mum being preggers announcement scooping last year's Worst News Award. Not only will I have to arrive at The Curry Cottage wearing clothes I've spent all day in, hair that seems to be getting greasier by the moment, and daylight slap (*everyone* knows that if you are going to be under electric lights in a restaurant you need to up the make-up if you are not to appear so washed out you look as if you're recovering from a bout of swine flu), my breath probably penks of Parmesan cheese. But just as serious as my sartorial crisis is my mode of arrival!

'I'm not turning up in this thing!' I shriek.

FB and me have agreed that I'll slip into The Curry Cottage as incognito as poss, just in case his parentals spot me. A blue and white van with ladders on the top and a plunger painted down the side isn't exactly an undercover mode of transport.

'Oh, pardon me,' Dad says sarcastically. 'I didn't realize you expected a limo to take you there. Should I wear a peaked cap as well?'

'And what if this Spanner bloke can't get the van going?' I say. 'What then? How am I going to get to The Curry Cottage?'

'It'll just be something simple,' Dad says. 'But if not, we'll get a minicab.'

I think Dad's being stupid not letting Phil come out and fix the van.

'I've got to phone Mum anyway as she'll be expecting us back,' I say. 'What if she suggests Phil comes out and takes a look? What should I say then?'

Dad bangs the steering wheel in frustration. 'Tell her we've broken down, but it's all under control,' he says.

Repairing the van might be under control but my hair and wardrobe certainly isn't.

'I'm off to a shop to find some mints,' I say. 'I've got vomit breath.'

Six o'clock and finally Spanos The Spanner pulls up in a monster breakdown truck with a row of flashing yellow lights pulsating across the top and a naked woman called Roxette spray-painted on the back. There's a snake in her right hand, her left hand is doing something rather rude to her huge left boob, and there's a speech bubble coming out of her mouth saying: *I Like Trucking*.

Jack looks as if he might wet himself with excitement.

'All right, Rob?' Spanner asks, staring at the van. 'What happened?'

'My daughter threw a Nintendo at me, I hit the kerb and then we lost power,' Dad explains.

'Why'd you throw the Nintendo?' Spanner asks me. I'm leaning against the side of the van trying to keep away from The Little Runt, who's pointing at Roxette and her boobs, squealing, 'Mega! Mega!'

I crunch down on another mint and just stare at Spanner or Spanos or whatever he's called. I don't have to explain my reasons for hurling computer hardware to a stranger.

Under instructions from Spanos, Dad starts the van up and the mechanic spends a long time with his head in the bonnet, shouting at Dad to press the accelerator, turn the steering wheel, put his foot on the clutch and so on.

Eventually he shouts, 'Turn her off.'

'So, what's the diagnosis, doctor?' Dad asks. 'A temporary illness or something terminal?'

'Could be so many things,' Spanos sniffs, rubbing his oily

black hands through his oily black hair.

'Could it be the timing belt?' I ask. 'Has it jumped?'

Spanner raises his eyebrows at me. 'That's the most likely thing. How did you know?'

I just shrug and look smug, and think how great it is to have a boyfriend who knows so many useful things, even if he doesn't send romantic texts.

'Did you try and drive it when you first lost power?' Spanos asks Dad.

Dad nods. 'My daughter said to step on the gas, floor it, so I did,' he says, as if he always takes driving lessons from me.

Spanos shakes his head and lets out a long whistle. 'Oh dear. Bad move. If you're lucky you might have just damaged the valves on one or two cylinders, but it's more than likely you've bent them, destroyed your camshaft and cam followers, bent your con roads and dented your piston crowns.'

'Which means?' Dad asks.

Spanos rubs his hands. 'A new engine, a big bill and a lift home.'

I'm used to disasters, plans going wrong, things not turning out as I imagined they would. Experience has taught me that when people say, *Cheer up, what's the worst that could happen?* I can usually tell them quite accurately. But *never* in my wildest dreams and shallow imagination could I have imagined that preparations for Big Date Night could go so spectacularly wrong.

It's almost seven and I should be on my way to The Curry Cottage with clean shiny hair, just the right amount of make-up, smelling fragrant after a long hot shower and a squirt of posh perfume, wearing a carefully chosen and artfully accessorized outfit, all ready for an evening of samosas and snogging with FB.

Instead, I'm sitting in the back seat of a monster pick-up truck decorated with a porno pic, wearing wrinkly-visiting rather than Hot Fox clothes, hours-old make-up and hair that's as greasy-looking as Spanner's, whilst behind me Dad's crocked van is being towed at a snail's pace.

I've done what few emergency repairs I could on the way.

I've hoiked up my bra straps, pushed a handful of tissues in the cups for added oomph, licked my hands and smoothed down my hair in the hope it will look sleek and shiny rather than greasy and grotty, sniffed my armpits, decided they might *just* be verging on ripe, licked my last remaining mint and rubbed it on my pits for a touch of minty freshness, sniffed my breath, worried about Parmesan so crunched the pit-rubbed mint, which now doesn't taste of mint but of deodorant, and finally slapped on masses of lip gloss.

'Please can you just drop me here?' I ask. We're getting dangerously close to The Curry Cottage and it's going to be hard to hide from Doc Burns and her hubby if I turn up in the dark in a monster truck with a naked woman down the side and yellow strobe lights.

'I'm not having you wandering around here on your own,' Dad says, turning round. 'You don't mind dropping her off at the door, do you, Spanos?'

'Can't be too careful,' Spanos says. 'There's some right weirdos about.'

As we pull up in the road outside The Curry Cottage, I'm relieved to see that there's no sign of FB, FB's parents or their dark-blue BMW. I can just slip out and slip in, go to the loos and emerge if not glam, at least oil-free.

'How are you getting back?' Dad asks.

'Lucy's boyfriend's mum is running me home,' I say, trying to find the door handle.

In front of us someone pips their horn. The pick-up is so enormous we've turned the two-way street into a one-way lane.

Unhelpfully, Spanos sticks his right hand out of the window, gives a V-sign and then sounds his horn back, except it's not a little pip, it's an ear-bleeding air horn that plays a tune and makes the cab vibrate.

The car replies by blaring its horn, which sounds a bit weedy in comparison to Spanos and his blaster.

For a moment there's just continual blaring of horns.

As if there's not enough noise, Dad leans out of the passenger window. 'All right! All right! Keep your wig on!' he shouts.

'It's a woman driver,' Spanos says, as if it's entirely usual for him to get into a *My horn is bigger than yours* contest with every woman on the road.

'You women in posh cars think you're the mutt's nuts,' Dad bellows out of the window. 'Well, let me tell you, lady, I've got more horsepower under my thighs than you can dream of!'

Chapter Six

FB's already at the table, sitting next to Josh, who's opposite Luce. When I see him, my heart leaps and my stomach churns, but perhaps that's from too many breath-blasting mints. He's looking nervous and awkward but totally hot in a green combat jacket with military badges dotted over the shoulders and down the arms.

'Hi!' FB says shyly, smiling when he sees me.

'Hi,' I say back.

He tries to get up but immediately sits back down again.

'I'm trapped by a bit of tablecloth,' he explains, looking flustered as he flaps his hands around his butt.

Just as he manages to free bum and fabric and I think I might be on for a welcome kiss, Luce turns round and sees me.

'You're here!' she shrieks, scrambling to her feet and smothering me with kisses. She pats the seat next to her with one hand and drags me to it with the other. 'Sit by me.'

I don't know why Luce was so keen I sat next to her, as the moment I sit down Luce and Josh start feeding each other poppadoms over the tablecloth.

I look across at FB.

He's studying his thighs, biting the cuticles on his thumbs, both digits rammed into his mouth at once.

What with Josh and Luce snogging and FB practically sucking his thumb, there's slurping in stereo above the cat-wailing-to-drum-and-bells music.

This is not going well. Not only am I inappropriately dressed for Big Date Night, my boyfriend is ignoring me *and* I'm completely starving.

FB sees me looking at him, takes his thumbs out of his mouth, wipes his mouth with the back of his hand, smiles, and leans across the table towards me. As he does so I can smell aftershave, though to be honest I'm not sure that he needs it yet as there's nothing really there to shave.

Oh. My. God.

He's going to kiss me!

I can't say I was keen on the thumb-sucking and mouth-wiping routine, but this was clearly just preparation for the big welcome snog. I'm not sure how he's going to lean over and actually plant his smackers on mine as the table is quite wide and neither of us are as tall as Luce and

Josh, so I'll have to lean in and help him. How terrible if he was puckering up in mid-air only to collapse across the mango chutney.

Hoping that I've still got minty breath, I run my tongue over my teeth, lean over, part my mouth in what I hope is a seductive glossy pout, close my eyes and wait for that first touch of his soft lips.

'What was wrong with the van?'

I open my eyes to find that I'm practically nose-to-nose with him.

'*What?*'

'Did you find out what was wrong with the van?'

I can't believe this! He's looking all eager, but to talk about engines, not snog my face off.

'Our piston crowns are dented,' I say, rolling my eyes. '*And* our camshaft is crocked.'

'So the timing belt *had* jumped!' FB claps his hands and sounds lottery-winning excited. 'I was right!'

I slump back in my seat. 'You were,' I say through gritted teeth, wondering if I started dressing like a mechanic FB might show more enthusiasm to snog me. Perhaps instead of stressing over what I was going to wear tonight I should have just borrowed some of Phil's AA gear. A fluorescent jacket and an adjustable spanner might have got him going.

'There's Naz!' Josh says, waving. 'Over here, mate!'

I turn round to see Naz Ashri loping towards us.

'Where's this Trisha bird?' Josh asks, as Naz hovers at the end of the table, looking first at FB and then at me, although because he has a wonky eye, he could have looked at both of us on opposite sides of the table at the same time.

'In the bogs,' Naz says. 'Fiddling with her hair or something.'

'You remember Electra, don't you?' Luce says, though from the look on Naz's face, I could be a curry-eating alien rather than the best friend of his best friend's girlfriend. 'And this is her boyfriend, Frazer.'

Luce and I both huddle together and giggle at the word *boyfriend*. It all sounds *so* grown up!

And then we both see the girl that has come up to the table and wrapped her arms around Naz, and stop giggling – *instantly*.

'What are you doing here?' Luce gasps, as we both look up the nostrils of Naz's date.

It's not a girl called Trisha. It's Fritha Kennedy, the total cow from Queen Beatrice's and the girl that gatecrashed my fourteenth birthday party and started trying on my mum's greying mega bap-packs. And for months Fritha Kennedy has been going out with James Malone after he dumped Natalie Price for her.

Fritha looks down her nostrils at us. 'I'm with Naz.' She clutches his arm as if she owns it. 'We're meeting friends.'

'These are my friends,' Naz says lamely. 'Well, Josh is.'

'Oh.' The Bra Bitch's voice is flat with disappointment. 'I thought you meant sixth formers,' she pouts.

'When did you and James break up?' Luce asks. 'He never said.'

Fritha looks a bit shifty. 'We haven't officially finished,' she says. 'But Naz is in the sixth form *and* in a band. He plays drums.'

Clearly going out with a sixth former at a comp with a wonky eye and a pair of drumsticks trumps a Year 11 lad with normal vision but at a posh school.

'You never said you were going out with someone else.' Naz looks put out. 'Who?'

'Oh, chill, Naz,' Fritha purrs. 'He was just some boy I was hanging around with for a bit. It was nothing major.'

'Just some boy!' Luce squeaks. 'He's not just some boy! He's my older brother and a bit was seven months!'

'So James knows you're here with him and he's cool about it?' I ask, scanning The Bra Bitch's wardrobe for style tips. She's wearing lots of jangly bracelets, hoop earrings, black top, tiny grey skirt, thick leggings and black fringed suede boots to die for.

Fritha looks rattled. 'I didn't say he'd be cool about it,'

she says, fiddling with her bracelets. 'But there's no law to say I can't go out with someone else, is there? It's a free country.' As a waiter hovers with some menus, Fritha does so much hair-tossing and pawing at the carpet with her feet, I wouldn't be surprised if she didn't start neighing and galloping around the restaurant. 'It's not like we're married or anything.'

My dad was married but it didn't stop him going out with someone else behind my mum's back.

'So where does he think you are?' Luce demands. 'What little story have you concocted about why you can't see him on Saturday night?'

Fritha bites her lip. 'He thinks I've got flu,' she mutters.

Seeing Fritha standing in front of me, all leggy and cocky in those fabulous boots, so sure she can get away with two-timing James, reminds me of Dad cheating on Mum and makes me so mad I want to sacrifice a poppadom and ram it in her mouth.

'You duplicitous sneaky rat!' I snap, rather proud of my use of the word duplicitous, the phrase being one of the less rude sentences Mum used to scream at Dad.

'Hang on, Electra!' Josh interrupts. 'This is between Naz, James and Trisha.'

'It's not between James and anyone because James doesn't know anything about it!' I say. 'And it's Fritha not Trisha, and if you'd paid attention to Naz you'd have known that!'

'Don't have a go at me!' Josh snaps. 'It's not my fault!'

'And don't you have a go at Electra!' Luce says. 'Fritha's the lying cow!'

'Don't you dare call me a cow!' Fritha barks at Lucy. She turns on Naz. 'I didn't realize you were friends with kids.'

'That's ripe, coming from you!' I say. 'You might be at a posh school but you're still in my year!'

A man in a dark suit comes over. 'I am afraid that if there is any more shouting, I will have to ask you to leave,' he says. He's polite, but I get the impression there's a man with a meat cleaver on standby in the kitchen ready to rush out if things get any more heated between us. 'You are upsetting the other diners.'

'Sorry,' Josh says as we all look round and realize everyone is watching us. 'We'll keep it down. Please could we have some samosas?'

Dark Suit scuttles away muttering under his breath.

'If she's staying, I'm going,' Luce says, pushing her chair back and trying to scramble behind me.

'Oh, sit down,' Fritha sneers. 'I'm off. I'm not spending my Saturday night with chavs and weirdos.'

Before I can hurl the chutney tray in her direction, she gallops out and Naz, looking worried, follows her.

84

'Poor James,' Lucy says, twisting her napkin into a knot. 'He'll be gutted.'

'Don't tell him,' Josh suggests. 'What he doesn't know won't hurt him.'

'I can't do that!' Luce gasps. 'I *have* to tell him. Wouldn't you want to know if I was cheating on you, not that I ever would, but say if I had the chance to snog Justin Timberlake?'

Josh laughs. 'I'd say if you had the chance to snog the Trousersnake, go for it, just don't tell me.'

The waiter returns and bangs a silver tray piled with golden battered triangles on the table.

'That's terrible!' Lucy cries. 'That's like saying you can be unfaithful as long as you don't get found out, isn't it?'

Luce looks to me for back-up, but I'm not sure I can give it. We only discovered Dad's affair with Candy Baxter by accident. Who's to say that if we hadn't found out, and Dad hadn't been forced to tell the truth, things wouldn't have just blown over and Dad would be back at home instead of being alone in a flat, whilst Mum is pregnant with a second-hand buggy in the front room.

'I'm not sure,' I say, nibbling the corner of a hot and spicy samosa. 'It's complicated.'

'I'd want to know if you were seeing someone else,' FB pipes up. It's the first time he's said anything after the engine overexcitement and, to be honest, with the whole James–Fritha–Naz thing I'd almost forgotten he was there. 'I'd want you to tell me, however hurt I'd be,' he says solemnly. 'I don't think couples should have secrets from each other.'

I look at FB. He's gone very red but I'm not sure if it's from embarrassment or because he's just popped an entire samosa in his mouth. He looks nervous and shy and hot all at the same time, and I feel an overwhelming desire to snog his face off, but I can't because I'd be too embarrassed, and if I lean over the table I'm likely to crush my elbows in the meat samosas.

'Well, that's not going to happen,' I say. 'I'd *never* cheat on you, even if I was offered a lush footballer on a plate.'

An image of David Beckham in tiny underpants sitting on a blue and white plate surrounded by onion bhajees pops into my head. Weirdly, I notice I grab the savoury snack before I go for Becks.

'You say that now,' FB says, gulping down some water. 'But one day you'll find me boring and go off with someone else. I've told you, you're out of my league.'

Josh looks fed up and hungry. 'Look, can we cut this who's going to be unfaithful to who first and with whom, and just order?'

* * *

We're staring at the menus, chatting about what to have. I'm thinking about going for a prawn biryani and FB is wondering about a chicken korma when Josh whispers across the table, 'Don't look, but there's some weirdo baldy bloke over there staring at us.'

So of course, we look.

And the weirdo baldy bloke is Dad.

I want to die of shame, right here, right now at the table. I've often thought spontaneous combustion would be a painless way to go, and never more so have I needed my body to suddenly ignite and turn into a pile of grey ashes smouldering on the red-velvet-covered chair as I do now.

Perhaps if I just pretend he's some perve after a prawn pilau and ignore him, he'll go away.

'It's Electra's dad!' Luce says. 'He's coming over.'

That's it. I am dead with shame.

'Hello, you four,' Dad says. I don't actually know who he's looking at because I'm studying the menu in forensic detail. 'Having a good time?'

'Yes, thank you, Mr Brown,' Lucy says. 'Josh, Frazer, this is Electra's dad.'

'I know,' FB says. 'I recognized you from when I followed you.'

'Followed me?' Dad queries.

I can't ignore Dad any longer and I have to stop FB from

revealing I got him to stalk Dad when I suspected him of having an affair.

'What are you doing here?' I hiss, as if I didn't know. I'm looking up through my fringe, and even without full-on vision I know Dad's looking between Josh and FB, trying to decide which lad is most likely to corrupt his little girl.

'We dropped Jack home, I borrowed a motor from Spanner and thought I'd just swing by for a curry,' he says unconvincingly. 'Fancied some tandoori chicken and a garlic naan or two.'

'I thought you were on a diet!' I growl, now employing the full eye-roll, tight voice and *Just get lost*-look combo. 'Since when was curry diet food?'

'Well, a man fancies something spicy occasionally,' Dad grins. 'You look like the sort of lad who goes for a gut-blasting vindaloo, not one of those girly kormas, eh?' He mega-embarrassingly playfully punches Josh on the shoulder. 'A real man's curry with butt-blistering chillies!'

No one says anything. I can't say anything because I am paralysed with embarrassment.

'Well, take care of my daughter,' Dad says awkwardly. 'Be a good lad and all that.'

If I thought I'd reached the pinnacle of embarrassment earlier, I was wrong. My ability to feel acute shame has hit new levels. This is because Dad gives the *Take Care of My Daughter* speech to Josh.

'Electra's going out with Frazer,' Lucy giggles from behind her hand as she nods across the table to FB. I can't look at FB because I'm glaring daggers at Dad. 'Josh is *my* boyfriend.'

'Oh.' If Dad's face could fall any further it would crash through the floor into the basement.

'I was the one who knew it was the timing belt that had jumped on your van,' FB says proudly. 'I read car manuals in bed.'

We all stare at FB, who looks embarrassed as even he realizes he's sent the nerdometer reading to its highest level.

'Ready to order?' a hovering waiter asks impatiently.

'I'll have a chicken vindaloo,' FB says. 'With extra chilli.'

'That was lush!' I say, shovelling the last forkful of rice, prawns and bits of unidentified veg in my mouth and wondering whether I can undo the button of my jeans if I keep my belly hidden behind my napkin.

Luce pushes away her plate, which she's hardly touched. 'I wish I'd had yours,' she grumbles. 'Mine was so spicy I've had to drink loads of water to get even a bit down.'

'You all right, mate?' Josh asks FB. 'You look a bit hot.'

FB looks hot all right. He's sweating so much his hair is

damp and curling around his face, and he's peeled his jacket off so he's just wearing a blindingly white T-shirt.

I haven't really been paying much attention to FB, as Luce and I have been dissecting the whole Fritha–James–Naz love triangle. Luce is in a right pickle over what she should do and how she's going to face James when she gets home. *She* thinks that she should tell James, but on the other hand he knows that none of us like Fritha, so he might think Luce is out to make trouble, especially if The Bra Bitch denies everything. I'm just keen to know where Fritha got her skirt and boots from. My legs are like tree trunks next to hers, but with careful use of coordinated tights, I think her look might work for me.

'I'm fine,' FB says, though his teeth seem a bit gritted, which is actually not a bad look as it makes his jaw look firm and square.

'You sure?' I say. 'Was the curry too hot for you?'

'Of course not!' He sounds snappy, but he looks even more gorge, sweaty *and* brooding.

'I'm going to the loo,' Luce says, kicking me under the table. 'It's all that water I've been drinking.'

'I'll come too,' I say, taking the hint.

We continue our love-triangle conversation in the loo, giggle about FB and Josh, I despair at how little make-up I'm wearing and borrow some of Luce's, there's a bit of hair-fiddling and then we head back to the table, where Josh is sitting on his own making a ghost puppet out of his red paper napkin.

'I thought you two had done a runner,' he says grumpily. 'I've been sitting here on my tod for ages. What took you so long?'

'We had stuff to do,' Luce says, sitting down and throwing me the sort of look that says, *lads!*

'And stuff to discuss,' I add, sitting next to her. 'Where's Frazer?'

'Gone to the bogs,' Josh says, sticking a finger up his puppet. 'Or so he said.'

'What do you mean, *or so he said*?' I ask as the waiter clears our table. 'Is he in the loo or not?'

'I've been for a pee and he's not,' Josh says.

'Well, where is he then?' Luce asks.

'Well, it's obvious, isn't it?' Josh mutters.

I flip open my phone. 'I'm going to ring him. Something must have happened.'

'I wouldn't,' Josh says. 'Not if you don't want to look a saddo.' He appears uncomfortable and not in a *I've just stuffed myself with too much lamb jalfrezi* type of way.

'Saddo?' I say. 'Why would I look like a saddo for ringing him?'

Josh shakes his head. 'Can't you see, you've been a victim

of the classic Date Great Escape? Lad pretends to go to the bogs. Lad legs it. Lad leaves lass at the table and his share of the bill with a waiter. It's what men do when they've had enough but don't have the balls to tell the girl they're with that they've gone off her.'

'You're saying FB's dumped me?' I gasp, closing my phone. 'He's climbed out the loo window or something, just to get away from me?'

Is it my greasy hair, my wrinkly-visiting outfit or my cheesy breath that's sent him running?

'He's probably just gone for some air,' Luce says. 'He'll be back.'

'His coat's gone,' Josh says, pointing at FB's chair, which no longer has his green jacket draped over the back. 'Doesn't that tell you something?'

'Frazer would never do anything like that,' Luce says confidently. 'He's much too polite.'

'Well, you two weren't,' Josh says sourly. He takes FB's napkin and makes another puppet. 'Me and him might as well have been somewhere else.'

'What do you mean, *you might as well have been somewhere else*?' Luce demands. 'What are you getting at?'

'From the moment Electra arrived you two have done nothing but giggle and gossip and huddle together,' he grumbles. 'You've hardly said a word to either of us!' He wiggles both puppets together as if they're nattering.

'But Electra's my friend!' Luce practically explodes. 'We've always got loads to talk about.'

'And I'm supposed to be your boyfriend,' Josh snaps back. 'I wanted this evening to be about the two of us and you ended up inviting half the school and ruining everything!'

'*I've* ruined everything?' Luce cries. '*I've* ruined everything? It's you who's ruined everything, not knowing it was Fritha and letting FB run off like that.'

Josh plays with his puppets. 'You're to blame! You're to blame!' he singsongs between the two.

'That's it,' Luce snaps. 'I'm getting Mum to pick me up. Electra, you coming?'

I've just been sitting amongst the poppadom crumbs and dirty plates, clutching my moby, waiting for FB to walk in or call or give me some sign to explain what's happened and why he's done a runner from The Curry Cottage. But however unhappy I felt before, now I feel absolutely desperate, and not just because I've been fingering my chin and can feel at least three mega lumps brewing, or because I've started to sweat a bit and my mint-rubbed armpits are sticking together or because Luce and Josh have just had their first blazing row in front of me and I can tell Luce is a nanosecond away from bursting into tears. I'm desperate because a waiter is hovering next to our table with a crumpled ten-pound note and a handful of change on a silver dish.

'Your friend. He left this and said he hoped it would cover his meal.' The waiter bows and places the dish on the table next to me.

'Is that all he said?' I croak. 'Nothing else?'

'I'm so sorry, miss,' he says, shaking his head and looking glum. 'So very very sorry.'

I stare at the crumpled dirty cash.

Josh is right.

I've been dumped on Big Date Night.

Frazer Burns has done a Date Great Escape.

Chapter Seven

After we bunged some money on the table, Lucy stormed out and I staggered after her, and then we both stood round the corner whilst she made the emergency Mum Taxi call. Waiting for Bella to arrive, Luce expected Josh to come out of The Curry Cottage and start looking for her, and I hoped FB would turn up or text, but we were left alone, shivering in the cold, sobbing into each other's arms. Luckily I was able to retrieve the tissues I'd stuffed in my bra so we could at least wipe our noses on something other than our sleeves.

When Bella turned up and we were safely inside The Beast Car speeding away from the wreckage of our date disaster, she gave us some speech about this not being the first time our hearts would be broken, and that there were plenty more fish in the sea, yadda, yadda, yadda. I then started wondering what sort of a fish most described FB and decided on a slippery eel because I was mad at being dumped, and it was the most revolting fish I could think of at the time.

After Bella dropped me home, I went in, slammed the front door and stomped up to my room, hoping that Mum would hear and come up to find me tear-stained and distraught, and then be all sympathetic and suggest we crack open a tub of Häagen-Dazs Cookies & Cream ice cream. But no one put their head round the door with frozen goodies or even a jar of pickled veg, so I had to march noisily up and down the stairs several times before anyone made a move from the kitchen, where the telly was blaring out.

Finally Mum popped her head up and said, 'Boy trouble?' to which I'd nodded and she'd given me the same fish-in-the-sea speech Bella had spouted, except that saying *fish* made her think of a new preghead craving so she sent Phil out to the twenty-four-hour Tesco to get a jar of pickled herrings.

Why don't people say things like, *There's more cake in the shop*? or *Clothes on the rack*? i.e. nice things that you might want. Why do boys have to be likened to smelly slimy scaly things with pouting mouths and staring eyes that are difficult to catch without tons of effort, and are usually disappointing when you eat them unless they're coated in light crispy batter and smothered in tomato sauce? And then I went to bed, fell asleep and had a brief but very satisfying dream about dipping FB in batter and plunging him in hot oil.

I spent Sunday morning drawing fish with hooks in their mouths all over what was supposed to be my history assignment, which is going to baffle an already confused Poxy Moxy when he marks it, whilst hoping FB would make contact (which he didn't) and then hoping he doesn't, as I never want to see the slimy eel ever again. In the afternoon I lolled about in Sorrel's egg on wheels discussing my boys equals fish theory with a weeping Lucy who had a text from Josh at midday, but not comparing her to twinkly stars or pleading for them to start again, but to tell her that we both owe him another two quid for the bill, at which point we christened him Herring Head.

Sunday evening was better. I spent it jumping up and down on FB's jumper so hard, Mum came up and told me to be careful as the ceiling might cave in.

Dad had dropped it off after tea. He'd been to Nana's to get it and I did feel a bit mean when he handed it over and I just stood there with my best *Like I care now!* look and took it like it was infected with a deadly virus.

And now it's Monday, I'm going back to school and Fish Boy will be there.

* * *

I'd been pretty quiet on the bus as I couldn't face a date post-mortem from Tits Out and Butterface. When Claudia asked how my evening with FB went I just said, 'OK' in a non-committal sort of way, and was saved from further grilling by Natalie showing us one of her geography assignments whilst she tried to convince us that all the crosses in the margin were not actually wrong answers, but Buff's attempt to give her secret kisses.

'It's not gym today, is it?' Claudia says, spotting my bulging bag as we head through the grey metal gates into Burke's. 'I need to forge another note from Mum if it is.'

I shake my head. 'It's not kit,' I say. 'It's just some skanky stuff that belongs to a creep.'

I'm scanning the crowd to see if FB is around. There's no sign of him or his bike at the bike racks, and I don't notice him until we're in first reg and Sorrel digs me in the ribs and whispers, 'There's Fish Boy.'

I make sure my eyeballs don't flicker even a millimetre in FB's direction, but Claudia's goss-antenna must be tuned into its highest frequency as she turns round and says, 'Fish Boy?'

'FB,' Sorrel explains. I try to glare at her, ignore FB and avoid Claudia's stare, all at the same time. 'Electra and him have issues. He's a freakin' eel.'

Around me I can feel girls perk up from their usual Monday-morning slump.

'What's he done then?' Shenice Jones asks. 'He disrespected you?'

I'm mad at FB but I *so* don't want Shenice and her scary sidekick, Shaz Kamara, brought into this. They could start a fight in an empty box let alone a packed classroom.

Luckily, Mr McKay comes in and screams at us to settle down, which we do until we leave to go to our first lesson. There's a crush by the door, and as we spill out into the corridor in a sea of bodies and bags, I find I'm shoulder-to-shoulder with Fish Boy.

'Electra?'

'Yeah?' I'm trying to give him my most withering sideways glare coupled with a sneery mouth.

'About Saturday night.'

'What about it?' Let him grovel.

'Oy!' Shaz Kamara pushes through the crowd and pokes FB on the shoulder. 'Did you disrespect Electra?'

'No!' FB looks alarmed. 'I mean, I didn't intend to.'

By now we've stopped at the junction of several corridors ready to split into our various maths sets. Luce and me are in the bottom class, Sorrel is in the middle and FB is a turbo-charged superbrain.

'So you did!' Shenice snarls. Claudia, Nat and Tam are

here, as is Sorrel and a miserable-faced Luce. Shaz pins FB against the wall not with her body, but with a giant pink bubble of gum slowly expanding from her gob. 'I don't like lads that disrespect lasses, do I, Shaz?'

'Nah, she doesn't.' Shaz lets the pink bubble explode over her mouth before gathering up the gum with her tongue and chewing again. I'd like to point out she's got some gum still hanging from her lip-stud like a pink bogey, but I daren't in case she pins me against the wall too.

'Just leave it,' I say. However mad I feel at FB, I don't want him bullied by this gruesome twosome whilst everyone else looks on. Also, I'm going to be late for maths, and since I decided to become a hotshot lawyer and earn lots of dosh so that I can afford clothes that are mint rather than minging, I can't afford a late mark from Mrs Chopley and miss the opportunity to claw my way up to the middle set. 'Honestly, it was fine. It was nothing.'

I try and give FB a look that says, *I'm mega mad at you but I don't want you humiliated even if you did humiliate me.* Trouble is, I've never had to give that look before, never needed to perfect it in the mirror, so I've no idea what it looks like.

'I don't call a Date Great Escape nothing,' Claudia says. 'He legged it from The Curry Cottage on Saturday night.'

I glare at Sorrel. 'She wouldn't leave the Fish Boy

comment alone,' she explains, though really I think it's revenge for my forgetting the meat samosa I promised her.

Shaz looks menacing, though because she has her hair pulled up and back in a really tight high ponytail, it always makes her eyes look hard and mean.

'You left a lass sitting alone like some Billy No Mates?' she growls in FB's face.

'She was with Lucy and Josh,' FB squeaks. He's practically melting into the plasterboard wall to get away from her. I know he stood up to Pinhead last term but girl bullies are *much* scarier. 'I can explain.'

'Oh, well, that's all right then, isn't it?' Shaz says. 'Leaving her perched like some freaking lemon.'

'Stop it!' I snap at the mob. 'Stop it, all of you.'

I glare at FB. 'Why *did* you leg it?'

He looks red, sweaty and embarrassed. 'I . . . I . . .' He pulls at the collar of his white shirt and then tries to grab the knot of his tie. 'I . . .'

'Go on, we're waiting,' Claudia urges. 'Give Electra one good reason why you left her sitting like a saddo.'

'My bro Rupert is always, like, breaking girls' hearts,' Tamara Lennox-Hill adds. 'But even he wouldn't, like, just leg it.'

FB looks anxiously at all the girls clustered around. 'I . . . I left some money,' he pants. 'And you were with Lucy.'

Some of the girls call him a tosser, others just shake their heads and walk away. Shaz and Shenice pretend to spit at him and walk off arm in arm. He peels himself off the wall and stands there looking shocked.

I stare at him and don't know whether to cry or belt him with my bag. I really really thought there might be some good reason why he'd left me. An emergency call from home to say something terrible had happened, like his collection of computer mags had been sent to recycling by mistake and he'd been lying in bed all day on Sunday too grief-stricken even to touch his moby. But nothing terrible had happened. The only reason he left was because he didn't want to stay.

'Electra . . .' he begins.

'Leave it!' I snap. 'I don't want to hear any more.'

I open my school bag and drag out the blue jumper.

This is yours,' I say, shoving the pile of wool in FB's chest so hard he staggers back a few steps. 'I don't want it any more.'

Chapter Eight

My moby rings, I see who it is, press *ignore* and go back to watching Friday-night *Hollyoaks*.

Then the house phone rings.

'Leave it!' I scream as Mum goes to pick it up.

'Who is it calling?' she says, totally ignoring my instructions not to touch it. 'Hang on a moment.'

'It's that Frazer,' she whispers, holding her hand over the receiver. 'For you.'

At first I'd given Mum only the briefest hint of what had happened on Saturday night, which was that due to an unfortunate incident, an event too upsetting for me to discuss in any detail, Frazer Burns, once known as Freak Boy, then Fit Boy, has now mutated to Fish Boy, and his name or any derivatives thereof are never to be mentioned again in my presence unless it's to tell me some good news such as his family is relocating to Siberia. Mum then became hysterical that FB had done something like interfered with me against my wishes, so, to avoid stressing a preggers woman, I told her it was much worse than that: FB had done a Date Great Escape.

'Tell him I've died,' I say, sticking my feet on the end of the sofa and not moving a centimetre towards Mum, who's holding the phone towards me. 'No, tell him I'm out on a hot date with an upper-sixth lurve god from a posh school.'

'She can't come to the phone at the moment, Frazer,' Mum says, as I wonder whether even if I did get a hot date with an upper-sixth lurve god it would end up with him climbing through a window and me paying the bill. 'OK, I'll tell her.'

'Don't speak to him again,' I order as Mum hangs up. 'And don't tell me what he said.'

'He said he needs to see you.'

'I said, don't tell me!' I shriek, putting a cushion over my ears, a big mistake as I've caught one of Sorrel's shell earrings in the tassels.

'Perhaps if you saw him and gave him a chance to explain you'd get back together,' Mum suggests. 'Look at Lucy and her young man.'

'She's easily broken down,' I sneer, untangling myself from the soft furnishing. 'I'm made of harder stuff.'

Yes, after a week of tears, tantrums and texts, Lucy and Herring Head are back together. He spent all week trying to impress her and she finally cracked.

He was waiting for her by the bike racks on Monday but she just ran out of the gates where her mum was waiting for her and jumped in the car. Josh saw me and asked me to tell her he was really sorry and that he would still text her every day at noon, but could I give him the two quid I still owed him?

On Tuesday he braved the lunch queue and tried to talk to Luce, but whilst some of the younger girls got all giggly and starting tossing their hair to attract his attention, Luce cold-shouldered him whilst choosing a cold chicken salad.

Wednesday evening about eight, Luce said, the doorbell rang, her dad went to open it and trampled on a massive bunch of flowers left on the doorstep. There was a card with something slushy written on it, but unfortunately James got to see it before Luce, teased his little sis with it, so in retaliation and because she was in a seriously bad mood, Luce spilt the fact that Fritha was two-timing him with a drummer boy. James rang Fritha, who must have confirmed it was true as he then threw his phone down and punched the kitchen wall so hard he put a hole in the plaster, which sent Bella absolutely mental as apparently she'd had the paint colour mixed specially.

But on Thursday, Josh was waiting by the school gates, legs astride his bike.

'Ignore him!' Luce hissed, as me, Sorrel, Nat, Tam and Claudia were walking towards him on our way to Eastwood Circle for a mooch about the shops.

But as we passed, Josh shouted out, 'I LOVE YOU LUCY!' Luce dropped her bag, Josh dropped his bike, and they ate each other's faces for so long, we left them to it and went shopping without them.

FB has also been trying to contact me but, unlike Josh, Fish Boy's attempts to get in my good books are toe-curlingly far too little and much too late.

He tried to come up to me on Tuesday but I gave him a withering stare, linked arms with Sorrel and sauntered off pretending to laugh hysterically at something, even though Sorrel hadn't said anything.

I got some texts on Wednesday, five actually, but I deleted them all without reading them, and pressed *ignore* when he rang me after school. If he thinks he can get round me by waiting four days – four days! – before bothering to use his moby, he can drop dead.

Thursday I had period pains and although they weren't mega bad, I pretended to Mum they were and whilst she went off to her business studies course at Eastwood Tech, I lay around watching daytime TV, wishing I'd gone to school and wondering why FB was no longer sending me texts I could then ignore.

And now he's using Mum to get round me.

'He's had his chance and he blew it,' I say to her. 'No lad disrespects me and gets away with it.' I'm not sure whether that sounds tough or just makes me sound like a Shaz and Shenice wannabe, two girls I definitely don't want to be.

'Are you seeing the girls later?' Mum asks, extracting a green gherkin from a jar with her fingers. This pregnancy stuff has got her craving pickles of every description, which is weird as usually she's a total carb-face.

'No.'

'What are they up to then?' she says, diving in for another mini cucumber.

'Dunno.'

I do actually. Luce is seeing Herring Head and Sorrel is going to some meeting with her mum about saving the allotments from being turned into trendy flats.

'Go and see him,' Mum urges. 'Sort it out.'

I get up, throw down the remote control and stomp towards the kitchen door.

'Are you going to see him?' Mum asks through a mouthful of green gherkin.

'I'm going to my room,' I say.

* * *

I'm lying on my bed, staring up at the skylight in the roof, watching stars twinkle and the lights of aeroplanes crossing the sky, thinking that this time last week I was mega excited about Big Date Night and how since then my life had gone spectacularly downhill, when I notice a very bright star coming towards the glass.

Clearly a meteor is about to crash through the window and kill me, which is a shame as there would be loads of publicity, my picture on the news and in the papers, and I would be too dead to see it all.

Rather than die and miss out on my five minutes of fame, it would be lush if the meteor could injure me just a teeny bit, a minuscule graze somewhere that doesn't show, but just enough to make the local news.

I can be *very* shallow.

I pull the leg of my jeans up and stick my mottled pin towards the window. I could always hide a thigh or calf graze with thick black tights or leggings. I wear those or jeans most of the time anyway.

There's a little thud as the meteor lands on the window, but doesn't smash it.

Opening windows in a roof conversion is very low-tech. For hot days and unexpected meteors, I have a long pole with a hook on the end with which to drag open the window.

But when I open it, a whole tree of dead leaves floats in, the meteor buzzes, jumps into the air, and then hurtles to the ground where it lands on a pile of abandoned underwear.

It's not a meteor or a fallen star.

It's a small remote-controlled helicopter with a note stuck to it.

This has all the markings of an FB attempt to contact me, though I have to admit I'm pretty impressed by his resourcefulness. Beats trying to ambush me in the lunch queue or buying me flowers any day.

I pick up the dead whirlybird, untangle a bra strap from its tail, peel off the sellotaped note and unfold it. FB's obviously had second thoughts about dumping me and this will either be to say he's sorry, in which case I'll fling the helicopter back out of the open window and hope it crashes on his head, or it will be some slushy sentimental stuff to win me back.

The reason I left you sitting at the table was because the vindaloo made me puke at one end and have the raging squits at the other.

Not quite the love note I was expecting then.

I take the heli and the note downstairs, open the front door and go out into the street.

From behind a parked car on the opposite side of the

road, FB appears holding a box in both hands.

'So why didn't you come back to the table to say you were ill?' I shout across the street as I stand on the pavement outside our house.

'I rang Mum to ask her to pick me up because I felt so rough,' FB shouts back. 'She said she'd be there in ten minutes. I was just coming back to the table to tell you, when I needed to go again. I couldn't get off the loo, then when I thought Mum would be outside I just bunged some money down and ran for the car. The journey home was terrible. I was ill all day Sunday.'

It all sounds plausible, except, 'If you could call your mum, why couldn't you call me to let me know where you were? I left you a message.'

'After I rang her, I dropped my phone in the loo when I pulled my jeans down,' FB says. 'It was in my back pocket. I fished it out but it didn't work, but I saved the sim card. I only got a new one on Wednesday and then I started texting you.'

'Why didn't you say something at school?' I say. 'You've had a week.'

'You never gave me the chance,' FB says. 'What was I supposed to do, announce in front of all those girls I'd lost most of my insides in The Curry Cottage loos and had to get my mum to rescue me? Hardly the grown-up date you wanted, was it? I kept thinking you'd give me the chance to explain but you wouldn't let me near you.'

My mind races back over the last week. All those times I'd seen FB coming towards me and I'd turned away or ignored him and now he's having to give me an account of his Saturday-night squits in the street.

'Your dad thought I was a wimp and I thought you would too,' FB says. 'I thought you might have phoned me.'

'Josh told me not to,' I say. 'He thought you'd done a Date Great Escape and dumped me!'

'Dumped you!' FB says. 'How could you think that? I . . . I . . . adore you!'

I hadn't really noticed but we've gradually got closer and closer until we're standing together in the middle of the road. And I only realize we're in the middle of the road when a car bears down on us, headlights glaring, horn blaring.

We jump out of the way and on to the pavement, laughing.

'I'd put my arms around you, except I've got a helicopter control box in my hand!' FB says.

'And I'm holding the helicopter!' I giggle looking down at it. 'Its rotor blades are a bit bent from where it crashed.'

'Shall we start again?' FB says, giving me a short but sweet kiss on the lips.

'I think we'd better,' I say, kissing him back.

'If I'd been able to tell Mum you were in The Curry Cottage, this could have been avoided,' he says. 'I'm sorry.'

'And if my dad hadn't come in to check you out and you hadn't been trying to impress him by ordering a vindaloo, it *would* have been avoided,' I giggle.

'So it's all the parents' fault!' FB laughs. 'Look, I'm going to tell Mum and Dad about you, then we don't have to sneak around.'

'Don't,' I say. 'If you tell your mum and dad and I tell mine it will become all stressy. Let's just be mates that date, you know, really good friends, but friends that snog.'

'Date mates!' FB laughs. 'I'd like that, but,' he looks worried under the street light, 'you don't have any other good friends that you snog, do you?'

'Just you,' I giggle. 'Where do your parents think you are now?'

'Perfecting my night flights,' FB laughs, a lovely deep laugh.

We have another little kiss, and then I hand him back the battered helicopter.

'Hang on a minute,' he says, pushing the helicopter hardware at me.

'What are you doing?' I giggle as FB starts doing a striptease in the street, taking off his scarf and his green

112

jacket and then his jumper. The jumper he'd given me and I'd thrown back at him.

'If you still want it,' he says, shivering in just a black T-shirt. He puts the soft mound of wool in my arms. 'I noticed one of the sleeves is a bit shorter than the other and there's a sort of food stain on the elbow too.'

'I do,' I say. I go to bury my head in it, but as I'm still holding the heli stuff, I've also snuggled into one of the rotor blades, which has almost gone up my nose. I look up at my lovely lush Date Mate and beam. 'I always did.'

Chapter Nine

'Ouch!' I feel a searing pain in my left ear and pull away from FB, who starts spitting something out of his mouth, spraying my cheek with gob juice.

FB and I have been snogging for just over fifteen minutes without a break. I know this because over his shoulder I noticed the clock on the wall of the shopping centre at Eastwood Circle said four-thirty when we started, and when I opened my eyes in agony, it's just gone quarter to five on a Saturday afternoon.

'Sorry,' FB says. 'I was trying to nibble your ear but got a mouthful of earring.'

He fishes something out of his mouth and hands it to me. It's one of the shells in the earrings Sorrel gave me, now crushed flat by FB's molars.

Claudia couldn't be more wrong about me and FB only lasting a couple of months. We're having too much fun – as

114

very good mates that don't so much date as just hang out together and snog – to ever get bored of one another.

We've been snogging all around town for the last three weeks: the bus stop after school; a seat outside Debenhams at Eastwood Circle when no one else is using it as a snogging station; randomly in the street whenever we can; outside the newsagent's; inside the newsagent's until Mr Patel shouted and threw a copy of the *Sun* at us, and on the bench in Victoria Park until it gets so dark we both freak. We've been so public in our snogging, I'm amazed that FB's parents haven't spotted us and dragged us apart. If we're not snogging, we're using our mobys to take pictures of each other doing daft things. Well, mainly me doing daft things, such as trying to sit in the bin outside BK and getting my butt stuck or pretending a Flake is a cigar and smoking it.

Mum knows about us, though I've kept it all very casual to prevent her giving me a Bella-type speech.

FB spits a bit more crushed shell on to the pavement and lunges at me, but I pull away.

'What's the matter?' he says, looking hurt that I've disengaged our smackers. 'What's wrong?'

'I'm starving,' I say. 'My tum's growling.'

I read somewhere that strenuous romantic activity burns shed-loads of calories, which must have something to do with me always being famished after marathon snogging sessions.

'I could get you some chicken dippers,' FB suggests. 'With tomato sauce.'

I really need some fuel if I'm to get back to serious snogging, so I tell FB that I'd love some chicken and he trots off towards Burger King.

I'm about to get my mirror out and make sure that all this snogging and slurping hasn't dislodged any zit cover-up near my mouth, when a girl with a pram stands in front of me and says, 'You're that girl from Burke's, aren't you? The one I met in the doc's when I was massively preggers and you'd been beaten up?'

It's Cassie Taylor, the Year 11 girl who got pregnant before leaving school and had a baby before Christmas. I couldn't possibly forget her *or* her huge stomach with its sunburst tattoo. It was a toss-up whether there were more stretch marks or sun rays beaming out of her sticky-out belly button.

'I walked into a door,' I remind her. I'd nutted myself on the mirrored wardrobe doors when The Little Runt caught me practising my kissing technique on my reflection.

'Look, you wouldn't watch Tequila-Becks for five minutes, would you?' Cassie asks. 'Just five, I promise.'

I get up and peer into the pram. I'm more of a puppy

person than a baby person, but even I can see that the pink-faced tot snuggled under the pink-and-white blankets is a smiling cutie.

'I really need some new jeans, but it's a right pain trying to get in one of them changing rooms with five garments and a baby buggy.' Cassie looks glum. 'She's no bother. Honest.'

I'm about to tell Cass that in a few months I'll have another baby to worry about and that I don't want to spend even five minutes of my Saturday afternoon sprog-watching, but as I'll be sitting on the bench munching on either FB's face or BK's best for at least five minutes, why not help her out?

'You angel!' she says, fiddling around the pram handles to unhook her bag. 'Won't be long.'

Cassie's off like a rat up a drainpipe, but the nanosecond I see her bum disappear into the entrance of Top Shop, little Tequila-Becks starts to yell.

And yell and yell and yell.

I look in the pram. Her little face isn't pink and cute any longer; it's red and scrunched up in anger.

FB trots up clutching a box. Amazingly he doesn't look surprised to find that in the few minutes between leaving me and coming back, I've gained a screaming sprog.

'Whose is she?' he asks, peering at the bawling babe and smiling.

117

'She that girl's in the year above I told you about,' I yell over the noise, not a bright move as Cassie's daughter takes this as a sign a yelling competition is underway and ups her volume to glass-shattering levels. 'Remember, the one who called her kid Tequila-Becks, after the drinks?'

Tecky-B carries on screaming, which makes *me* want to scream.

'What do we do now?' I say.

'I don't know,' FB replies. 'Perhaps she's hungry.'

He goes to offer her a bit of chicken, which just sends her even more mental, so I take it from him and pop it into my mouth not just because I'm starving, but to stop me from yelling too.

I scan Top Shop hoping that, like some wild animal, Cassie will have heard the call of her young and come running out to see what's happened, but there's no sign of any female galloping towards her distressed child.

I try Mum at home and on her moby. She's bound to know what to do, or at least I hope she does when baby number three arrives or I'll never get any sleep with this racket. But both the house phone and Mum's mobile go to answerphone, and I don't want to leave a message saying, *I've got a baby and I don't know what to do*, a phrase guaranteed to send any parent into a manic mental meltdown.

I ring Sorrel. I have to admit, with seeing FB, and Luce spending all her time with Josh, neither of us have been paying much attention to her recently, but she'll know what to do. 'I've got a baby that won't stop crying!' I yell above the noise. 'Advice! Now! Please!'

'Whose baby?' Sorrel asks.

'Just tell me!' I snap. 'You've got sprog-minding experience.'

'Trying rocking the pram,' Sorrel says, as I pass on the instruction to FB.

It doesn't work, probably because FB's rocking the buggy so hard, Tequila-Becks is in danger of being catapulted out of the buggy and on to the pavement.

'Trying walking round with the pram,' Sorrel suggests when she hears the rugrat still yelling. 'Keep moving.'

'She says, start walking around,' I shout at FB, who sets off with the pram, circling the seat.

Amazingly Tequila-Beck's cries grow less and less until on about the fifth circuit, she's fast asleep, looking pink and angelic, but with two huge yellowy/green bogies oozing from her nose.

'It's defo more than five minutes,' I say, pushing the pram round again. We haven't dared stop in case T-B starts yelling again, but the turning circle is quite tight and too many

119

times round the seat makes me dizzy, so we've been taking it in turns. 'If you take over, I'll go into Top Shop and find AWOL mum.'

FB takes the pram and I head off to the mini Temple of Style. But despite looking round the store and hanging about the changing rooms, there's no sign of Cassie. I come out, notice FB's still marching round with the pram, and go into New Look.

Nothing. But I do notice the fringed boots that Fritha The Bra Bitch wore at The Curry Cottage and try a pair on. They're fabulous and they fit, so I blow my entire month's allowance on them, even though it meant I had to queue up and be served by Sorrel's snotty sister Jasmine, who works there on Saturdays.

I head back to FB, swinging the bag with my new purchase inside.

'She's gone,' I say. 'Not in Top Shop, not in New Look, wouldn't be seen dead in M&S jeans, but I bought a fab pair of new boots.'

'Unless you think she's abandoned her daughter, she'll be back,' FB says confidently. 'We'll keep going for a bit.'

As I take the pram handles, FB reaches in and tucks the blanket around the sleeping baby.

'When we have kids, what shall we call them?' he says. 'How do you feel about Oliver and Fleur?'

I'm rooted to the spot. I couldn't be more shocked if a spaceship landed outside M&S and little green men with antennae marched in to buy prawn sandwiches and a three-pair pack of pants.

When we have kids? *When?* That's years away, if at all. I can't even make plans for next weekend without wanting to change them all the time.

I look at FB cooing over the baby and suddenly feel panicked and smothered. I thought we were having fun hanging out as mates that dated, but in his mind FB has me down the aisle and up the duff with Oliver and Fleur. My heart begins to race and I feel my chest tighten. This wasn't part of our deal to be mates that date! Somehow I've got to let FB know, gently, that I do want to go out with him, I think he's gorgeous and lovely and there's no one else I'd rather go out with, but I get more excited about suede boots than baby names.

'Hello.'

We both look up to see Dr Fiona Burns next to us, weighed down with M&S food bags.

'Mum!' FB smiles. 'I thought you were working.'

'And I thought you were studying.' Glam Doc twists her face as if she's also found a bit of Caribbean shell under her tongue. 'Clearly not.'

She looks me up and down. 'Hello, Electra.'

'Hi, Doc Burns, I mean Mrs Burns, I mean Doctor Burns . . .' I'm gabbling.

FB's mum leans into the pram.

'And who do we have here?' she says, her face finally cracking a smile. 'She's adorable.'

'Tequila-Becks,' FB says. 'We've only just managed to get her to sleep.'

'She was yelling,' I add. 'Driving me mad. I don't know how I'm going to cope in the future, but I hope Mum will know what to do, having had two carpet crawlers already.'

Doc Burns straightens up. 'Looking after a baby is a big responsibility, Electra.' She's glam but scary.

'I know,' I nod, thinking it's no wonder Cassie's done a runner. I've only been looking after Tecky-B for twenty minutes or so and I'm fed up.

'But I've been helping out,' FB beams. 'Pushing the pram and tucking her in.'

Doc Burns looks at me and then at FB. 'Frazer, is there something I should know?'

I notice Doc Burn's horrified face and realize she thinks Tecky-B is *my* baby and that FB is somehow involved. I thought we'd got over that misunderstanding at Christmas.

'Oh, she's not mine!' I say, pushing the pram away slightly. 'I was looking after her for a friend, well, not really a friend, just a girl in the year above me actually. She used to hurdle for the school until she got preggers, of course then she had to stop putting her leg over . . .' I manage to stop myself babbling. 'It's my mum that's having a baby, but she's never hurdled, as far as I know.'

'Actually, Mum, there is something,' FB says as the baby begins to snuffle and struggle beneath her blanket. I've an awful feeling that now we're not circling the seat, Tecky-B is going to start inflating her little lungs again.

'Electra and I are seeing each other.'

I look up from baby-watching to see Doc Burn's face tighten.

'We have been for forty-five days, twenty-one hours, forty-five minutes and twenty seconds, haven't we?'

'Have we?' I say, realizing I haven't actually been counting the hours, let alone the seconds.

'I set the timer on my watch the moment you said you'd go out with me on Christmas Day,' FB explains. 'Well, not the moment, but an approximation of the moment. I took it as eight o'clock, when you texted me back.'

He starts rocking the pram with one hand and puts his arm around my shoulders with the other, and even I can see that Doc Burns must be freaked at the sight of her teenage son playing happy families with a borrowed baby and a girl she thinks is out to corrupt him. I'm freaked that FB wants to have children with me, has chosen their names and is timing our life together.

I take a step away from the pram *and* from FB.

Doc Burns does not look happy, but before she can explode, Cassie arrives, huffing and puffing but without any sign of shopping bags.

'Soz!' she says. She looks in the pram. 'Told you she'd be good as gold, didn't I?'

'That was the longest five minutes in history!' I say through gritted teeth. 'Where've you been?'

'I just ran into some mates and we had a coffee,' she says. 'Not a problem, was it? Anyway, I'm back now. Ta!' She loops her bag over the pram handle and then she's off, pushing the buggy through the shopping centre, her phone clamped to her ear.

'That was fun,' FB says to me. 'Wasn't it?'

I just want to get home and put my new boots on.

'Frazer . . .' Doc Burns starts.

'Mum,' FB says firmly. 'I know you think Electra is a bad influence on me, but there's nothing you can do to stop us seeing each other. We're totally in love and it's *very* serious.'

'Is it?' Doc Burns asks me.

I'd like to have run out of Eastwood Circle, hijacked the nearest car and screamed, 'Take me to the airport!' where'd I try to get on a flight to Australia. But as that's not going to happen without a passport or ticket and I've only got my bus pass and just blown all my money on boots, I stand there *horrified*.

Doc Burns takes my silence as a *Yes*.

'Then I think it's about time I met your parents, don't you, Electra?'

Chapter Ten

'Josh told me he loves me,' Luce says. 'I think it's sweet.'

'We know,' Sorrel says rolling her eyes. 'He did it in front of half the school.'

'Well, this isn't sweet!' I say, pacing around my bedroom, picking my way through discarded knickers and the odd bra. 'It's terrible!'

After the *In love and it's serious* speech I convened an emergency meeting on Sunday afternoon with Luce and Sorrel, and specifically chose my bedroom to prevent Luce dragging Josh along. They're spending so much time together Sorrel and I have started calling them LuJo.

'So you've never given FB the *I love you too* speech?' Luce asks.

I shake my head. I've said I love Cadbury's Flakes or I love Edward in *Twilight*, but I've never so much as whispered the L word in connection with FB.

'And what's with the whole meet-the-parents routine?' I shriek. 'What's that all about?'

Somehow I've agreed that Doc and Mr Burns can pop round early on Monday evening to meet Mum, presumably to check that she's not a drug addict and I'm not living in a twenty-four-hour crack den, or whatever it is they're worried about.

'It's totally understandable,' Sorrel says. 'Given that FB has given them the impression you're about to get married and start sprogging Oliver and Fleur.'

Luce and Sorrel giggle. I'm not giggling. I am totally freaked, not just by FB assuming that we're serious, but by the thought that at any moment he can look at his watch and tell me how long we've been dating, down to the nearest second.

'Stop it, you two!' I shout. 'Stop it! This is doing my head in and you're not helping!'

'I don't get it,' Sorrel says. 'You wanted FB to fancy you and now he clearly fancies the pants off you, you don't fancy him.'

'I do,' I say. 'I just don't want him to be that keen. It's scary!'

'Perhaps it was just the thrill of the chase,' Luce suggests. 'You know, he was more exciting before you got to know him than when you really did know him.'

'And there's still Tits Out and her prediction,' Sorrel reminds me. 'She said you'd be finished in two months.'

'She said we'd be finished because I'd find him boring,' I say, 'not because he wants to get married and I don't.' I hunt around and find a piece of paper and my four-in-one coloured pen. 'I need to make a list of FB pros and cons.'

I click on the black button, make two columns, write *For* and *Against* at the top, and draw a line down the middle.

'He's kind; he's thoughtful; he's a super snogger; he's always there for me; we spend hours talking . . .' I start writing things in green on the *For* side of the list.

'Sounds more like me and Sorrel than a boyfriend,' Luce interrupts.

'Except we don't snog you,' Sorrel points out.

'OK, *Against*,' I say, writing *Too Keen* at the top of the right-hand column in red capital letters.

'He's boring,' Sorrel says. 'Go on. Admit it. You're getting close to a boredom break-up.'

'Just because he doesn't ride a jet ski doesn't mean he's boring!' I say, jabbing the pen in her direction. 'He just needs to chill a bit, that's all.'

'I think FB is the human equivalent of your burgundy ankle boots,' Sorrel says. 'You saw them, you lusted after them, you dreamt about them, you were really excited when you got them on Christmas Day, but now you've got them, you've gone off them and have fallen for flashy fringes.' She flips the soft suede strips with her hand as she examines my new footwear purchase.

I don't know what to say. Sorrel comparing FB to a pair of boots is scarily accurate, right down to the fact that I got both of them for Christmas. But she's missing one thing out.

'My feet must have grown since I got them as they don't fit me any longer.'

'Perhaps you've grown out of FB,' Luce suggests. 'Already.'

'So, tell me again,' Mum says, as we wait for the family Burns to descend on 14 Mortimer Road. 'You are sort of but not really going out with Frazer Burns, but he thinks the two of you are serious, which you say you're not, and his parents think you're both serious *and* a bad influence on their son?'

'That's about it,' I say, wondering whether I've overdone the make-up. With my complexion it's a fine line between looking pasty or tarty, and that third coat of lash-lengthening mascara might have been a mistake. 'FB's got a bit keen and his mum's got a bit angsty.'

'So she said on the phone,' Mum says. 'Isn't this a bit over the top if you're just friends?'

'Well, a bit more than friends,' I say, not wanting to go into any snogging specifics with my mother.

The doorbell rings and Mum and I go upstairs into the hall. Phil's gone out for a drink with some of his AA chums and Jack is already in bed, so he's one less problem to worry about. The Little Scroat rushing in and telling Mr and Doc Burns that he caught me snogging myself in the mirror would just about finish me off.

'Mrs Brown.' Doc Burns is standing on our doorstep, her hand outstretched. 'Pleased to meet you. I'm Fiona Burns.'

'Call me Ellie,' Mum says, shaking Doc B's hand.

FB beams and steps forward. 'I've brought you some piccalilli, Mrs Brown,' he says, handing Mum a jar with something alarmingly bright yellow in it. 'Electra told me about your cravings so I thought you might appreciate a range of pickled vegetables in a lightly spiced mustard sauce.'

Josh bought Bella some expensive blooms, but Mum looks delighted at her salty snack in a jar. 'That's very thoughtful of you,' she smiles. 'Come down to the kitchen, it's warmer in there.'

It's a bit of a tight squeeze getting Doc Burns and FB past a five-months-preggers Mum, through a hall full of junk and downstairs to the kitchen. Mum asked me if I'd prefer to clear the front room and we could sit in there, but that would just mean moving the pram and the cot (another card-in-the-newsagent's-window purchase) and various bags of baby clothes Phil brought down from the loft, not to mention the piles of old magazines and newspapers that are a permanent fixture in the front room, which seems too much effort for the parents of a boy I have no intention of marrying, only snogging.

'I'm afraid Frazer's father, Duncan, couldn't come,' Doc Burns explains as Mum leads the way and I follow up the rear. 'He's entertaining clients.'

This is a bummer as Duncan Burns is such a Hot Dad I'd hoped that seeing him might remind me that FB has amazing potential and is a keeper, even if he is freaking me out with his long-term plans for blissful coupledom.

'Electra's father can't be here either because he was always off entertaining people too!' Mum laughs. 'We're divorced.'

I think Doc Burns thinks Mum is suggesting FB's dad is having an affair under the smokescreen of work, as she says rather tightly, 'However, he will be back tonight.'

'Coffee?' Mum asks, flicking the kettle on when we're in the kitchen. 'Or something stronger? And do sit down.'

'Nothing for me, thank you,' Doc Burns says, sitting on the sofa, but jumping up again very quickly as she seems to have speared her butt with one of Jack's plastic dinosaurs.

She puts it on the coffee table in front of her. 'Frazer told me you were pregnant but I hadn't realized how far along you are. When are you due?'

I go to the fridge, get a couple of Diet Cokes and throw one across the room to FB, a mistake, as he drops it, picks it up, opens it and showers his face with sugar-free froth.

'Well, I hadn't realized I was pregnant so I'm only going by the hospital,' Mum says, biting into a whole pickled egg. 'They say early June but I was late with the first two.' As FB and I sit at the kitchen table, Mum perches on the arm of the sofa and finishes off her pickled egg, licking her vinegary fingers before wiping them on her black trousers. 'Now, from what you said on the phone, you're concerned about Electra and Frazer. I've talked to Electra and I really don't think you have anything to worry about, Fiona.'

'You do know they're only fourteen?' Doc Burns points out.

'I'm fifteen next month,' FB butts in. 'On March the fifteenth.'

'Don't you think fourteen is a little young to get serious?' Fiona Burns presses.

Mum smiles. 'I think perhaps Electra isn't quite as serious about your son as he is about her, but that's often the way, isn't it?'

'Aren't you?' FB says, looking at me. I can hardly shatter

his illusions sitting at our kitchen table in front of his mother, plus, being Diet Coke damp, he looks cute, so I just shrug, feel embarrassed and mutter, 'Dunno.'

Mum swivels her head around and raises her eyebrows at this apparent change of heart. She turns back to Doctor Burns. 'I don't think that you need to worry about them. I know Electra has her moments, but really she's very sensible, and from what I've seen of Frazer, he's very . . .' Mum seems to be searching for a word to describe FB, 'straightforward.'

'I know, I know,' Doc Burns sighs and nods. She seems to be relaxing in the warmth of our kitchen. 'It's just, well, you must remember when you were young and your hormones were racing?'

'Of course!' Mum laughs. 'I met Electra's father when I was sixteen. That's how I ended up being a teen mum myself.'

The kitchen suddenly doesn't seem so cosy any more. Doc Burns is sitting ramrod-straight on the sofa, something I thought was superhumanly impossible given how saggy the cushions are.

'Oh, not until the sixth form,' Mum assures her. 'Well, actually, the summer holidays *after* the sixth form, or was it the last week of sixth form? Sorry, my hormones are all over the place and I've a memory like a sieve.'

Doc Burns's face is a picture and not a very pretty one.

'I had to leave university in the first term to have Electra, which I why I know she won't make the same mistake, although,' Mum pats her tummy, 'of course I did! Who says lightning never strikes twice!'

I look at FB, who's fiddling with his watch. I start to wonder if he's about to hit the *Stop* button as this clearly is the point when Doc Burns forbids her son to see anyone in the Brown family ever again, and instead of feeling upset, I feel a strange sense of relief at the prospect of it all being taken out of my hands.

The doorbell rings again.

'I'll get it!' I say, pushing back my chair and racing upstairs. I could do with a break from the tension downstairs.

'Dad!'

My father, wearing a baggy grey tracksuit, is standing red-faced and panting on the doorstep, clutching his chest as if he's having a heart attack.

'What's wrong?'

'Water. Need water,' he gasps. 'Might have overdone this keep-fit lark.' He gobs over the low wall on to Ethel and Frank Skinner's front step, which must hit their mega-moggy Tiny as it yells and darts into the road. 'I'm having a heart attack.'

'Come in,' I say, pulling him into the hall by a wodge

of grey material. It strikes me that if Dad *is* about to have an exercise-induced middle-aged heart attack, it's an amazing stroke of luck that we have a doctor in our kitchen basement. 'Phil's out but Mum's in. We're in the kitchen.'

Dad staggers down the stairs in front of me, heads straight for the sink, turns on the tap, sticks his head underneath the running water and guzzles it.

'This is my dad,' I announce over the noise of great watery gulps. 'He's taken up running.'

Dad stops his gulping, turns off the tap, swipes a green-and-white tea towel from a hook on the wall, wipes his face with it, blows his nose on it and then sticks it back on the hook.

'Phew! That's better,' he pants. Then just when I think the father humiliation is over, he grabs a handful of grey material around his crotch area and does some rearranging. 'Haven't done any sort of sport since school and even then we used to stop off for a fag and a can of cider during cross-country running.'

'Rob, this is Frazer Burns and his mother, Fiona,' Mum says sounding tense. 'Electra and Frazer are,' I will her to say something casual, 'good friends.'

Dad looks at FB. 'I know, we've met. You were that lad in The Curry Cottage.' He pulls a kitchen chair out, turns it round and sits facing Doc Burns with his legs spread-eagled.

'Electra was at The Curry Cottage?' Doc Burns queries, raising an eyebrow at her son. 'You didn't say she was there. Whose idea was it not to tell me?'

Clearly the implication is that it was mine.

'Actually, it was Frazer who disappeared and left my daughter sitting there,' Mum says tightly. 'Electra thought he'd dumped her.'

'He did what?' Dad turns to glare at FB. 'You did the Great Date Escape?'

'I had diarrhoea!!' FB says. 'Terrible squits.'

'Vindaloo too much for you?' Dad asks sarkily. 'I expect you're more of a wimpy korma kid.'

'How dare you speak to my son like that?' Fiona Burns snaps. 'He's only fourteen!'

'He's old enough to have designs on my daughter!' Dad retorts.

'I'm nearly fifteen,' FB says lamely. 'And I've explained about my digestive disaster.'

This doesn't seem to be going well and if FB thinks I'm going to want to marry him after he's discussed his curry-induced bowel habits with my tracksuited father, he's *so* wrong.

'All right, all right, keep your wigs on,' Dad says. 'I was only saying.'

Fiona Burns gets up from the sofa, puts her hands on her hips and glares at Dad. 'We've met before,' she says, sounding suspicious.

'I don't think so,' Dad snorts.

'You shouted at me in the street outside The Curry Cottage. What was it you said? Let's see, something about women in posh cars thinking they're the mutt's nuts?'

Oh. My. God. Doc Burns was Horn Woman!

'I seem to remember you started it!' Dad snaps.

'Look,' Mum says, baring her teeth at Dad. 'Fiona came round because she's worried about Electra and Frazer going out together.' She turns to Frazer's mum. 'I hope you feel more comfortable having met us.' She gets up from the arm of the sofa and starts walking towards the door, which is clearly a sign for everyone to get out of her kitchen, *now*.

'I'm sorry, Ellie, but I don't think that either of you are taking this seriously enough,' Doc Burns says, not moving a millimetre towards the door. 'Clearly Electra is a lovely girl and I can see why my son is smitten with her. However, the fact remains that your daughter seems to attract trouble as well as boys. Let's just say she's sassy and streetwise whereas Frazer is more serious and sensitive.'

In other words, the snobby Doc is saying I'm common and FB's posh!

Dad makes a grunting noise but Mum points a finger at him and snaps, 'Rob, I'll deal with this.'

She rounds on FB's mum. 'Now listen here, Fiona. We are both extremely proud of our daughter and the way she's handled our marriage breaking up, not to mention the prospect of a surprise new baby, aren't we?' She looks at Dad, who nods. 'It's not been easy for her and she's shown maturity and understanding all the way along, hasn't she?'

I think they must have another daughter as they've never said any of this about me before, in fact quite the opposite.

'It wasn't Electra's fault that I started playing hide the gherkin away from home,' Dad says. 'Her brother started nicking tampons and playing up, but Electra's been fine.'

Hide the gherkin? Pinching sanitary supplies? Perhaps I should just climb into the fridge and shut the door behind me. I may be having second thoughts about FB but I don't want my family to be branded as liars and thieves.

'So you're just ignoring the fact that because of Electra, Frazer got excluded from school last term, are you?' Doc Burns flashes. 'Had it skipped your mind or are you going to blame *that* on your hormones?'

'Oh, there's nothing wrong with my memory of that day,' Mum retorts, her voice laced with acid or possibly pickled-egg vinegar. 'Perhaps *you* need reminding that it was *your* son that hit that other boy. Our daughter had nothing to do with it.'

'So she was hauled in front of the headmaster for nothing?' Doc Burns laughs sarcastically. 'And what about the bet then? Your daughter used *my* son to win a bet!'

'I knew nothing about a bet.' Dad turns to me. 'What did you win?'

'She won a designer handbag,' FB says glumly.

'Nice one,' Dad grins putting his thumbs up.

'And what about the time Electra was found semi-naked in the gutter on Christmas Day?' Doc Burns says. 'She turned up at our house in a terrible state, crying about being pregnant!'

'I had a miniskirt, a pinny and a paper crown on!' I mutter, thinking that hardly counts as starkers in the street. 'And I was crying because Mum was preggers!'

'Yeah, that ruined Christmas Day,' Dad chips in. 'Rotten timing, Ellie.'

If this was happening in the school playground we'd all be standing around chanting *Fight! Fight! Fight!* until a teacher came to break it up.

I lean across the table to FB. 'Aren't you going to say something?' I whisper.

FB just smiles at me as if he's totally unaware that around us the two families are trying to score points off each other.

I've had enough of this.

'Stop it!' I yell, getting up from the table. 'Stop it, all of you.'

The grown-ups look sheepish and FB looks shocked.

'You're all arguing about nothing!' I say. 'Doctor Burns, I can see why you're worried about Frazer and me but there's nothing to stress about, honestly. Frazer and I are just really good friends. We know we're far too young to be serious.'

'We do?' FB says, his bottom lip quivering.

'We do,' I say firmly.

'Well,' Doc Burns says. 'I'll say one thing for you, Electra. You're certainly spirited.' And for the first time all evening, she smiles.

'Sorry if I came on a bit strong,' Fiona Burns says as we leave the kitchen. 'Teenagers can be such a worry, and when you have an only child . . .'

'I understand,' Mum says, patting Doc Burns sympathetically on her shoulder.

'And then there's the geography trip next week. The two of them away, in the fresh air . . .'

Doc Burns clearly thinks we're going to be up to no good, despite the school sending a letter to say the girls and boys would be housed in separate blocks and supervised at all times, making it sound as if the field trip is being held in a prison.

'We all just want the best for our children, don't we?' Mum says soothingly as we troop along the hall. 'It's up to us to act as role models.'

Mum ushers Doc Burns towards the door and opens it.

There's a thud, a groan, an overpowering smell of alcohol and a clearly plastered Phil rolls into the hall and spontaneously voms over the doormat.

'Who on earth is that?' Doc Burns gasps, sidestepping the river of puke.

'That,' I say, 'is Mum's boyfriend. The father of her baby.'

Chapter Eleven

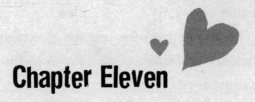

'So just because you don't want to be serious, it doesn't mean you want to go out with someone else?' FB asks as we wait in Tesco's car park for the coach to take us on our GCSE geography field trip, two nights and three days in an outdoor centre to study coastal erosion. 'If you'd gone off me, you would tell me, wouldn't you?'

'Course I would,' I say as I watch a succession of cars, parents and bleary-eyed kids arrive. Phil's on an early shift so he offered to run me and Sorrel here, meaning I was one of the first to arrive, other than FB who must have been up at the crack of dawn to get here before me.

'So we're OK? There's nothing for me to worry about?' FB presses.

'Course not,' I say.

It's been over a week since the parental kitchen summit, and FB and I have had this *Are you going off me?*

conversation about a million times. Quite frankly, it's getting on my nerves, especially when he does it at school, in the corridor, between lessons and in front of my friends. I asked Paul Cottismore if he'd done his history homework, just because I wanted to know whether I was the only one who hadn't, as if so I wouldn't feel quite so bad telling Poxy Moxy it would be late, and it sent FB into a frenzy of, 'Why didn't you ask me?' 'I could have helped you.' 'Why were you asking Paul before you asked me?' yadda yadda yadda, even though I explained I didn't ask him because he *never* hands his homework in late. It's like FB's watching my every move, not to mention his watch timing it.

'So you don't find me boring,' FB continues. 'You still want to go out with me.'

'Course I do,' I say, nudging him in the ribs and trying to force a smile. 'I gave you a Valentine card this morning, didn't I?'

FB beams at the thought of the card I'd given him. It had taken me about an hour in Clinton Cards to choose the right one, one that was more jokey than romantic. In the end, whilst Lucy got one for Josh that had a red padded heart on the front and a verse so long and sugary I lost the will to live halfway through reading it, I plumped for one with two budgies in a cage saying, *You're So Tweet*.

'And you liked your present, didn't you?' FB sounds

anxious. 'You'd say if you didn't, wouldn't you?'

'She loved it,' Sorrel chips in. 'Didn't you?'

I can't look at her.

'It's just, you didn't want to bring it with you on the trip.' FB looks worried. 'I thought you might have thought it a bit over the top.'

I look across at Phil's titchy blue Toyota parked under a street lamp, a life-size pink teddy bear with a white bow round its neck strapped into the front seat by the seat belt.

'It wouldn't fit in my luggage,' I say. 'That's all.'

'So you definitely still want to go out with me? I mean, I know I keep asking but you would tell me if you didn't, wouldn't you?' FB grabs my hand with his leather-gloved mitt. I don't feel as if I'm holding hands with my boyfriend, I feel as if I'm being pawed by Freddy Krueger.

'I still don't understand what the problem about becoming serious is,' FB says as we watch Josh and Lucy having the sort of goodbye that is just about acceptable if your boyfriend is going off to war, but completely inappropriate for a two-night three-day school trip. 'Lucy and Josh are serious.'

'Luce had already been out with that French lad, Pascal,' Sorrel growls. 'He was her practice boyfriend.'

'So you're saying I'm Electra's practice boyfriend?' FB

144

sounds alarmed. 'A sort of trial run before she moves on to the real thing?'

'She didn't mean it like that,' I say, throwing Sorrel a look. 'Did you?'

Sorrel just shrugs and stamps her feet to keep warm.

FB grips my hand. 'You know it's my birthday on the fifteenth of March? I thought it would be great if we could all go out for a meal. You know, me, Mum, Dad and you.' FB smiles, and for the first time his smile doesn't make my heart melt. It makes me want to put a bag over his head so I can't see it. 'I thought we could all go to The Galloping Greek, you know, the one Angela Panteli's father runs?'

'It's ages away,' I say.

'And maybe your mum and Phil might like to come too,' FB says. 'It would be great if we could all get to know each other better.'

Despite being splashed with partly digested lager and pork scratchings, Doc Burns seemed pretty cool over Phil vomming on the doorstep, but she's still scary and the thought of sitting eating a plate of stuffed vine leaves with FB's mum makes *me* want to vom.

'I'll ask them,' I mutter, catching Sorrel's eyes, which are rolling so much they're practically spinning out of their sockets.

At last the coach trundles into the car park and pulls up

next to the trolley bay, and with a last wave at Phil, I climb on board. FB clearly wants to sit next to me, but I want to sit next to Sorrel so I push her into a seat and plonk myself next to her.

He hovers for a moment, and then gets carried along the coach by a tide of kids wanting to get in out of the cold.

'Mr Butler!'

I wince as Sorrel practically pierces my eardrum with her shriek. She's hanging over the headrest of the seat and waving at Buff, who's at the front of the coach, holding a clipboard and looking totally gorge, despite it being six-thirty in the morning, and wearing a nerdy red anoraky-type coat. 'Mr Butler!'

'Yes, Sorrel, what is it?' Buff calls back.

'Can you tell the driver to switch the engine off? He's wasting energy keeping it running.'

Several people, including me, groan. I'm all for this saving-the-planet stuff, but Sorrel went from not caring whether the planet burnt itself out as long as it didn't do it whilst she was alive and able to eat burgers in Macky D's, to being a total eco-warrior and, to be honest, a right pain. She tells us off for using plastic carrier bags; came round to my house one night and gave Mum a lecture about how she'd stood on the street and seen light coming out of just about every window; is always going on at Luce about

Bella's 4x4 and fishes stuff out of the bins to put in the recycling. The weird thing is, she wants to go back to Barbados (which I think is more to do with seeing The Jozster than helping marine conservation in the Caribbean), which of course means going on a plane, which means increasing her carbon footprint to at least size twenty, but when I've pointed this out, she just says, 'Joz says we all have to start somewhere.' She's even decided she'd rather be a marine biologist than in the police, though I think she only wants the marine bit if it involves the warm and blue Caribbean rather than the freezing grey Atlantic.

'The driver says he needs to keep the engine running to keep the heater going,' Buff shouts, before carrying on studying his list.

Sorrel slumps back in her seat. 'Joz says everyone should try turning their heating down' she grumbles, which is great advice if you're living in the West Indies rather than the UK. She elbows me in the ribs. 'I thought you'd want to sit with luvver boy.'

'I'd rather sit with you,' I say. 'I see FB loads.'

'What's going on with you two?' she asks. 'You seem a bit angsty around him at the mo.'

I look around to see where FB's sitting. He's further back, next to Paul Cottismore, probably giving *him* the third degree over what he said to me about my history homework.

'It's that whole Oliver and Fleur stuff,' I say. 'He's suffocating me. I feel he's practically stalking me.'

'Well, at least the next few days will give you a breather,' Sorrel says. 'I can't see Buff and Hammy Chops allowing him to stalk you on the sands.'

'Did you see that?' Butterface cries as she heads down the coach and sits opposite me and Sorrel, and next to Claudia who's filing her nails. 'Buff pushed himself right up against me!' She's dressed as if she's going to a nightclub and is in triple-churned mode she's got so much slap on. She must have been up at the crack of dawn this morning to trowel it on.

'He *so* did not!' I say. It's not just Tits Out who's getting fed up of Nat's Buff fantasy. We all are. 'You pushed past him and he pushed you down the coach.'

'He did so,' she says sulkily. 'The moment I leave school, I just know he's going to ask me out.'

Given that legally we're not able to leave school for nearly eighteen months, Nat's got a long time to wait for her teacher-date.

'I think he's got the hots for Miss Rogers,' Claudia says, stopping her early morning mani for a moment. She points her nail file at The Hamster, who's at the front of the coach, huddled over Buff's clipboard. 'I think he goes for little women with puffy cheeks.'

'He can't fancy her,' Nat pouts. 'That woman doesn't know the meaning of the word *blusher*.'

'Come on, Lucy!' The Hamster calls out of the coach door. 'Get a move on.'

Luce gets on the coach and makes her way towards us, waving at Josh all the way down before sitting just behind us, next to Tam.

Josh appears at the window, blowing kisses and waving.

'I think it's so unfair we're away for Valentine's Day,' she moans as the coach finally pulls out of the car park. 'We wanted to spend it together.'

'There'll be loads of cards for me when we get back,' Claudia says confidentially. 'There always is.'

'I bet Jon would send me a card if he could,' Nat sighs.

'I hope they're all made out of recycled paper,' Sorrel grumbles.

'Well, that was a big disappointment.' Claudia dumps her bags on one of the six blue-and-white-checked-duvet-covered beds. 'Zero chance to wear a bikini.'

'It's a field trip in February!' I point out. 'When did you think you were going to be able to use a tiny triangle?'

'The timetable said we had a day on the beach,' Claudia says. 'I brought a matching cover-up and shaved my bits and pits specially.'

'I think it's been cold and boring,' I moan, dumping my bag on a bed and wondering whether doing GCSE geography has been the right choice after all, even if we are taught by top Teacher Totty.

So far we've spent three hours on a coach; been shown around a bit of bog by a man with a wiry grey beard; had lunch in a wooden hut with humungous spiders running around; spent another hour on the bus and then the afternoon being lashed by a freezing wind as we clambered over rocks by the coast looking for fossils in limestone.

Luce nearly fell in the bog when Josh's text arrived at bang on midday; Sorrel's moaned that there are no jet ski trips to go on; Pinhead's been making us cringe by telling filthy jokes and boasting that he's smuggled some booze in his bag; Claudia's life has been ruined over breaking a nail on the rocks; Tam's coat isn't warm enough so she's been shivering all day; and I've been trying to ignore the fact that every time I look up, FB's staring or smiling at me.

'What's the situ with you and FB?' Claudia asks, lying back on her bed and examining her split ends. 'You seemed kinda cool to him today.'

'It was a cool kinda day,' I remind her.

'You know what I mean,' she says. 'I still give it two months max, which means you've got about three weeks to go.'

'I think Buff and The Hamster are going to get it together,' I say, lying back on a lumpy pillow, flicking through hundreds of shots on my camera, trying to change the subject. 'They seem pretty close if you ask me.'

I've gone mental with the camera today. I've been snap-snap-snapping anything and everything, which has made Miss Rogers and Buff think I'm well keen on putting together a great project.

'They are so not,' Butterface snaps.

'Well, they were this arvo,' I say. 'I've got evidence!'

In one of my snapping frenzies I've got a picture of Buff on the beach with his arm loosely around The Hamster's shoulders.

'Let's see.' Sorrel puts her notes down, comes over to my bed and sticks out a mitt.

I hand her my camera.

'Practically snogging,' Sorrel agrees before gently lobbing the camera on to Claudia's bed. Claudia looks at it, says, 'Defo,' hands it to Tam, who nods but doesn't even have to get off her bed to give it to Nat, as Nat is at the side of Tam's bed with her hand outstretched.

'Give it here then,' she says urgently. 'Let's have a look.'

She takes the camera, peers at the screen, and her brow furrows.

'He could have just been stopping her from falling on the

151

rocks,' she says. 'That doesn't prove anything.'

'Er, spot the rocks,' Sorrel says. 'They're on flat sand. They'll be at it after lights out tonight, no doubt.'

'So it looks like Hammy Chops is going to get the Buff Body rather than you, Nat!' Claudia teases. 'If it's teacher-action you're after, you could always bat your lashes at Mr McKay and see what happens. He's probably desperate for anything with a pulse.'

We all collapse with laughter at the thought of *anyone* fancying The Ginger Gnome.

'So if he's with The Hamster, why is Jon sending *me* steamy texts?' Nat says indignantly. She's standing with her hands on her hips, her chin jutting out. 'Explain that one!'

The room falls silent.

Claudia's the first to speak. 'Buff's been texting you?' She sounds as amazed at this bombshell as I am. 'Straight up?'

'Straight up,' Nat confirms.

'Saying, like, what?' Tam asks.

Nat chews her bottom lip then goes over and shuts the dorm door. 'You've all got to swear on your life that you won't tell anyone,' she says. 'If you do, you'll die.'

We all nod and mutter stuff under our breath.

'OK.' Butterface sticks her hand down her top and pulls out her moby. After furious key-pressing she hands it to Claudia. 'Read it,' she orders. 'Read it out loud.'

'What's it say, Claudia?' Tammy Two-Names asks, practically panting with excitement. 'Go on!'

Claudia peers at Nat's moby. 'It says: "So want you. So need you. Will arrange a lesson in lust ASAP I promise. Love J", and there's,' she taps on the screen with a French-manied talon, 'eight kisses.'

'Eight!' I shriek. Even FB in his new guise as master stalker only manages three, four at most.

'God, that's, like, so hot!' Tam gasps. 'When did you get it?'

'Today,' Nat says, looking smug. 'When I was fossil-hunting.'

Claudia is still holding Nat's moby, flipping it from one hand to another. 'How do we know it's from Buff?' she asks. 'It could be from anybody. That fat lad with the stutter who works in the park has the hots for you. I gave him your number. It could be him.'

'Ring the number,' Sorrel suggests. 'Then we'll know.'

'Don't!' Butterface shrieks. 'I don't want Jon to think I'm harassing him, not during school time.'

'I'll do withheld number,' Claudia says, pressing the keys. 'I'll put it on speakerphone. Don't say anything.'

The noise of the phone ringing vibrates around the silent room. Then, 'Jon Butler. Hello? Hello?'

Claudia presses the *Off* key as the rest of us press our

hands to our mouths to stop us gasping and shrieking.

'I've been telling you for weeks he was giving me the look of lust,' Natalie says, beaming from ear to ear. '*Now* do you believe me?'

'What's the problemo?' I whisper as I meet FB in the dark, by the equipment shed. After dinner we had an hour in a classroom to go over the day and neaten our notes before some free time before bed. I'd been hoping to have a good goss with the girls about the whole Nat and Buff situation, but then I got a text from FB to say he had to meet me as there was an emergency.

'I just wanted to see you, that's all,' he says, kissing me. 'I've missed you.'

'*That's* the emergency?' I say, irritated. 'We've been with each other all day.'

'You were in a different group to me,' he says. 'You were limestone and I was chalk, remember?'

He leans in for another swift snog but I pull away. 'Frazer, I can't stay. I've got to go. There's loads of stuff going on with Nat.'

'What stuff?' FB asks.

'I can't tell you,' I say. 'I'm sworn to secrecy.'

'You can tell me,' FB says. 'I don't blab, you know that.'

I know he doesn't, he's the one person in the world I

would trust one hundred per cent with a secret, but I've sworn on my life not to.

'Can't,' I say. 'I promised the girls. And if I do, I die.'

'But I thought we weren't going to have any secrets from each other,' FB says in a slightly whiny tone of voice. 'The girls are obviously more important to you than me.'

I blow air out of my mouth and it rises into the night as if I'm some fire-breathing dragon. I want to get back to the girls, not spend time with FB interrogating me, and everyone knows that spilling a secret doesn't really mean you're going to peg it.

'Mr Butler wants to sleep with Nat!'

I wait for FB to gasp with shock at this pupil–teacher hook-up, but after a moment's silence he bursts into laughter.

'Natalie Price? Our Natalie? Butterface Nat?'

'It's not funny!' I hiss. 'It's deadly serious.'

'Come on,' FB says, putting an arm around my shoulder and kissing me on the nose. 'She's making it up. Mr Butler wouldn't look twice at her. I don't want to sound mean about your friend, but she's as thick as all the make-up she wears.'

'I've seen evidence,' I say.

'Like what?' FB asks.

'Like a *really* hot text message from him about wanting

her and arranging a lesson in lust. *And* there were loads of kisses at the end. Claudia rang the number back and Mr B answered. She's been telling us for ages he had the raging hots for her but until now, we didn't believe her.'

Chapter Twelve

'Rise and shine! Time to get up, girls!'

It's the sound of The Hamster banging on our dorm door.

I can't believe it's morning or that I've slept even so much as a tiny wink, but it is and I have. I thought we'd all be up all night gossiping about what it might be like to snog a teacher, but I think the sea air must have knocked us out, as one minute I was climbing into my bed worrying about who else had slept in it and whether bedbugs were teeming below the bottom sheet and my bod, grateful that Mum had bought me a new pair of PJs with pink pigs on them, as at least I'm covered from ankle to neck, and the next old puffy chops is shouting at us to get our butts out of bed. I say us: looking around, I seem to be the last one up. There's no sign of Luce, Sorrel, Nat or Tam.

I reach over and look at my moby. Five texts, *all* from FB. I don't even bother to open them. There was a time when I longed for texts from him. Now my heart sinks slightly when I see them piling up in my inbox.

Claudia is sitting on her bed in jeans and an alarmingly red lacy bra, pushing a couple of chicken fillets in the cups. I suppose that if she does fall into the sea they'll act as floats. She pulls on a cream jumper and then starts swirling bronzing powder over her face with a big fat brush.

'Where are the others?' I say, swinging my legs out of the bed and padding across the floor.

'Nat and Tam are in the bathroom, Luce is phoning Josh and I expect Sorrel's hugging a tree,' she says, peering into a little mirror.

'What do you think is going to happen with Nat and Buff?' I say, climbing on the end of Claudia's bed.

Tits Out swirls the brush over the powder and blows on it, sending brown dust into the air. 'Nothing,' she says, starting again on her face. 'Not a thing.'

'What? She's going to knock back Buff?' I'm amazed after all the lusting Nat's done. 'I thought she'd be well up for it.'

Claudia shakes her head. 'Nothing's going to happen because nothing *has* happened.'

I'm confused. 'Has Nat fessed to fibbing?' I ask.

Claudia's on her eyes now, doing the whole eyeliner and eyeshadow routine.

'Nope, she swears it's true,' she says. 'But I know for a fact it isn't.'

'How come?' For an awful moment I think the reason she knows Buff can't be lusting after Nat is because he's lusting after *her*.

Claudia looks round and leans towards me.

'I saw the text. No way was it from a grown-up. It was in teen text. Buff's the sort who would put commas in his texts.'

'You're saying she sent it to herself?' I gasp. 'How?'

'Dunno,' Claudia shrugs. 'Must have got hold of his phone or something.'

'But why didn't you say something last night?' I ask. 'Why didn't you say you thought the text was dodgy?'

Claudia rummages in her bulging make-up bag and pulls out a tube of mascara. 'I didn't want to humiliate her in front of you lot,' she says, pumping the brush up and down in the tube. 'It's just some little fantasy of hers, which is why none of us must breathe a word of this until it either blows over or she admits she's telling porky pies. OK?' Claudia brandishes her mascara wand towards me in a very aggressive way. 'You haven't told anyone, have you, even though you swore on your life? Not even Razor Burns?'

'Course not,' I say, thankful that FB is the one person in the world I can trust totally. 'As if!'

'Good,' Claudia says. ''Cause if this gets out, Nat could get in loads of trouble if she's lying, and Buff could lose his job if she's not.'

'Frazer, can you come back and study rocks rather than your girlfriend?' Buff calls across the beach. Everyone except me giggles. 'You're supposed to be in *my* group!'

'Electra, I need to talk to you!' FB hisses. *Again.*

'You heard what Mr Butler said,' I say, turning my back and studying a limpet clinging to a rock.

'Frazer!' Buff calls out. 'I won't tell you twice!'

We've had breakfast, a slideshow about rock formations, spent an hour on the coach, and we're now split into groups, standing in our wellies in a rocky cove looking at exactly the same rocks that we saw in the slideshow, which rather makes me wonder why we needed to freeze our butts off and risk drowning in a rock pool when we've already seen the things on screen. And whether we've been eating or travelling or doing stuff with crustacean-covered rocks, FB has been hanging around, trying to get my attention and it's getting on my nerves so much, I'm having a mean fantasy about him slipping on a rock, twisting his ankle and having to be taken home.

As FB takes the hint, I watch him walk across the sand towards the rocks where Nat is bent over a clipboard.

She's in the group that Buff is supervising, whereas I've got Miss Rogers.

Something long, thin and slippery flicks across my forehead, so naturally I scream and spin round. Lanky Pinhead is dangling brownish-green slimy seaweed in front of me with one of his bony hands. I can smell cider on his breath and wonder if he's poured it on his cornflakes instead of milk this morning. He goes to slap me with it again so I scream and push him away.

'What's going on?' The Hamster asks, puffing her little cheeks out.

'Pinhead's assaulted me with seaweed,' I say, picking up the notebook I've dropped with shock. 'Look at my notes. They're ruined!'

'Stephen,' Miss Rogers snaps. 'If you spent the same amount of time studying as you do larking around, you might actually find you get decent marks for a change.'

Pinhead's sunken little face peers out from under his hoodie hood like a tortoise popping out of its shell. 'But to get really good marks I'd have to sleep with you, wouldn't I?' The Grim Reaper says, leering at the teacher.

First Miss Rogers looks shocked. Then she looks nuclear furious.

'You've crossed the line, Stephen Prescott,' she snaps, trying to wag a finger in his face, but, as she's so short and he's so tall, wagging it somewhere around his belt buckle instead. Her cheeks puff in and out. 'You've crossed the line, even for you.'

'It's not me that's crossed the line,' he sniggers, looking sickenly smug. 'Everyone knows that to get a decent mark for geography you've got to put out with the teacher. Ask her.' He dangles slimy seaweed in my direction. 'She knows all about being a teacher's pet.'

'Me?' I squeak. 'Don't drag me into this. What's it got to do with me?'

Several of the others have stopped staring at rocks and are now gathered round, staring at me.

'Go on. Tell her. Tell her all about having an affair with a teacher!' The Grim Reaper says, and I feel so sick I wonder if I can just jump over the rocks, race down the beach, rush into the sea and drown myself.

'It's not me!' I shriek, as people gasp and giggle. 'Don't look at me.'

'Electra?' Miss Rogers's little hammy chops are quivering with indignation. I expect that if there was a nearby wheel she'd be on it and running at top speed. 'What's going on?'

'I don't know what he's talking about, miss.' I glare at Pinhead. 'Everyone knows he's nuts.'

Pinhead snorts. 'Me, Gibbo and Spud heard you and Frazer B talking last night. We heard you say Mr Butler and

Natalie Price were getting it on. Didn't we?'

He nods at Gibbo and Spud. Spud starts giggling and snorting behind his hands but Gibbo says, 'Mr Butler sent Natalie a text about giving her shagging lessons.'

'You know nothing!' I snap. 'So button it.'

'But you said Mr B wanted to show Gormy Girl more than just a bit of old rock,' Pinhead sneers at me. 'Didn't you?'

'What's going on?' Claudia has wandered over with Nat. 'Are we missing something?'

'Nat and Buff are sleeping together,' someone helpfully fills her in. 'Been at it like rabbits for ages apparently.'

I look at Nat. Even the thick yellow slap can't hide the fact she's gone deathly white.

'Natalie?' The Hamster asks. 'Shall we discuss this in private?'

Nat just stands like a heavily made-up rabbit paralysed by car headlights.

'You lucky cow having a bunk up with Buff,' Shenice says to Nat. 'I bet he knew what to do.'

'The texts were porno!' flaky little Spud adds excitedly. 'Red hot!'

'They rang the number back and Bonking Butler answered,' Pinhead says. 'It was defo him.'

FB pushes his way through the crowd towards me. 'I

163

tried to warn you they knew!' he hisses. 'They were swigging cider in the bushes and overheard us.'

I think of all the texts FB sent and the way he kept trying to come up to me this morning. For telling FB, for ignoring FB, this is my fault, and now I'm going to die for spilling the secret when I swore on my life I wouldn't.

'Do we have a problem, Miss Rogers?' Buff calls out as he strides towards us.

'You do, sir,' Shaz sniggers.

'We need a word,' The Hamster says, motioning to Mr Butler. They walk across the sand and, in a huddle, stop to talk.

As I hear Buff shout, 'WHAT?' and stare at Nat with the look of disgust rather than the look of lust, Claudia grabs Natalie's arm.

'Did Buff really send you that text?' she demands.

Natalie just stands there looking white and shocked and defiant.

'Nat?' Claudia shakes Nat's arm. 'If he did then we'll get the letch out of our school and away from you, but if you're not, you've got to fess up *now*.' She gives Nat another strong shake. 'Did Mr Butler send that text?'

Nat stays silent for a moment and then begins to cry.

'I saw his moby on the coach seat and pinched it,' she sobs. 'I sent the text.'

Chapter Thirteen

'So what are we doing tomorrow?' FB asks, unlocking his bike from the racks. 'I could meet you in the morning and we could spend Saturday together.'

'I'm going shopping with the girls,' I say. 'And Luce has promised not to bring Josh.'

'What about after shopping?' FB says. 'How about the cinema?'

'OK,' I shrug. 'If there's something worth seeing.'

'And what are you doing on Sunday?' FB asks, as I wonder whether I should give FB a timetable of my week so that he doesn't have to question me on my plans *all* the time.

'I'm helping Phil clean up his house before people start seeing it,' I say. 'I've promised Mum.'

The estate agent said Phil's place needed a bit of tidying up, the furniture rearranging and stuff like that, before it officially goes on the market. Mum wanted to go over but Phil thinks it would be too much for her, so I'm going with The Little Runt.

'Well, why don't I come and help you?' FB says. 'It would be great to spend the day together.'

If I had the energy I'd point out that we spent practically all day *every* day last week together because it was half-term, and with LuJo doing stuff, Sorrel helping out at the café and everyone else blanking me because of the Nat–Buff incident, I didn't have anyone else to hang out with. We wandered around the shops, went to the cinema, ate far too many burgers and practically set up home on a bench in Victoria Park. We're now back at school and I'm still being given the cold shoulder from Claudia and Tam, which has made mornings at the bus stop really difficult as me and Tits Out just stand there in silence as I study the bus timetable and Claudia examines her nails. Nat is still suspended from school and the rumour is the suspension might become permanent. Claudia told Shenice who told Shaz who told Angela Panteli who told me that Nat's being home-schooled until everything is sorted out, but that she's defo failed her geography GCSE because she couldn't finish the field trip.

'So how about it?' FB says, as he wheels his bike out of the school gates with his right hand, holding my hand with the other. 'Shall I come over on Sunday?'

'If you want,' I shrug.

FB perks up. 'That's great. But what about tonight? What are you up to tonight?'

The interrogation *never* ends.

'Sorrel and I are going to The Codfather for chips and a goss.' I say this in a tone of voice that I hope conveys it's just me and Sorrel and there's no room for anyone else, particularly clingy boyfriends.

'I could come with you,' FB suggests, my *Stay away* tone of voice clearly lost on him. 'I fancy a bit of battered haddock.'

'Frazer,' I say, trying not to sound narked. 'I hardly saw Sorrel last week, and what with me and you and Lucy and Josh, I think she's feeling a bit left out. I'm seeing you tomorrow aft—'

Ahead of me I see something – or rather someone – who stops my conversation dead in its tracks.

Just along from the school gates parked at an angle on the pavement is a small red Mini and, leaning against it, a tall lad. He's using one hand to push his floppy brown hair out of his eyes, but his other arm is around Tammy Two-Names's shoulders and they're both laughing. Clearly Tam's bagged herself a new boyfriend during half-term. With being practically sent to Coventry I haven't got all the up-to-date goss. He looks older and posher than any of the Burke's lot and he can't be in the sixth form at King William's as they wear grey suits and red ties. This lad is in jeans and a big black jacket with the collar turned up. With his high cheekbones and square jaw, he's not just beautiful, he's absurdly beautiful. Tam's done well bagging herself such a hottie.

'Who's *that*?' I say. 'I haven't seen him around before.'

'Dunno, but he's badly parked,' FB says primly as Absurdly Beautiful lights a skinny cigarette. '*And* he's damaging himself with free radicals.'

The little car is old, quite battered and has an American flag painted on its roof. I must tell Maddy.

'What are you staring at?' Claudia snaps as we get level with Tam and her beautiful new boyfriend. Tits Out is trying to look frosty at me and foxy at Absurdly Beautiful, which just makes her look absolutely mental.

'Nothing!' I say, not realizing I'd been staring.

Despite not wanting to speak to me, Claudia is clearly *desperate* to prove she's first with the goss. She bats her eyelashes at Absurdly Beautiful, wiggles her chest and says breathily, 'This is Tam's brother, Rupert.'

So Tam isn't going out with this long-limbed high-cheekboned beautiful boy after all!

'Hi! Rupert smiles and waves with his cigaretted hand.

With his sleepy eyes and ruffled hair, he looks as if he's just rolled out of bed.

'Rupert's down from boarding school,' Claudia says. If she can push her tits out any further she'll be slapping him with them.

'Sent down,' he corrects her in a posh drawl. 'There's a humungous difference.' He gives a lazy smile and raises one eyebrow.

'Oh,' I say. 'What?'

Rupert takes a drag on his fag, blows a smoke ring into the air and gives a cute snorty laugh. When he tips his head back I notice his nose is bent and has a little bump in the middle. 'Sent down means I've been kicked out for being a very *very* naughty boy.' He takes another drag on his skinny fag. 'Again.' He laughs, a deep and dangerously sexy laugh.

'What did you do?' Claudia pants, wide-eyed. She's been constantly pouting and puffing beside me. 'It must have been something *really* bad.'

'Hop in and I'll tell you,' Rupe says, and I feel disappointed but hardly surprised that yet *another* boy has fallen for Claudia and her obvious charms. Then he looks straight at me with green-grey hooded eyes and says, 'And where do you live?'

'Me?' I squeak, feeling flustered and looking around to check that Absurdly Beautiful really was asking me and not

169

some sixth-form blonde stunner who's been lurking nearby. 'Um . . . Mortimer Road. Off Talbot Road.'

'Then I'll give you a lift home too,' Rupe says, fishing some car keys out of the front right-hand pocket of his incredibly tight faded jeans.

I manage to tear my eyes away from the key-retrieving routine to see Tam and Claudia glaring at me, obviously hoping I'll drop dead rather than get in the car.

'We're fine, thanks,' FB says. 'I've got the bike.'

Rupe throws his cigarette on to the ground and grinds it into the tarmac with a long slim foot clad in dirty red Converse trainers. 'Sorry, mate, I wasn't offering you a ride.' He smiles and tosses his keys in the air. 'Coming?'

He looks directly at me again and I have to look away as his gaze beneath his low eyebrows is so, I don't know, *intense*.

Claudia's already in the back seat adjusting her bra. Tam's standing at the door shooting me evils. FB's arm is round my shoulders, holding me so tightly he's practically slicing me in two.

'My girlfriend doesn't need a lift,' he growls. He increases his grip and I feel as if I'm being strapped into a straitjacket. I'm also absolutely nuclear-furious that FB has answered for me.

'It's OK, mate,' Rupe says to FB. He glances at me for a

170

nanosecond with smiling naughty eyes before looking back at FB. 'You've well and truly marked your territory.'

'Thanks anyway,' I mutter, wriggling my shoulders to try and get FB to loosen up.

'Another time then,' Rupert says, smiling and giving me a wink. At least I think it's a wink. I thought for ages Naz Ashri was winking at me but it was just his dodgy eye.

Rupert folds his long legs into the little Mini, starts it up and roars off leaving me, FB and the bike standing on the pavement.

'Did you see that?' FB fumes. He's uptight and angry. 'He flirted with you in front of me! What an arrogant public school brat. Just who does he think he is?'

I get off the bus on Talbot Road and start stomping home.

I am seriously narked with FB and I mean *seriously*. Firstly, as Sorrel and I got to The Codfather last night we saw FB hanging around outside, obviously lying in wait for me. Luckily Sorrel saw him first, so we scuttled off and ended up buying a bucket of KFC and going back to mine, because although Yolanda is mega relaxed about Sorrel bringing girlfriends or boyfriends back to the caravan, she draws the line at battered poultry. We'd barely put a foot through the door of Mortimer Road when FB rang my moby, so I just said that we'd decided to stay at Sorrel's instead of going out, my theory being that whilst he might turn up on my doorstep, he wouldn't dare come to Sorrel's. I was so mad that he'd tried to gatecrash my evening, I got the mega pink bear he'd given me and kicked it into the front room where it landed on its head in a pile of old *heat* magazines.

Secondly, unless we say otherwise, FB knows that lads are banned from girly shopping. It's our chance to wander around the shops, gossip, try things on we've no intention of buying or things we'd love to buy but can't afford, sit in Starbucks, do more gossiping and generally have a good time. Even Luce told Josh to do something else this afternoon. But did FB pay any attention to what I said? Did he heck! There he was, sitting on that seat outside Debenhams, the one where he gave me the Oliver and Fleur speech, waiting to ambush me.

Luckily he was tying his shoelace just as we saw him, so we ducked into Mothercare, I hid behind a display of breast pumps whilst Sorrel and Luce took it in turns to see whether he was outside, which he was, for half an hour, until I stormed out, told him that shopping time with the girls was sacred and that I'd see him later at the multiplex, before consoling myself with a flame-grilled Whopper and double chips in Burger King.

I don't know what to do. FB's lovely, he means well, but

he's driving me absolutely nuts.

As I turn into Mortimer Road, a car zooms past me and then stops with a screech of brakes, before reversing back and neatly parking between a couple of cars. As I realize who the car belongs to and who's driving it, my legs turn to jelly and my chest starts to tighten, which isn't good as I've already got the air bra on its tightest bap-enhancing setting.

Rupert Lennox-Hill gets out of the car, shuts the door and leans against it. I can't decide whether he's thrusting his bits towards me or it's just the way he's leaning on the red metal.

'So,' he says, smiling, 'I meet the Princess again.'

'Me?' I squeak, trying to remain cool, which is practically impossible when I've just been called a princess by an absurdly beautiful lad and my underwear is cutting my circulation off.

'Yes, you, Electra Brown,' Rupe says. 'You were named after mythological Greek royalty, weren't you?'

'Actually after a hotel in Faliraki,' I say. 'Anyway, how do you know my name?'

'I *forced* my little sister to tell me.' He puts a denim leg up on the front bumper and from a little orange packet pulls out a white cigarette paper and lays it on his slim thigh. 'What have you done to upset Tamara and her busty friend?' He takes a pinch of tobacco from a tin and sprinkles it along the paper. 'Something about being a sneaky lying rat?'

'Oh, that,' I say as my stomach sinks. Just for a nanosecond I had this wild and wonderful fantasy that Rupert Two-Names had driven to Mortimer Road in the vague hope of catching a glimpse of me, when really it was to track me down and stick up for his stuck-up sister. 'One of our friends was having an affair with a teacher, except she wasn't, she was just pretending to, but because of me it got out and now she's suspended, maybe for ever.'

'Who's a naughty girl then?' Rupert teases. He fixes his eyes on me as he licks the edge of the cigarette paper and then smoothes it down. 'Don't stress. It'll blow over.'

'You sound very sure,' I say. 'I wish I could be. Any more mornings of icy silence with Claudia Barnes and I might have to drag myself out of bed to get an earlier bus.'

'No need to leave a warm bed early,' he smiles. 'Things always blow over. Believe me.'

'Even being kicked out of boarding school?' I ask.

'Ah, that,' Rupert says furrowing his thick brows. 'Growing weed in the school greenhouse doesn't blow over quite as quickly as girly cat fights, at least not as far as my parents or the police are concerned.'

I giggle as Rupert pulls a face.

'Anyway, I was completely fed up of the whole

conformist routine of school,' he adds. 'I'd had enough of sixth form before they'd enough of me.'

'Lower or upper?' I ask.

'Well, I'm not in anything and I hate labels,' Rupe says, lighting the cigarette with a purple lighter. 'But if you have to pigeon-hole me, upper.'

Absurdly Beautiful goes to hand me the glowing roll-up but I shake my head.

'Ah, Little Miss Innocent,' he says. 'Just like my sister, sweet fourteen and probably never been kissed.'

'You are so wrong!' I snap. Rupert Lennox-Hill may be absurdly beautiful and dangerously sexy with his floppy hair, hooded eyes and sinewy body but, as FB pointed out, he's also arrogant. 'I'm fifteen in a few months and I have a boyfriend.'

'What? That nerdmeister you were with yesterday? The boy with the bike?' He laughs but, instead of the sexy laugh, it's a sarcastic patronizing laugh and it *really* annoys me. 'Does he always cling on to you like a limpet or just when other blokes are around?' He takes another drag on his skinny ciggy.

'Don't you dare laugh at him!' I snap back. 'He's lovely, he's loyal—'

'And I bet he bores you to tears,' Rupe says. 'Go on, admit it. He won't let you out of his sight. He certainly didn't want you in my car.'

'Didn't your parents ever tell you not to get in a car with strange men?' I say. 'He was just looking out for me.'

'He was terrified of losing you,' Rupert says. 'You can't cage a free bird without making it unhappy. I saw the way you looked when he answered for you.'

'Oh, get lost,' I say. Rupert Lennox-Hill reminds me of Jags: gorgeous to look at but completely up his own backside and probably a terrible kisser, not that I'd let Rupe get anywhere near me with his smoke-filled mouth. 'You don't know what you're talking about. You don't know anything about me and FB!'

'Well, tell me then,' Rupe says, throwing his roll-up to the ground, taking a step towards me and fixing me with those dangerous eyes. 'Tell me what's so special about him.'

I take a step backwards. 'It's nothing to do with you!' I squeak as Rupe comes closer.

I move away again but feel cold metal on my butt. I seem to have backed into the car bonnet.

'I know one thing,' Rupe says softly. 'I know he doesn't kiss you like this.'

He leans forward, holds my face in his hands and kisses me and kisses me and kisses me until I'm bent backwards over the bonnet of the Mini and he's on top of me. I'm glad I'm lying over the bonnet because if I didn't have something solid underneath me I'm sure I would faint, because Rupert Lennox-Hill, dangerously sexy but dreadfully arrogant, is right. FB has never kissed me like that. No one, not even in my raciest dreams, has ever kissed me that way. Had I known that it was possible to be kissed like that I would have added another level or ten to my old five-point Snogability Scale. It's like he's kissing me all over. I don't even care that he tastes of stale tobacco or that he's slightly stubbly.

'I was right, wasn't I?' Rupe whispers into my ear before nibbling it, artfully managing not to tug at one of my dangly earrings or get a gob full of glittery bits. 'Bike Boy was just a warm-up for the real thing.' He kisses me again but this time, as knee-tremblingly wonderful as it still is, a few thoughts start popping into my head such as, *What if Mum sees us? Does my breath smell of the burger I've just had at BK?* and, *Do my thighs look huge flattened on a car bonnet?*

In my hip pocket my moby rings and vibrates, and I'm both thrilled and alarmed to feel Rupert's hands digging into my jeans.

'It's Bike Boy,' Rupe says, waving my moby at me as FB's smiling face looks out from the screen. 'Shall I answer it?'

'Stop it!' I gasp, pushing Rupert off me and straightening up. 'Give me my phone!'

'Shall I tell him his girlfriend's been bent over a bonnet

with a stranger?' Rupe taunts. 'Or will you?'

The phone stops ringing. Rupert holds on to it. 'He'll ring again,' he says. 'It's up to you whether you answer it.'

I rearrange my clothes and try to look as if it's every day a beautiful stranger snogs me on the street and turns my bod to jelly.

'Give it back,' I say, holding my hand out and trying to look coolly angry at being taken advantage of.

Rupe hands it back to me, I turn it off and tuck it back in my pocket, wondering what happens next.

What happens next is that Rupert gets back in his car and winds the window down.

'Just get in touch when Limpet Boy finally bores you to tears and you want some uncomplicated fun,' he says, starting the engine. 'I'll be there.'

Chapter Fourteen

'You OK, Electra?' Phil asks as we pull away from Mortimer Road very early on Sunday morning to start the big clear-up. 'You seem very quiet. Boyfriend troubles?'

'I'm fine,' I say as we pass the spot in the road Rupe and I snogged and I feel my face burning at the memory, not just of what we did but how I felt.

After Rupe drove off and I'd stopped gasping and my legs began to work again, when I looked at my phone there were four missed calls and two answerphone messages from FB, all in the space of about five minutes. The messages rambled on about how sorry he was to have gatecrashed my shopping trip and he knew he'd narked me but it was just because he loves being with me blah blah blah. But instead of feeling irritated by him, I just felt unbelievably sad and guilty that whilst he was ringing me, worried that he'd upset me and wanting to make things right between us, I was bent over a bonnet snogging a drug-growing ex-sixth former who hardly knows me, and not only that, I was enjoying it more than I've ever enjoyed a snog before. And even though the last thing I wanted to do was sit snuggled in the dark with FB and a bucket of popcorn watching some daft rom-com, freaked that I might have *Unfaithful* tattooed across my forehead, I felt I had to go. But the worst part of going out with FB post-steamy-bonnet-snog with Absurdly Beautiful wasn't sitting in the cinema knowing that I'd cheated on my lovely, kind, gentle boyfriend who worships the ground I walk on. No, the worst part was when FB and I kissed and I realized that kissing FB is now like kissing my brother.

I glance at Jack who's in the back seat, picking his nose.

Oh, what am I going to do?

'If you want to talk about anything, I'm always happy to listen,' Phil says as he turns Mum's silver Ford Focus into Compton Avenue to pick FB up. 'Many moons ago, I was your age.'

I glance across at Phil and find it hard to believe that he once had hair and no designer stubble.

'I said I'm fine,' I mutter as I see FB standing outside his drive looking smiley and cute, waving.

That does it for me. I'm not going to treat FB like a pair of unwanted ankle boots. He deserves better. I've had a brief but thrilling snog with Rupert, a lad I met less than forty-eight hours before, whereas I've secretly and not so secretly fancied FB for months. I know masses about FB, his life, his family, even his dog, but all I know about Rupert is that he's at least seventeen because he drives a car, is Tam's brother, has been expelled from school for growing drugs, is sexy and dangerous and a fabulous earth-moving nerve-jangling kisser.

'Here we are. Home sweet home,' Phil says as he stops the car.

'Is this it?' I ask, looking out of the window.

When Phil said he lived in the country I had visions of a cottage with roses around the door, rolling fields and little lambs gambolling in his garden. The house is certainly in the country – the smell of ripe animal poo is coming through the air vents – and there are green fields, but Phil's house isn't a pretty cottage with cute animals playing on the lawn. It's a grey pebble-dashed bungalow with a rusting van standing in the paved front garden. Quite frankly, it looks more like a scrap yard than a home and makes the Callenders' drive seem positively posh.

I get out of the front and let FB and Jack out of the back. The Little Runt makes a dash for the old van, which has no doors or windows.

'Cool!' he shrieks as he climbs into the driver's seat.

'Jack! Be careful!' Phil shouts, undoing a series of locks on the front door. 'There's all sorts of stuff in there!'

FB and I pick our way through bits of metal strewn on the front path and follow Phil inside.

'It's a bit of a mess,' Phil says, picking up a pile of post from the mat. 'You can see why the estate agent says it could do with some tidying up.'

A bit of a mess! That's an understatement! As FB and I wander through the downstairs rooms it's clear the entire house is one huge junk yard decorated with seventies-style psychedelic swirly wallpaper. This isn't a case of just throwing out old magazines, bunging stuff in cupboards or kicking shoes under the bed and spraying some perfume around, which is what tidying up in my bedroom amounts to. This is serious slinging-in-a-skip stuff.

The kitchen sink is filled with dirty mouldy coffee mugs, and there are towering piles of newspapers and magazines, and bundles of carrier bags littering every surface. Through the window I can see the back garden, totally overgrown, but with a few rusty things sticking out of the grass.

Further down the hall, towards the back of the house, resting against the wall there's a guitar (without strings), several tennis rackets (stringless), and a heap of old trainers (laceless). When I see the tennis rackets I have a sudden

182

image of Rupert dressed in tight white shorts lobbing a ball across a net at me, but unfortunately instead of me expertly whacking it back, it hits me on the forehead and brings me back to my senses and the appalling state of Phil's house.

'Electra, look at this!' FB gasps, his head poking out of a door leading off the hall.

It's the living room, but instead of a cosy sheepskin rug to lie on in front of the fireplace (another Rupe flash!), there's a red and silver motorbike.

'Phil,' I say, going back into the hall where he's still reading the post. 'Do you know you have a motorbike parked in your lounge?'

'Oh, yes,' Phil says. 'The estate agent mentioned I might have to move it, but it's without its engine at the moment.'

'Well, where is its engine?' I ask as we both go into the living room and stare at the bike as if it's some amazing modern sculpture rather than an oily lump of metal.

'In the bath,' Phil replies, looking sheepish. 'I stripped it down and haven't had time to put it back together.'

'Has Mum ever been here?' I ask.

Neither Mum nor I are the tidiest people in the world, in fact, we compete for the title Queen of the Grubs, but never *ever* would we be able to live in this mess. On second thoughts, neither does Phil. No wonder he spends all his time at our place.

'Not since we first met,' Phil admits. 'And it was tidier then.'

'We don't just need bin liners,' I say, noticing tools piled on the brown leather sofa. 'We need a skip.'

Phil looks horrified. 'I'm not throwing any of this out,' he says, picking up a long screw from the floor and putting it on top of the television, which is already home to a number of other screws. 'It just needs moving around a bit.'

'Phil!' I shriek. 'No one is going to buy a house with a motorbike in the front room and an engine in the bath! And even if they do, they'll have to go once the house is sold.'

Phil shakes his head. 'No, no, it's all coming with me,' he says, as if it's been decided. 'It'll all come in useful one day.'

I am *horrified*. It's bad enough that I'm going to have to share my space with baby stuff, but I'm not going to live my life next to a motorbike that doesn't go anywhere. 'Anyway, there isn't room,' I add pointedly.

'We'll make room,' Phil says, practically flouncing out.

I'm about to have a major strop when I realize Phil and his junk could strengthen my argument that I really need to live in a caravan on the street. Perhaps Rupert could hitch it up to his car and we could go away at weekends? I suddenly feel terribly gut-wrenchingly guilty that my tennis, rug and caravan daydreams have so far excluded my actual boyfriend, and that it is FB, not Absurdly Beautiful, who's got out of bed ridiculously early to roll up his sleeves and help my family sort through piles of greasy junk.

'It would be great to have a house like this one day,' FB says. He's on his hands and knees picking up screws and bits of unidentified metal from the beige carpet. 'What do you think?'

'You want a house like *this*?' I say, amazed. I can't believe that anyone brought up in a house like 7 Compton Avenue could aspire to live in what is basically a pebble-dashed shed rather than a place oozing granite and steel with a swish plant-filled conservatory and startling green lawns.

'Oh, yes,' FB says. 'Somewhere in the country that we could do up. A nice place in the fresh air to bring up Oliver and Fleur.'

It's wretched Oliver and Fleur again!

I no longer feel guilty about the love triangle. I just feel trapped and desperate that not only has FB named our children, he now knows where we're all going to live.

Jack is in heaven. Not only is the house full of bits of old car and bike but the cupboards are packed with Pot Noodles so it's the only thing we can have for lunch.

Whilst Phil and FB discuss the finer points of pistons or something, Jack sits on the motorbike in the front room and makes roaring noises and I go outside with a Chinese

Chow Mein and sit on the front step surrounded by bin bags. It's not exactly warm, but the step is probably cleaner than Phil's sofa.

I've taken some photos of the mess before we rearranged it into another constellation of mess and I'm going to send them to Mum so that she can see that she's having a baby with King Grub.

I'm just scrolling through my address book to find Mum, when just before the Ms I spot a new L, just after Lucy.

Lust

Someone has put a new number in and called it *Lust*. Someone has got hold of my phone. It wouldn't be FB; it's just not the sort of thing he would do. It could be the girls mucking around on Saturday when we were shopping or it could be . . . I think of Rupert holding my phone yesterday. I was so flustered after the butt-on-the-bonnet incident, could Absurdly Beautiful have done it without me realizing? And if he put the number in, does he want me to ring him? 'Just get in touch,' he'd said as he left.

Abandoning my half-eaten Pot Noodle, I get up and go into the house. FB, Jack and Phil are in the bathroom, bent over the engine in the bath, putting it back together as if it's a massive metal jigsaw.

I go back out into the front garden and walk towards the end of the drive. Feeling sick with excitement and guilt I press *Lust*. It rings and rings and just as I'm about to chicken out, a male voice answers, 'Yah?'

It's him! It's Rupe! He is *Lust*!

I cut the call and stare at my moby as if it's burning red hot in my hand. Within seconds *Lust* is flashing on the screen.

I can't answer it. I mustn't answer it.

After letting it ring for ages I answer it.

'Hello?' I croak.

'Dumped Boring Bike Boy yet?' Rupert asks. 'Is that why you rang? To tell me the good news?'

'I rang because I found a strange number,' I say, trying to sound cross. 'And don't call him boring.'

'Just let me know when you finally prise Limpet Boy away,' Rupert says teasingly, and the line goes dead.

'Who was that?' FB says, making me jump. I hadn't heard him come up behind me. 'Who were you on to?'

'Lucy,' I say, putting my phone back in my pocket. 'Just Lucy.'

'Are you sure you're OK?' Phil asks as we pull up outside our house, having dropped FB at his. He'd suggested coming back with me but I said I had stuff to do before school tomorrow.

I shake my head. 'Not really.'

'Remember, I'm happy to listen.'

I give a deep sigh. Phil's not the ideal person to discuss my love life with, but he's here and I'm desperate to talk about Rupert and FB. I don't need to go into specifics.

I wait for The Little Runt to get out of the car and rush up the steps.

'What if, in theory, you were going out with someone and they're really lovely and totally into you, but after a bit you find them, well, limpet-like?'

'Simple?' Phil asks.

'Clingy,' I say.

Phil scratches his non-beard and blows air between his lips.

'Well, if the relationship is going nowhere then it would be better to let them down gently now, rather than string it out for months when they'll be even more hurt,' he says. 'If you do it now, they'll have more time to get over it before exams and stuff.'

'But what if I can't bear to hurt him?' I say, close to tears at the thought of FB's crumpled face. I remember how hurt he looked when he found out I'd used him for a bet. This is going to be a billion times worse. 'What if he's done nothing wrong? He'll hate me for ever and I'll lose a friend.'

'Are we talking about Frazer?' Phil asks and I nod. He touches my arm. 'Electra, Frazer's young, he'll get over it.

He'll have his heart broken many times in his life. You both will, but these things always blow over.'

'That's what Rupert said,' I say, and just saying his name out loud feels thrilling.

'Rupert?' Phil asks. 'Who's Rupert?'

'Just this lad,' I say. 'But he won't go out with me while I'm seeing FB.'

'And you like this boy?' Phil asks. '*Really* like him.'

I nod so enthusiastically I can feel my head is bobbing around like a nodding dog in the back of a car.

'He's totally different from FB,' I say. 'He'd never be a limpet. He just wants fun. He's not the serious sort.'

'Then follow your heart,' Phil says. 'Just be kind when you do it.'

Chapter Fifteen

I've tried really hard to put Rupert out of my mind this week. I've even thought about formulating one of my famous plans to stop me thinking about him, but so far the only option has been either a coma coupled with a full-frontal lobotomy in the hope that I'll wake up and say, 'Rupert who?' or straightforward death. That's a pretty serious plan, even for me.

But despite trying to think of everything except Rupert, I'm a total smitten kitten. I can't get him or that steamy bonnet snog out of my head. I keep running through everything he's said to me, thinking about what he wears, how he looks, staring at his phone number on my moby, desperate to ring it again, terrified of what will happen if I do and terrified that if I don't he'll get fed up of waiting for me and go off with Tits Out who's on an all-out offensive to snare him.

On Monday morning at the bus stop she accosted me with, 'So, what do you think of Tam's bro then?' clearly forgetting in her Rupe excitement that she's not supposed to be talking to me.

'Her brother?' I'd queried, trying to sound ultra-casual whilst hoping my face wasn't looking steamy-snog guilty.

'The posh lush lad with the red Mini,' Claudia had gushed. 'You saw him on Friday. Isn't he *total* hottie?'

I did a bit of hair-tossing and said something like, 'Oh, *that* lad in the Mini,' as if our school gates are packed solid with sexy expelled sixth formers picking up their kid sisters. 'I didn't really notice him because I was with FB.'

Claudia then launched into her plan, something that seemed to involve lots of perfume, eye-popping cleavage and regular wearing of her bumster jeans and lucky thong; told me he was eighteen (*eighteen!*) and that Tam had warned her off him because he was always getting into trouble.

'But I like bad boys,' Tits Out had said with a coy smile. 'And I *really* like posh bad boys.'

There was no sign of Rupert on Monday or Tuesday, but today, Wednesday, as I was on the way home on the bus at the back of the top deck with Sorrel, I heard the thud of rock music from a car outside, looked down at the heavy traffic and saw an American flag on the roof of the car below.

'Look,' I whisper, elbowing Sorrel in the ribs and pointing at the window. 'Rupe's down there.'

To be honest, I can't actually see him, just a long arm in a white shirt tapping on the roof of the car in time to the music, a rainbow of coloured rubber bands circling a slim wrist.

Just the thought of him being near me has my tummy doing somersaults.

Sorrel leans over me and peers down at the stationary Mini in the lane next to us. 'You're obsessed with him, aren't you?' she says, sitting back in her seat. 'You've really fallen for Rupert Lennox-Hill hook, line and sinker.'

'I'm trying not to,' I say, and meaning it.

The bus moves forward a few metres and so does Rupe's car.

'He's eighteen, Electra,' Sorrel points out.

'Joz is nineteen,' I reply.

'But he's in Barbados and I'm not going out with him,' she retorts. 'You're going to get hurt, believe me.'

I'm still looking down at the car. 'I just want some uncomplicated fun,' I say. 'I don't want anything heavy. I've had that with FB.'

'Er, newsflash!' Sorrel says. 'Wrong use of tense. You've *still* got Frazer, or in this sudden rush of lust hormones have you forgotten about him?'

I haven't forgotten about FB. I just don't know what I'm going to do about him. Whilst I got on the bus, he's ditched his extended maths class, cycled home and we're meeting up at the newsagent's. Lovely, kind, gentle, reliable Frazer Burns, who, compared to Rupert with his sexy smile, ruffled hair and sleepy eyes, now bores me to tears.

'When did Claudia say you and FB would be finished?' Sorrel asks.

'By the seventh of March, latest,' I reply.

Sorrel taps her watch. 'It's Wednesday the fifth of March,' she says. 'Not long to go then.'

FB's waiting for me outside the newsagent's, sitting on a bench covered in graffiti.

'Where've you been?' he says, getting up to kiss me. 'I wondered what had happened to you.'

'You know where I was. On the bus with Sorrel,' I say as we sit down. I'm irritated, not just by FB's questioning but by the fact that he'd texted me several times during the journey to ask me the same question. 'The traffic was murder. A lorry was blocking the bus lane.'

'You should get a bike,' FB says. 'We could cycle to and from school together every day. That would be great, wouldn't it?'

'I like going on the bus with the girls,' I say. 'It's our goss time.'

'But you hardly speak to Claudia nowadays and Natalie's not on the bus any more. I'll see if I can find you a second-hand one.' He clearly isn't listening to me.

'I don't want a bike.' I shrug off FB's arm, which is around my shoulder. 'I *want* to go by bus.'

'There might be a postcard in the post office window. If not, I'll look in the local paper.'

'I'm not getting a bike.'

'I could get you one as an early birthday present. What about that? A bike would mean we could spend an extra hour together a day, and there's so many health benefits—'

'DON'T YOU EVER LISTEN TO ME?' I yell, jumping off the bench. 'I DON'T WANT A FREAKIN' BIKE! STOP TRYING TO CONTROL ME!'

FB looks shocked, I feel shocked and a scruffy little dog who was cocking his leg against a tree wobbles with fright.

'I'm sorry,' I say, slumping down beside him. 'It's just – sometimes I feel I can't even go to the loo without you wanting to know what I'm up to. You're suffocating me. I need some space.'

There, I've said what I've been thinking for the last few weeks. Maybe now FB and I can go back to just having fun, being the mates that date we always meant to be.

'I just want the best for you,' FB says, his voice shaking. 'For us.'

'I know, I know.' I put my arm around him, though as I do it I realize it feels as if I'm comforting a really good friend, not my boyfriend. 'I'm sorry. It's just – when you go on about our kids being called Oliver and Fleur and what sort of house we're going to live in, it all feels far too much, much too soon.'

FB sighs, leans forward, rests his elbows on his thighs and runs his hands through his hair. 'I know I've been a bit full-on with all this stuff, but there's no one else I'd rather be with.'

'I know,' I say, rubbing his back. 'And it's lovely. It's just, as Rupert says, sometimes you're like a limpet clinging to me, not letting me move.'

'Rupert?' FB sits up sharply. 'That lad with the car? What's he got to do with this?'

'Nothing,' I say. I hadn't meant to bring Rupert into this, but his name just sort of slipped out and I *so* wish it hadn't.

'When did you see him?' FB asks.

'I just ran into him in the street.' I'm trying to sound casual but I can feel my throat tightening. 'It was nothing major.'

'You never said,' FB says accusingly.

This is what irritates me. The need to account for my every move.

'I don't have to discuss everything with you,' I snap. 'I do have a life without you.'

'But you're obviously discussing me with him!' FB says. 'Telling him how I suffocate you, how I won't let you do anything without me. And for your information, Rupert is incorrect. Limpets move, barnacles don't.'

'It wasn't like that,' I say, now thinking of FB as Barnacle Boy and wondering just how much longer I can go out with a lad who gives me a lesson on crustaceans instead of someone like Rupe who probably doesn't know one end of a bit of shellfish from another, unless it's grilled and smothered in garlic butter.

'So what was it like?' FB asks, looking straight at me. 'Go on, tell me!'

I think back to being bent over the car bonnet and Rupe's steamy kisses and the way he nibbled my ear and whispered into it, the way he called me a princess and the word *Lust* he'd tapped into my moby.

'Oh. My. God!' FB jumps up as if he's been scalded. 'You've been with him, haven't you?'

'I . . . I . . .' I'm trying to think what to say as it's obvious my face has given the game away.

'You've been seeing him behind my back, haven't you?'

FB gasps, jumping around as if he's walking on hot coals. 'You've been two-timing me!' He's waving his hands in the air, clutching his head in total panic. 'What is he, seventeen, eighteen, what?'

'Eighteen,' I mutter. 'And I haven't been seeing him. Not really.'

FB stops pacing and jumping and stands in front of me. 'But something happened, didn't it? Something's gone on between you and him, hasn't it?' Looking up at him, he no longer looks like the lush lad I've spent hours snogging on benches and behind bus stops and in the cinema. In his school uniform looking down at me with hurt, frightened green eyes, he looks like a heartbroken school kid.

I have to look away. I can't bear what I'm doing to him. I'm tearing him apart and it's tearing me apart.

'That time in The Curry Cottage, I told you I'd rather know the truth than be kept in the dark.' He squats down and grabs my hands. 'Tell me, Electra. TELL ME!' He's shaking and practically hysterical.

I feel *terrible*. I never meant to hurt FB. I never want to hurt FB. But it's too late; I have done and there's no going back.

'He kissed me,' I admit, pulling my hands away and hanging my head. 'Just the once.' No need to say it was twice, it went on for ages and was out of this world.

'And did you kiss him back?' FB says.

I nod. 'Yes.'

'Oh, God!' FB lets out a moan as if he's been stabbed in the heart. Then he suddenly gets up and says, 'We can get over this. I mean, it was just a kiss, wasn't it? Just one of those things? It meant nothing, right? Like when you kissed Jags or that French-exchange kid before you met me?'

I feel terrible, and being reminded of my previous disastrous snogging history doesn't help.

'He wants to go out with me,' I say swallowing hard. 'But not whilst I'm seeing you.'

For a moment, neither of us says anything. We just look at each other as the enormity of what I've just said sinks in for both of us.

'And you, do you want to go out with him?' FB croaks. He slumps back on the bench, hanging his head. 'Should I stop my watch?'

I look sideways at him. I can tell from his contorted face that he's willing me to say *No*, to admit that snogging Rupert has all been a terrible mistake and that it's shown me that it's him I want.

I want to hug him, make it all better, take his pain away and wipe the grief from his kind and lovely face.

But I can't.

Even if I said the things FB wants to hear, we'd both

know I didn't mean it, and at some point in the next few weeks or months, we'd be reliving this scene, even if Rupert didn't exist.

'I'm so sorry,' I say as we both start to weep. 'You need to stop your watch.'

Chapter Sixteen

'Whatever's happened?' Mum says as I barge through the front door, sobbing.

'FB and I have broken up,' I say, dumping my bag at the end of the stairs and slumping on the bottom step. I can feel snot running down my top lip and start to rummage in my bag for a tissue. Mum digs into her cleavage and hands me one. I think back to what has just happened. 'Oh, Mum, it was terrible.'

Through tears I'd tried to say that we could still be friends, still see each other just as I see Luce and Sorrel, and that he'd soon find someone else, but FB was distraught.

'Friends?' he'd cried. 'Friends? You don't treat friends like that! You don't go sneaking around behind friends' backs! I love you and you've just trampled all over my heart! I'll *never* find anyone else!'

And then he'd rammed his helmet on his head

and cycled off, leaving me sitting on the bench worrying that he was going to die under the wheels of a passing lorry either because he was crying so much he didn't see it, or deliberately, just because life wasn't worth living without me.

From upstairs comes the noise of Phil decorating the study, turning it into a nursery, or at least that's what he says he's doing. I'm not convinced he's not making room for his own stuff and instead of a duck mobile and ABC wallpaper, the baby will have to sleep beside an old motorbike and car parts. I showed Mum the photos of Phil's house and the mess but all she said was, 'I remember liking the wallpaper.'

'Budge up,' Mum says, as I shuffle along the step and she squeezes beside me. What with her being six months pregnant and me being on the meaty size, I'm slightly concerned that we may end up wedged between the wall and the banisters, unable to move. She used to store her moby in her cleavage but now it's so huge she could keep an entire network down there. 'So what happened?' She pats my knee.

'I don't really know,' I sniff. 'One minute everything was fine and the next it wasn't. I think it was Oliver and Fleur that started it.'

'Friends of yours?' she asks.

I shake my head and feel snot flying. 'It was the name FB

201

was going to give our children,' I say.

'Oh, love.' Mum tries to put her arm around me, but manages to slap me in the face by mistake. To prevent more inadvertent daughter abuse, she gives up and holds my hand. 'The first time someone finishes with you is always the worst,' she says. 'You'll get over it, I promise.'

'*I've* not been dumped,' I say indignantly, wondering why my mother thinks I'm the one who's been binned. 'I was the dumper. FB's the dumpee.'

'Then why the tears?' Mum asks.

'Because I've hurt him and I didn't mean to and I didn't want to,' I say. 'Just because I didn't want him as a boyfriend doesn't mean I don't want him as a friend.' This sets me off on double-snotter sobs even more. I've also started to wonder who's going to help me with my homework when I'm stuck. FB was just down the road and round the corner and knew *everything*. Somehow I don't think Rupert is going to be any good at solving quadratic equations. 'What if I've made a terrible mistake?'

Mum squeezes my hand. 'If it didn't feel right it was probably never going to feel right,' she says. 'Don't get me wrong, Frazer is a lovely boy, but he was a bit, well . . .'

'Boring?' I finish Mum's sentence off.

'I was going to say intense,' Mum says. 'Perhaps a bit serious. It's maybe just as well things have come to an end.

202

At your age you should be having fun, not planning your future together.' She tries to get up, but as I predicted she's stuck between my arm and the wall. I wriggle free and haul her to her feet. 'You'll both find someone else and then perhaps you can be friends again.'

'I already have,' I say, brightening up at the thought of Rupert. I take my coat and blazer off and bung it over the banister. 'Well, we're not officially going out at the moment, but now I'm not seeing FB we will.'

Even though I'm desperate to see him, I'm going to leave it a day before letting Rupe know FB and me are history. Somehow it would feel wrong to be straight on the moby, pressing *Lust* and announcing, 'I'm free!' when a few roads away, I'm pretty sure that FB will be sobbing his heart out, assuming he's not in hospital with lorry-related injuries.

'Oh, Electra!' Mum laughs as we go down to the kitchen. 'That didn't take you long.'

'Rupert's defo not anything like FB,' I say. It's such a relief to be able to talk about him instead of keeping it all to myself. 'He's a total Lurve God and *totally* not the serious sort.'

'Rupert?' Mum says. She opens a tub of olives and I go to the fridge and take a slurp straight out of the orange juice carton whilst her back is turned. 'That's a name I haven't heard before.'

'Rupert Lennox-Hill, Tamara's brother. He doesn't go to our school; actually he doesn't go to any school.'

'Well, what does he do?' Mum asks, popping a couple of green orbs in her mouth.

'Nothing at the mo. He did go to a posh boarding school, but he had to leave.'

Mum isn't laughing now and I wish I'd missed out the bit about being kicked out of school.

'What was he expelled for?' she asks, still troughing the olives.

Better not tell the truth or Mum will freak. 'Oh, he wasn't expelled,' I say, trying to sound convincing and pretending to rummage in the fridge so Mum can't see my face. 'He didn't like boarding school. He missed his parents too much. His dad had a breakdown with the pressure of work and lost his job as some global sales manger, that's why Tam came to our school, remember?'

That was good. Use his dad's meltdown to get a sympathy vote for the Lennox-Hill family.

'And how old is this Rupert?' Mum says. There's only so much rearranging of cold sausages and bags of wilting watery salad you can do, so I've had to take my head out of the fridge and now I have done, I notice Mum is wearing her Mega Suspicious Mother face.

No point in saying sixteen if Rupe comes to pick me up

in the car or Mum will think he's driving illegally, plus I really don't want her to inhale an olive with shock and choke to death.

'Seventeen.' I say. 'He drives an old Mini.'

What's a year between mother and daughter if it keeps the peace?

'Seventeen!' Mum explodes. 'Seventeen! You're riding around in a car with a seventeen-year-old and I know nothing about it!'

Thank goodness I knocked a year off. If I'd told the truth, Mum might have gone into labour right here in the kitchen. The cannabis in the school greenhouse confession would defo kill her off.

'I'm fifteen in July,' I point out. 'And I haven't been in the car yet.' *Just over it*, I think.

'You're fourteen,' Mum snaps, 'and there's a vast difference between going out with someone your own age and a lad like him.'

'You don't even know him so don't judge him!' I snap back.

'Well, perhaps I should,' Mum says. 'I think I should meet this Rupert Lennox-Hill and his parents.'

This is horrifying for so many reasons, firstly because Mum will find out Rupert is an eighteen-year-old smoker with a flair for illegal gardening, but mainly because I remember how freaked out I felt when FB's parents wanted to meet mine. Also I can't decide whether the roll-up and sexy-smile routine would charm or horrify her.

'You didn't want to meet FB's parents!' I shriek. 'You thought Doc Burns was OTT coming round here and grilling you about me!'

'Frazer was your own age, a lovely boy and I had no worries there,' she says, ramming the pickled snacks in her mouth. 'No worries at all.'

'A lovely boy!' I yell. 'A lovely boy! One minute ago you were pleased we'd split up because you thought he was too serious for me.'

'That's before I knew what the alternative was!' Mum snaps, her mouth full of green stuff.

'You know nothing about the alternative,' I shriek, thinking I don't really know much about Rupert either.

'What on earth is going on?' Phil arrives in the kitchen wearing a grey sweatshirt spattered in golden-yellow paint. 'I could hear the yelling in the nursery.'

'Electra's got a new boyfriend,' Mum says raising her eyes.

'Phil knows!' I say. '*He* was the one who told me to ditch FB and go out with Rupert!'

'Did you?' Mum rounds on Phil. 'Have you been giving relationship advice to my teenage daughter?'

206

'Well, I didn't know he was called Rupert,' Phil says. 'But I suppose I did.'

'And did you know he's seventeen and drives a Mini?' Mum demands. 'What do you think about that?'

'Lucky lad,' Phil says. 'Driving a classic car at his age.'

It's almost midnight, the house is quiet and I'm lying in bed fuming so much I'm surprised my swirly patterned duvet cover hasn't caught fire.

First Frazer turned into a clingy shellfish and tried to stop me living my life, and now Mum wants to do the same. I've got rid of Limpet Boy and gained Mollusc Mum. How *dare* she tell me who I can or can't go out with? Like I had any say in what happened between her and Dad or her and Phil. Nobody asked me whether I wanted a new baby sister or brother, did they?

Well, *no one* is going to stop me or tell me what to do. I'm not going to pass up the chance of going out with someone as hot as Rupert, even if I have to do it in secret.

I drum my legs on the bed in an anger-frustration combo and wonder what to do next. I'm much too wound up to go to sleep.

I reach for my moby. It's by the side of my bed. I've been clutching it all evening, sending texts back and forth to the girls, telling them about FB and me splitting up and Mum going mental over Rupe.

I scroll through the texts and then through my contacts and see the word *Lust*.

`Is that offer of a lift home from school still on?` I stab out defiantly.

I'm not going to send it. Yet. Like I said, it wouldn't feel right to do it so soon after dumping FB.

But then I think of Claudia and her Rupe-baiting plan. What if she gets to Absurdly Beautiful before me? What if he falls for a red thong and fake baps? What if he never asks me to fill his passenger seat because Claudia's bumster-clad butt is already there?

I press *Send* and then gasp at what I've done.

I wait for a text back.

And I wait and I wait and I wait.

But nothing happens.

Perhaps he's asleep or, more likely, he feels freaked that a kid he hardly knows has sent him a text at midnight. Perhaps he was just teasing me and never really fancied me at all. Maybe he does this to all the girls he meets just to see what power he has over them.

After about fifteen minutes of praying for a response, I give up, feel *totally* embarrassed, hope that I never see Rupe again and have to explain my midnight texting and put the phone back on my bedside table. I've just switched off the light when the moby vibrates. Once, twice.

It's a text!

Three, four, five . . .

It's a call!

I grab it and see *Lust* flashing on the screen. Absurdly Beautiful is calling me!

'Hello?' I whisper.

'Why wait until tomorrow?' Rupert says.

'What do you mean?' I ask.

'Come outside and I'll show you,' he replies.

'This is mad!' I giggle, as Rupert pulls the car away from Mortimer Road, turns into Talbot Road and races through the eerily empty streets. 'If Mum finds out, she'll ground me for life.'

'So don't tell her,' Rupe says, changing gears. 'What she doesn't know, she can't worry about.'

I'm not sure that's true when it comes to my mum, though perhaps even *she* couldn't guess that instead of sleeping in my bed having sweet dreams, I'd managed to creep out of the house and now be zipping around the streets in a beat-up old car wearing just my piggy PJs.

'Do you always drive around in the early hours of the morning on a school night?' I ask, wondering if that's why Rupe has permanently sleepy eyes.

'It's not a school night for me,' Rupe says, slowing the car down. 'Now, where do you want to go?'

'Surprise me!' I giggle, putting my feet up on the dashboard, even though I'm wearing a pair of pink furry pig slippers.

'Oh, I think that can be arranged,' Rupe says, putting his foot down. 'I'm good at surprises.'

We drove to London.

We actually drove to London!

Even thinking about it makes me want to shriek with excitement, though I'll only be able to shriek silently, inside my head, as if Mum finds out she'll be doing a different sort of shriek and it *defo* won't be silent.

We saw Piccadilly Circus, Big Ben, Buckingham Palace, the lot, all whilst I was wearing my PJs and slippers. As we were driving along there wasn't that constant chatter about strange facts and odd figures like there was with FB. It was just Rupe driving, us both listening to music, me thinking that this is the best night of my life, even though I've got no make-up on and am wearing unsuitable footwear for an unplanned visit to Britain's capital city.

On the way back we stop at a petrol station, Rupert buys a can of Red Bull for him and a Diet Coke for me, and after driving a bit further we pull off the motorway, go down another road and stop, put the seats back, Rupert has a cigarette and we both lie looking up at shooting stars in the sky.

After I've realized the shooting stars are actually aeroplanes, I whisper, 'What happens now?'

It might be the best night of my life, but suddenly I'm a little freaked that it may turn into the worst. At the end of the day, or rather in the early hours of the morning, the fact is I'm fourteen, on the side of the road down an unlit lane in a car with an eighteen-year-old lad I hardly know, dressed in my pyjamas, a couple of plush porkers on my trotters and not wearing a bra or knickers. In my rush to get outside and see Rupe, I'd forgotten about the little matter of underwear.

'I take you home,' Rupert says, putting his seat up. 'That's what happens.'

As I put my seat up I feel a stab of disappointment mixed with a nanosecond of relief. I'd been rather hoping for a repeat of the bonnet snog, but this time *inside* the car. Clearly I've bored Rupert. This was probably a test to see how witty and entertaining I could be. Saying nothing whilst wearing a porcine-inspired wardrobe has obviously put him off. I expect he's used to girls wearing slinky little slips not brushed cotton pigs.

* * *

We pull up in Mortimer Road and park just along from my house, under a street lamp. It's five o'clock in the morning and for the last half-hour I've been praying for two things, one – that Rupert will kiss me and two – that Phil isn't on an early shift and comes out to find me snogging in a car, barely dressed.

Luckily there's no sign of Phil, but neither is there any sign of a steamy snog coming my way.

'Well, thanks for a lovely evening,' I say, unclipping my seat belt. 'Or morning, or whatever it was.'

'My pleasure,' Rupert says. 'Any time.'

'Really?' I say. 'You mean that?'

'I don't say things I don't mean,' he replies, pulling his seat belt free and turning towards me. He sweeps his hair out of his eyes. 'But don't you have to check with Limpet Boy first?'

'I thought you'd realized,' I say. 'He's out of the picture. We broke up.'

I try to push the image of a hysterically sobbing FB out of my head.

'He wasn't right for you,' Rupe says.

'And you are?' I tease.

'I didn't say that,' Rupert laughs. 'I'm known as seriously bad news by girls all over the country.'

'I'll take my chance,' I giggle.

'You sure?' he asks, tracing my lips with his finger. 'You're absolutely sure?'

'I'm sure,' I say.

And *then* Rupert kisses me.

Chapter Seventeen

Standing at the bus stop in my school uniform in bright sunshine watching Claudia Barnes marching towards me, I can hardly believe that last night happened. It's as if someone else slipped out of the house and raced up to London in the middle of the night. I'm not even tired as proof of my adventure, in fact I feel more alive than I think I've ever done in my entire life. As I'd left the front door on the latch, I managed to get in and back upstairs without anyone noticing I'd ever gone. Mum wasn't around for breakfast as Phil said she had a bit of a headache, so unless she brings the Rupe row up, I'm not going to. I'm also not going to mention anything about him to Claudia, even though I'm *desperate* to tell her. I want the girls to be the first to hear the full glorious details of my night-time adventure.

The only cloud on the horizon is that I'll see FB at school.

I'm hoping he doesn't cause a scene, beg me to go back with him in front of everyone or throw himself at my feet and wail. And what if he sees me with Rupert? What if he does something stupid like punch him in the face? He biffed Pinhead because of me, so it's entirely possible he might punch Rupe's lovely lights out, and Rupert looks more of a lover than a fighter.

'Well, I hope you're pleased with yourself,' Claudia practically spits at me. 'I've only just heard.'

'What are you talking about?' I say, thinking that actually I am pleased with myself. *Very* pleased.

'You just couldn't leave him alone, could you?' she snaps. 'You just had to sneak around behind my back. If only you'd told me the truth. I'm *totally* devo.'

Oh. My. God. Rupe must have gone straight home, told Tam about me, Tam's texted Claudia and Claudia is devastated I've whipped him from under her nose, so wrecking her thong and cleavage plan. Still, I can't help but feel thrilled that I've finally beaten Tits Out to a boy without the need for chicken fillets and peroxide.

'It just happened,' I say. 'I didn't mean it to and I'm sure he didn't mean it to, but it did. And FB and me are over. Your two-month prediction came true.'

Instead of being smug that she was right, Claudia looks close to tears. I've never seen Tits Out cry *ever*, but I'd be fascinated to see how much make-up floats off if she does blub. She must have really had the hots for Rupe to be in this state.

'That doesn't make things right,' Claudia sniffs. 'Nat's practically suicidal,'

'Why's Natalie upset about me going out with Rupert?' I ask. 'Did she fancy him too?' I don't blame all these girls for falling for Absurdly Beautiful. He is *totally* dreamy but he's *mine*!

Claudia stares at me.

'*You're* going out with Rupert?' she gasps. 'Tam's bro Rupert?'

'Yeah,' I say. 'What were you talking about?'

Tits Out starts to sob proper springing-from-the-sockets tears. 'I was talking about the fact you scuttled off to tell your now-ex-boyfriend about Nat and Buff and now Nat's been excluded from Burke's. *Permanently*. She's being sent to Osborne Grange.'

'Osborne's the pits!' I gasp. We used to play them at hockey but, after they started a mass fight on the pitch and two of our lot had to go to hospital with stick-induced injuries, they've been banned. '*And* it's miles away.'

'I know,' Claudia sobs, her eye make-up floating down her cheeks. 'But it's the only place that would take her.'

Poor Natalie. I feel mega sorry for her. I mean, I know

she lied and nicked the phone but I don't think she meant to and I'm sure she had no idea how much trouble she'd be in. Nat's Claudia's best friend, so no wonder she's in bits. If it was Sorrel or Luce who'd been excluded, I'd be in bits too.

'I'm so sorry, Claudia,' I say, trying to put a hand on her shoulder as the bus arrives. 'I really am.'

She shrugs me away and when the bus arrives, instead of coming upstairs with me and Sorrel, she stays downstairs with the office-bound wrinklies.

FB didn't cause a scene and plead with me to go back out with him because he didn't come to school on Thursday; nor was Rupert waiting for me at the gates that evening like I'd sort of assumed he would. I didn't get a text or a call or anything, but I did get a good night's sleep as I was exhausted and only narrowly managed not to drop off in history because Sorrel kept poking me with a sharp pencil to keep me awake. It worked, but the left arm of my white shirt now has loads of grey dots on it.

When FB still wasn't at school on Friday I became a bit worried that he'd thrown himself in a ditch or something, but I guess if he had, Doc Burns would have been straight round to blame me, so actually I'm more angsty that I haven't heard anything from Rupert. I'd like to know what

217

we're going to do this weekend and when we're going to do it. Absurdly Beautiful might not have to fit homework in around his plans, but I do, and there's also the small matter of coming up with excuses to be out with Rupe without Mum finding out.

'Do you think I should text him?' I say as we head towards art, the final lesson after a particularly gruelling double period of poetry in English lit.

'Who? Rupert or Frazer?' Lucy asks.

'Rupe,' I say. I have wondered about trying to see if FB is OK, but I don't want him to think that there's a chance we might get back together.

'Makes you look a bit keen,' Sorrel says. 'You don't want to turn into Limpet Girl, do you?'

I don't, but I *so* want to see him.

'But he did give Electra his number, so he must want her to use it,' Lucy points out. 'I'd go for it.'

'Limpet Girl,' Sorrel hisses as we enter the art studio.

'Why not ask Tam what he's up to?' Lucy suggests. 'She might know.'

I look across to where Tam and Claudia are setting up their stuff, a strange installation made out of magazines and coat hangers. Despite telling Claudia I'm seeing Rupert, neither Tits Out nor Tam have said anything about it, but now Nat's been officially expelled, the chill factor towards me has been turned up to max.

'I'll think about it,' I say, unable to think of anything else.

Guttingly, there's no sign of Rupert's car at the school gates. Lucy is wandering out hand-in-hand with Josh, excitedly making plans for the weekend and I'm with Sorrel, who's planning another eco-crusade, this time in Sainsbury's car park.

'Why don't you come sticker-slapping with me tomorrow afternoon?' she says. 'After we've done the shops.'

'No, thanks,' I say, scanning the road, hoping that a little red car with an American flag on the top will zoom into view. 'It's not really my thing.'

'It's good fun,' Sorrel presses. 'People get narked, then when they're trying to peel it off you spring up and tell them their car is murdering the planet.'

It doesn't sound like my idea of a fun afternoon, not unless I was sticker-slapping with Rupe. He'd make *anything* seem fun.

As I'm looking for the Mini, ahead of me I see Tammy Two-Names, on her own, heading along the road, bag slung over her shoulder.

'I'm going to have a word with Tam,' I shout at Sorrel, as I sprint after Absurdly Beautiful's sister.

'Tam!' I say, out of breath from the sudden burst of

energy. 'Do you know what your bro is up to this weekend?'

Tammy Two-Names might have been at Burke's for a while, but she can still look down her nose like the snooty Queen Bee bitch she used to be. 'Like, I'd tell you,' she says icily.

'It's just, I haven't seen him for a few days. Not since we went to London.'

'It's nothing to do with me,' Tam shrugs.

For a moment I think she's going to turn on her heel and stalk off, but then her face suddenly softens.

'Electra, I love my bro,' she says. 'He's fun and girls find him cute but he's, like, *really* bad news. Don't get involved with him. He'll, like, totally break your heart.'

'We're just having fun,' I say. 'It's nothing serious.'

'They all say that,' Tam says. 'Don't say I haven't warned you.'

'I can handle it,' I say confidently. 'It'll be fine.'

'They all say that too,' Tam says. 'But it never is.'

I stomp down the steps of Mortimer Road, head towards the bus stop and feel annoyed with myself that I've totally wasted a perfectly good weekend.

After the most exciting night of my life, the last few days have been the most crushingly boring *ever*.

There were no texts or phone calls or late night visits

from Rupe, not even a long-distance sighting, despite spending *hours* wandering around the streets in full make-up hoping for a glimpse of his car zooming around. I thought of going to see where the Lennox-Hills live, but I couldn't find them in Directory Enquiries and although I know roughly the area they're in, I couldn't risk running into Tam and having to pretend that I was just passing when she'd know it would take me three buses and a walk to get there.

I had my moby tucked into my bra 24/7 so that I could answer instantly if he called, even wearing a bra to bed because I daren't put the phone on loud and risk waking the house, but although there were one or two false vibrates around the boob area – a wrong call, a few texts from girls at school who'd included me on some boy-related goss – there was nothing from the posh boy with the sexy not-yet-been-to-bed eyes.

Now I'm back to school and it will be another four sleeps or five days until the next weekend.

I know I shouldn't be stressed and that this is all supposed to be a bit of fun, nothing serious, no hint of either of us acting like a limpet or a barnacle or any other rock-hugging crustacean, but as I lean against the bus stop and check my moby is working for the trillionth time in seventy-two hours, I can't help thinking, *Where the hell is he?*

And then in a screech of tyres, a car pulls out of a side road, pulls in at the bus stop, the driver leans across, winds the passenger-side window down, and above the sound of rock music says, 'Hello, gorgeous,' and winks.

It's Rupert.

I want to be really angry with him for not being in touch at the weekend, but seeing him smiling with those gorgeous eyes, his square jaw stretched across his face, all I feel is absolute lust.

'You'll get a ticket!' I say, crouching at the window and pointing up at the sign. 'Only buses can stop here.'

'I'll tell them I'm a minibus!' Rupert laughs. 'What are you up to?'

'Er, look at me,' I say pointing at my minging outfit. 'It's Monday morning and I'm in school uniform, what do you think I'm up to?' It occurs to me that despite spending years perfecting my look, my most successful boy-luring outfit has been my school uniform and my penguin PJs.

'What lessons do you have today?' Rupert asks, turning down the music.

It's hard to think of your timetable when you're face to face with an absurdly beautiful boy and it's eight-twenty in the morning, so it takes a bit of thought before I remember. 'English lit, geography, maths . . .'

'I can teach you all those things,' Rupert says. 'Hop in.'

'I can't!' I gasp, though I *so* want to.

'Have you lost the use of your legs?' Rupe teases. 'Is that why you're crouching? Your legs have fallen off and you can't hop?'

'Stop it!' I say, practically wetting myself with laughter. 'I can't hop anywhere other than school.'

I see Claudia in the distance. The bus can't be far behind.

'Why can't you?' Rupert asks. 'What's stopping you other than the desire to conform to a rigid system imposed by narrow-minded bureaucrats?'

I want to say it's not bureaucrats stopping me jumping in the car with Rupert and skipping school, it's the thought of one very pregnant mother being nuclear angry if she finds out I'm being taught things in a Mini that are not on the GCSE syllabus.

'So are you coming or not?' Rupert asks. 'Last chance. Say yes or I drive off for ever.'

I look at him, all bed-head hair and hooded eyes, a faint smell of sweet smoke coming from the inside of the car.

Both Claudia and the bus are approaching. She's cut it a bit fine this morning and is jogging towards the bus stop, hands over her boobs to stop uncontrollable bap-bounce, looking back every few seconds to see how close the bus is.

I open the car door, fling my school bag on the back seat and climb in.

'Let's go,' I say.

'So, did you have a good weekend?' I ask Rupe, giving him a sideways glance as we drive along.

'Great, thanks. You?' he asks.

'Good,' I lie. '*Really* good. I just hung out with friends, did some homework, you know, the usual stuff.'

'Sounds like my weekend,' he laughs. 'But without the dreaded homework.'

We drive on without saying anything. I don't mind not saying anything. I love just sitting in this tiny car next to Rupe, seeing his arms outstretched towards the steering wheel and watching his thighs move as he presses the clutch, or the accelerator or whatever pedals are under his feet.

'You don't wear a watch,' I say, noticing that his left wrist is full of coloured rubber wristbands but there's nothing on his right hand. 'Aren't you late or early for everything?'

'A clock is just man's attempt to harness time,' Rupe says. 'I prefer to go with instinct.'

I can just see our school secretary's face if I told her the reason I was late was because my instinct and their clock didn't agree.

'And what are all the bands for?' I say.

He starts to counts them off: black and white against racism; white for stopping poverty; pink for breast cancer— 'What's the red one?' I ask, interrupting him as I point at one much slimmer than the rest.

'That came around the post,' he says.

I get out my moby and text Sorrel and Luce to say that I've taken a day off and am spending it with Rupert. Then I switch my phone off and put it back in my bag. I don't want to see texts coming through from the girls telling me I shouldn't be doing what I'm doing. I know that I shouldn't be doing what I'm doing but I'm doing it anyway.

We turn off the road at a sign that says Copse Hill.

I haven't been here for years, even though it's only about a half-hour drive from Mortimer Road. The last time we went, Jack took a stunt kite he'd got for his birthday. It all ended in tears because, even though it was Jack's kite, Dad wouldn't let him fly it so The Little Runt ended up having a tantrum. He jumped up and grabbed the strings, which made Dad lose concentration, causing the kite to plunge to the ground, smashing into a group of people who were having a quiet picnic and spearing their pork and pickle pies.

But that was at a weekend.

Early on Monday morning, Copse Hill is quiet except for a few dog-walkers and random joggers.

Rupert parks in the car park at the bottom of the hill and we both get out. It's bright but windy and quite cold for the tenth of March. Rupe opens the boot of his car and gets out his coat, a huge blue-grey thing with shiny brass buttons, the sort of coat I can't imagine anywhere round here selling.

He notices me staring at it.

'It came from an Army surplus shop in Oxford,' he explains, putting it on. 'It's actually an ex-Air Force coat and warm as toast. Come on.'

He takes my hand and we walk up Copse Hill, into the wind. I'm out of breath, sweating a bit despite the cold, my hair is whipping about my head like an epileptic octopus and I've probably got a red face. But for once I don't care. It's me, not a girl like Claudia, here with Rupert. Me with the mottled stocky legs and wide face and not-as-uneven-as-they-once-were-but-still-small boobs. And I don't care, because being with Rupert makes me feel as absurdly beautiful as he looks.

'There you are,' he says as we stop at the top of the hill and admire the view spread out below us. 'That's your geography lesson.'

Instead of rolling hills and lovely countryside or a rocky

beach full of fossils and limpets, I'm looking at a sprawling mass of grey industrial buildings with smoke rising into the air.

'And you live . . .' Rupert drops my hand and starts looking round. 'About there.'

He points to somewhere in the distance. All I can see is a green blob. It must be Victoria Park near our house. The park where FB's dog, Archie, tried to hump my leg and covered me in stinky goose poo; the park where FB and I sat on a bench snogging for hours.

I glance at Rupert in his oversized airman's coat, trying to light a cigarette in the wind, cupping his hand around his mouth, flicking his lighter and cursing every time the flame blows out, his floppy hair flipping about in the wind. And looking at him I know for a fact that it's Rupert I love, and that compared to FB Rupert is exciting and dangerous and incredibly sexy. But I miss FB, not as a boyfriend but as a friend. In a strange way, I want to tell FB about Rupert as much as I want to tell the girls, not to show off but just to share my excitement.

'You OK?' Rupert asks.

For a moment I don't feel OK. I feel scared at what I'm doing here, what I'm getting into, how I've hurt FB, going behind Mum's back, but then Rupert puts his arm around me and, as I snuggle into his chest and almost take my eye out on one of the brass buttons, everything feels not just right, but perfect.

'And English lit?' I say. 'How are you going to teach me English lit? Mr Farrell is doing poetry with us.'

Rupert bends down and gently kisses me. 'Soul meets soul on lovers' lips,' he says softly. 'Shelley.'

I think I'm going to die of happiness. 'What else?' I whisper.

'I was out on a drive, on a bit of a trip,' he says.

'Shelley again?' I ask.

'No, AC/DC,' he replies. 'Fancy some breakfast? I saw a snack van in the car park.'

'Breakfast!' I say. 'Haven't you had some already?'

'I haven't been to bed yet,' Rupert laughs.

The sun has come out, we've found a sheltered spot on the other side of the hill, and we're lying on the ground, stuffed with bacon, eggs, beans, sausage, the works. Rupert paid, which is just as well as I've only got a few coins on me.

I turn to Rupert and prop myself up on my elbow.

'I don't know anything about you,' I say. 'Not really.'

Rupe is using my school bag as a pillow, his eyes closed, the sun making his mass of tousled golden-brown hair shine. 'There's not much to tell,' he says. 'I'm not really that interesting.'

'You are,' I say, thinking I find him fascinating. 'Go on, tell me something.'

'Like what?'

'Like, how you got that bump on your nose.' I run my finger down it. 'Playing rugby?'

Rupert smiles into the sunshine. 'The old man of some girl I was seeing hit me,' he says, and I'm not sure whether he's joking or not. 'I probably deserved it though. Anything else you want to know?'

There's loads of stuff, like how many girlfriends he's had; why did he choose me instead of Claudia; who his friends are; what his favourite colour is; can he eat hot curries without getting the squits; does he like aubergines, aka the vegetables of the devil; what makes him laugh on the telly? I want to know *everything* about him but I don't want to interrogate him the way FB used to question me, so I just say, 'Do you have a middle name?'

'Oliver,' he says. 'After my grandfather.'

'That is *so* weird!' I shriek. 'That's one of the names my ex wanted to call our kids.'

Rupert lets out a long whistle. 'Poor Limpet Boy must have had it really bad if you and he were having those sorts of conversations.'

Before I can stop myself I ask, 'What kids' names do you like?'

Rupert opens one eye and raises an eyebrow and I suddenly panic that I've said the wrong thing and he's now having an Oliver and Fleur moment.

'I told you Mum's preggers and she's always going on about names,' I add quickly. 'I'm supposed to help choose something but I haven't come up with anything yet.'

Rupert closes his eyes again and says, 'Laa-Laa and Po,' which clearly wouldn't go down well at home.

'You've never really asked anything about me,' I press. 'You don't really know much about me either.'

He rolls over to face me. 'All I need to know is right here in front of me,' he says, stroking my hair. 'I don't stress about the past or worry about the future, I just live in the now.'

That's easy for him to say, I think, as he rolls on his back again. I'm stressing about skipping school, worrying about whether there's a loo near here and wondering what Rupert has been up to all night.

I'm about to ask him when I hear snoring.

Absurdly Beautiful has fallen asleep.

I leave Rupert snoring and have a wander, hoping to find a proper loo at best, or a bush with no one around at worst.

Unfortunately, it's the worst.

I'm just squatting behind something sharp and prickly,

hoping that my bum isn't on show to all the joggers and dog-walkers on Copse Hill, when I hear the sound of heavy breathing. I'm about to yell that there's a flasher about, when a woman shouts, 'Come on, just a few steps more!'

I pull up my knicks so quickly I manage to give myself a wedgie, and crouch behind the bush as two people run towards me.

It's an unfit panting man and a sporty-looking woman in a white tracksuit. And – Oh. My. God! The unfit man is Dad.

What do I do now?

If they run past they might see me. How I wish I'd chosen a bush with leaves to pee behind, not one with prickles. I could really do with the extra coverage.

But then they stop just a few metres from the bush, by a rubbish bin and after Dad has a coughing fit and looks like he might collapse *into* the bin, they snog. Or at least I think it's a snog; it could be mouth-to-mouth resuscitation and the woman with *Instructor* across the back of her top is trying to revive my father. But then – oh, gross! Dad slips his hands down the back of her tracky bottoms. I mean, I know I encouraged him to go for it, but I hadn't intended him to go for it in full view of me with his personal trainer. And what is it with this man that he can't hire a professional without having an affair with them? First his dental hygienist, then his solicitor and now the woman in white! Is no one safe?

I have to look away.

Luckily the next time I look up they've started jogging back in the direction they came, but I can't risk them finding me here, on a hill, in my school uniform or, worse, lying on a coat snogging Rupert when I should be in maths.

I stay behind the bush for a bit and then, when the coast is clear, race back to Rupert, who's still lying in the spring sunshine, now wide awake, smoking.

'I thought you'd left me,' he says, giving a sleepy smile and taking a drag on his fag. 'Gone back to school.'

'No, but we have to go,' I say, trying to drag my bag from underneath his head. 'I've just seen my dad!'

Rupert looks totally unconcerned. 'And did he see you?' he says, squinting at me. 'Should I expect another whack in the nose?'

'No!' I say. 'He was too busy feeling his personal trainer's bum!'

'Good man!' Rupert drawls.

'We have to go,' I say, standing over him.

'We haven't started your biology lesson,' Rupert says, a naughty smile creeping across his face. 'I thought we could time how long someone can kiss before coming up for air.'

'I don't have biology today,' I say as Rupert holds

his hand up and pulls me to the ground and next to him. 'I have art.'

'Then we need to practise the art of kissing, don't we?'

We amble down the hill, Rupert with his arm draped over my shoulder, me wondering just how red my face is from all that snogging. As Rupe hadn't been home and hadn't shaved, his face was getting more bristly by the hour and for the last half-hour it's been a bit like being scrubbed by a nail brush.

The other thing is that there has been plenty of snogging and over-the-blazer stroking, even under-the-blazer feeling, but absolutely no move to go elsewhere. His hands haven't hovered by my bra strap or tried to push my skirt up or any of the things I'd been led to believe a sixth former might actually do, which is all rather a disappointment as although I'd have defo slapped his hand away – well, eventually – I think he might at least have tried to get his evil way with me. Maybe he respects me too much to try it on too soon.

We cross the car park to the car and get in. Reality is starting to bite as I begin to wonder what I'm going to tell the school, whose notes I'm going to borrow, how I'm going to get the dirty grassy marks out of my skirt and blazer elbows and how I'm going to face Dad knowing what I know.

Rupert chooses a CD and I switch on my moby, which starts vibrating and bleeping as if it's having an electrical meltdown.

There are several texts from the girls and fifteen missed calls from Phil. There's also a message from him. Something must have gone wrong.

With shaking hands I ring the answerphone.

'Electra, it's Phil. Where are you?' He sounds panicked. 'I've tried the school and they say you didn't come in. Your mum's blood pressure has shot through the roof and they've taken her in. We're in the General, Halstead Ward.'

Chapter Eighteen

When I arrive at the hospital Phil's outside the ward, sitting on a chair in the corridor, hunched over, wringing his hands and looking terrible.

'Is Mum going to be OK?' I ask, feeling as panicky as Phil looks. 'What about the baby? What have the doctors said? What happened?'

'They're doing tests,' he shrugs. 'That's all I know. She was at the doctor's for a check-up and mentioned that she kept getting headaches but this latest one wouldn't go away, and next thing is they're taking her in as an emergency case. Her blood pressure was rocketing.'

'And Jack,' I say. 'Who's looking after Jack?' I might not always like my little bro, but I don't want him standing outside Hilmartin Junior School sobbing his heart out because no one has come to collect him.

'Mrs Skinner will get him from school and give him his

tea,' Phil says. 'I couldn't get hold of you. Where were you? The school said you didn't come in today.'

'I didn't feel like it,' I mutter.

Phil's face is too full of worry over Mum and the baby to look angry at me. Instead he says, 'How did you get here?'

'A friend dropped me off,' I say, remembering how Rupe zoomed to the hospital at top speed and screeched into the car park. 'I'd better just go and say not to wait.'

I give Phil a hug and leave him to watch people shuffle along in slippers and gaping gowns as they push drips on sticks along the corridor.

It's a big car park but a bright-red Mini with stars and stripes painted on the roof should be easy to spot. But there's no sign of Rupert.

I ring his moby, but it just goes straight to answerphone and I don't bother to leave a message. For some reason, I'm not surprised he isn't waiting for me, but I'm too worried about Mum to stress about it.

As I'm heading back to the main entrance, walking towards me is Doctor Burns dressed in pale-blue scrubs, a stethoscope looped around her neck. Even in shapeless stuff she looks glam and glossy and frighteningly efficient.

We can't avoid each other without either swerving into a flower bed or knocking over an already fragile person tottering along, so we have stop.

'Hello, Electra,' Doc Burns says. 'Is everything all right?'

'Not really,' I say, shaking my head. 'They've brought Mum in. There's something wrong with her blood pressure. They're doing tests and stuff.'

'I'm sorry to hear that,' Doc Burns says, sounding genuinely concerned. 'When you see her, give her my best, won't you?'

'I will,' I say, standing to one side to let her carry on saving lives.

She begins to walk past, but I call out after her, 'How's Frazer? How's he doing?'

Doc Burns turns back. 'Not so good, but he's getting there. It was his first day back at school today. How did he seem when he saw you?'

'I didn't go in,' I say. 'Is he really upset?'

Doc B folds her arms across her chest. 'Electra, I knew this would happen. I knew you would break my son's heart sooner rather than later. It wasn't personal; I was just trying to protect him. He takes things very seriously and reacts badly if they go wrong.'

Clearly FB has been howling like a wolf in his room since we broke up.

'Will you tell him I was asking after him, and wish him happy birthday for Saturday?' I say.

Doc Burns stares at me. 'Are you still seeing this older lad, the one involved with drugs?' she asks.

I didn't know FB knew why Rupe had been expelled and, put that way, it makes him *sound* terrible, but now doesn't seem the time to start defending my current boyfriend to my ex-boyfriend's stroppy medic mother, so I just nod.

'Well, that can't be helping your mother's blood pressure,' she says, pursing her lips.

'She doesn't know,' I admit.

From the look on Doc Burns's face she clearly thinks that even if her son was still locked in his bedroom doing wolf impressions, he's better off without me.

'Probably just as well,' she says tightly. 'Good luck with your mum and the baby.'

As I watch her go off to do important things with her stethoscope I can't help but think that, unlike Rupert, FB would have stood outside all night in the cold if he had to, just to make sure me and my family were OK.

By the time I get back to Halstead Ward there's no sign of Phil. I immediately start panicking that Mum has taken a turn for the worse and that Phil is by her bedside, watching her die, whilst I've been in the car park searching for a missing boyfriend and battling with my ex's mum. But before I start yelling for a nurse – which is what freaked rellies do on telly – Phil appears, beaming from ear to ear and looking mega-relieved.

'Is everything OK?' I ask. 'Are they both going to be all right?'

'They've done the tests and it's not as serious as they thought it was.' Phil's breathless with relief. 'They're going to keep her in for a week or so to be sure. I expect you'd like to see her?'

I nod. 'Yes, please!'

'She's in there.'

He points to a door on the left and I head off, but he calls me back.

'Electra! Hang on!'

I stop and turn round. Phil's caught up with me.

'The person that dropped you off here, it was that boy, Rupert, wasn't it?' he asks.

My heart starts to hammer in my chest and I'm not sure whether it's because I'm about to see my mum in a hospital bed, just the mention of the word *Rupert*, or the fact that, now he's out of panic mode, Phil's on to me. I try to arrange my face into its most sullen blank look, something I used to excel at, but an expression I haven't used much recently.

'Was that why you bunked off school today, to spend the day with him?'

I'd like to lie my way out of this one, make up some

plausible excuse as to why I wasn't at school, such as unexpectedly being asked to meet the Prime Minister, but it doesn't feel right to lie when Mum isn't well, plus, if I'm going to tell the truth I might as well do it here, in public, where Phil can't go ballistic without a security guard intervening and throwing him out.

'Yeah,' I say, biting my lip. 'I spent the day with him.'

I wait for Phil to explode, read me the riot act and ground me for life, but all he says is, 'Your mum's blood pressure is already high. She must never know about this *or* him, OK?'

'Electra Brown, come up, please,' Mr McKay barks as he spots me at first registration on Tuesday morning.

I push my chair back and, trying not to catch Luce or Sorrel's eye as they know the real reason and full steamy details for my Monday no-show, make my way to The Ginger Gnome's desk. I'm also wondering if Tam and Claudia have guessed what I was up to as, despite furious rubbing with Vanish and a wet cloth, my blazer elbows are dirty.

As I weave my way to The GG's desk, I see FB hunched over his, doodling on a bit of paper.

'So where were you yesterday, Miss Brown?' Mr McKay growls, his bloodshot eye looking particularly gross

240

this morning. 'And do you have a note to back up your no doubt wildly unlikely explanation for your unplanned absence?'

'My mum was ill,' I say. 'They took her to hospital. She's still there.'

'*I* know,' Mr McKay says, breathing his toxic breath straight at me. 'Someone phoned to tell us to tell you, but you weren't here to tell, were you?'

I shrug. 'I'd stayed off because I knew Mum was ill. Her boyfriend didn't realize.'

'And the note? Why haven't you brought a note in?' I'm getting the full force of The Ginger Minger's bloody stare and rank breath.

'Er, Mum was too ill to write a note,' I say in a tone of voice that I hope is just the right side of *What a stupid question* not to get me further teacher grief. '*That's* why she's in the General.'

Mr McKay glares at me. 'I don't know what you've been up to, Miss Brown, but I suggest whatever it is doesn't interfere with your schoolwork in future. Do I make myself clear?'

I nod and scurry back to my desk.

After more droning by The GG, the bell goes and the class surges through the door. I hang back so that I don't bump into FB. He's obviously trying to avoid me as we both end up hanging back together.

It's the first time I've seen him properly since that awful day I dumped him. It's only been just under a week, but already but he looks thinner, smaller, sadder.

'How's your mum?' he asks, staring at the ground, not me.

'She's fine, thanks,' I say as we walk down the corridor. 'She might come out at the weekend, but she'll have to stay in bed until the baby arrives. Did your mum tell you she was ill?'

'Mum?' FB sounds surprised. 'No, I overhead you telling Mr McKay. When did you see my mum?'

'At the hospital, yesterday afternoon,' I say. 'I bumped into her. I did tell her to say hello to you but . . .' I let my voice trail off as I remember Doc Burns's stony reaction to seeing me. 'I guess she didn't.'

'No, no, she didn't.' FB gives a slightly sarky laugh. 'Look, I've got to go,' he says awkwardly, 'or I'll be late for physics.'

'Me too,' I say, 'but for French. Mademoiselle Armstrong already has it in for me.'

FB smiles. 'I'm glad your mum's OK,' he says. 'If I'd known she was so ill, I'd have been in touch, despite everything.'

'Thanks,' I say. 'I know you would.'

And as I watch him go, bag slung over his shoulder, his head down, I suddenly wonder if I've made a terrible mistake in letting him go, because despite Rupert burning rubber to get me to the General, he's not been in touch to find out whether Mum is dead or alive.

Chapter Nineteen

It's raining fat cats and overweight dogs as Luce, Sorrel and me dart out of Flora Burke's on Thursday afternoon, the three of us huddled under Lucy's pink frilly umbrella, giggling and screaming as passing cars drench us with dirty puddle water.

We're off to Sorrel's caravan to eat pizza, drink Diet Coke and compare our geography field trip projects. The written stuff has got to be in next week, but because of the whole Nat–Buff–Hamster excitement, I'm not sure my note-taking was up to scratch. I'm also having trouble with my closing paragraph, the one where I have to summarize my findings. I want to write that amongst the limestone rocks and fossils I found out that Natalie Price wasn't having a steamy affair with Jon Butler after all, but I'm not sure that's the type of summarizing the examiners are looking for. But I've got to buckle down and get on with it as the whole bunking-off with Rupe or sitting-dreaming-about-him stuff has meant I'm behind with *masses* of homework and I'm in serious danger of getting a crappola report and a bollocking from the parentals.

It's been a weird couple of weeks since the day that began on Copse Hill with Rupert and finished in the General with Phil and Mum, as since then I've been living a double life.

After a week in hospital and a cocktail of drugs, the docs sent Mum home with strict instructions to keep a baby bag packed and ready to go, spend the rest of her preggers life either in bed or on the sofa, not to drive, watch any horror films or listen to bad news, and to avoid stressful situations such as doing Sudokus that are too hard, which is why by day I am Delightful Daughter, on hand to stick a frozen lasagne in the oven or whizz the Hoover around and make sure Mum doesn't lift a finger, but by night, or rather odd afternoons after school and one evening where I pretended I'd been at the cinema with the girls, I turn into Deceitful Daughter, the daughter who has a secret life with Rupert, a lad who never texts or arranges dates, but just drives in and out of my life whenever he feels like it.

Like now.

I haven't heard from him since he whisked me off to watch the sun going down over the gasworks on Tuesday (when I pretended I had to go to a history lecture), but here he is, parked outside the school, two wheels on the pavement, two wheels on the road.

I duck and knock on the wet window.

He winds it down.

'What are you doing here?' I ask, trying to sound cool and uninterested, whilst being very interested despite being sopping wet.

'Waiting for you,' he says, flashing me that heart-stopping smile. 'Hop in.'

'Ow!' My left arm is practically yanked from its socket as Sorrel drags me up and back before I have the chance to hop anywhere.

'What was that for?' I say, rubbing my shoulder as I shelter under the pink parasol. 'You could have disabled me for life!'

'A little reminder that we're going back to mine,' she says darkly. 'You promised.'

'Even *I've* told Josh I can't see him,' Lucy says.

I look at the car. Not only is it warm and dry, it's got hot Rupe sitting in it.

'I could come round tomorrow,' I suggest. 'It doesn't *have* to be tonight, does it?'

'Yes. It. Does,' Sorrel snaps. She looks wet, fed up and angry. 'Electra, you've got to put a stop to this *now*. *He's* the one always calling the shots, never you. He just turns up when he feels like it. Can't you see he's just using you when it suits him? Stand up to him for a change. Tell him you'll see him at the weekend, but not now.'

'You're just miffed he's here and Joz is over there,' I say, throwing her what I hope is a friendly yet decidedly sarky look. 'You'd be the same if it was The Jozster's jet ski parked on the pavement.' I'm starting to get stressed that Rupe will drive off without me and find a rain-soaked Claudia to keep warm.

'Sorrel's right,' Lucy says. 'You either don't make plans in case Rupert turns up, or if you do and he does, you break them.'

'And you can't mess up this project,' Sorrel reminds me. 'This isn't just homework, it counts.'

Rupe beeps his horn and looks out of the window. 'Coming or not?' he calls out.

'Look,' I say to the girls. 'I'll have a word with him and see if I can arrange to see him at the weekend or something. Don't move.'

I dive from under the umbrella and run to the car.

'I'll hop in but I can't go anywhere,' I say, getting in and shaking my head, sending water flying everywhere. 'I've got loads of work to catch up on.'

Rupert pulls away, the car's windscreen wipers squeaking as they scrape across the glass.

'I've told you!' I say, half laughing, half annoyed that he's ignored me. 'I can't go anywhere. I've got work to do.'

'Work!' Rupe snorts. 'Don't let your life be dominated by work!'

We're now racing along the wet main road.

'It's OK for you!' I say, texting a *Soz* to the girls. 'You're old enough to have left school.'

Rupe carries on driving. The car is small, the road is wet and we're going *very* fast.

'Rupert, I mean it,' I say, irritated and putting my seat belt on. 'I can't go anywhere with you tonight. What about the weekend? We could do something then. I'll make up an excuse to slip away.'

'Got plans at the weekend,' Rupert says. 'Sorry, E.'

'But we *never* make plans,' I moan, realizing I'm whining but unable to stop myself. 'The girls are right, you just turn up when you want and expect me to be there.'

'Well, you always are,' Rupert laughs. 'So that's OK, isn't it?'

'Can't you cancel your plans?' I ask. 'We could go for a meal or to the fair that's on the common.'

'Can't,' he replies. 'Sorry.'

'But why?' I whine. 'What's so important that you can't find time for me?' I can hear myself sounding pleady and needy and it shocks me. In three weeks of seeing Rupert only a handful of times I've turned into Limpet Girl.

Rupert pulls the car over and stops in a lay-by by the side of the dual carriageway.

'Electra, that's just how it is,' he says gently. He cups my wet face in his hands and as he kisses me all the anger and irritation and disappointment I feel melts away.

'Look,' I say, after we've kissed for so long, my hair is practically dry. 'If you can't do this weekend we've got the Easter hols coming up in a couple of weeks. We can spend every day together. I'll sort out a cover story to keep Mum off the scent.'

'I'll be living in Oxford then,' Rupe says casually.

'Oxford?' I practically shriek. 'What will you be doing in Oxford?'

'Oh, God, it's an absolute nightmare,' he drawls, pushing his hair out of his eyes. 'Ma and Pa have found some poxy crammer to force me through my sodding A levels.'

'But I thought you'd had enough of school!' I say. 'You told me you'd finished with it.'

Absurdly Beautiful rolls his eyes. 'Last-ditch attempt by the old folks to get me into uni and make paying for all that education worthwhile,' he says with a grimace. 'A few weeks of concentrated hell in the hope I'll scrape the odd grade.'

I'm confused.

'What happened to all that non-conformist stuff?' I ask. 'What happened to not sticking to the system?'

Rupert looks a bit uncomfortable. 'Well, the deal was I either finished my A levels and went to uni, or moved out and got a job, and I'm not ready to become a little cog in a big wheel lining the pockets of corporate fat cats.'

In other words, he's lush but lazy, I think to myself.

'But what will we do?' I ask. My mind is whirring about what this means for me, for us, other than the fact I'm not going to get any lifts in a Mini after school. And how often will I be able to see him? I don't think my bus pass will take me anywhere near Oxford.

'What do you mean, what will we do?' Rupe asks. He pushes my hair back from my face and tucks it behind my ears, and I'm momentarily freaked that after three weeks he'll suddenly realize he's been going out with a girl with a face the width of a satellite dish.

'I mean, will you come back here at weekends?' I say. 'I can't see Mum letting me stay with you overnight.'

'I don't think Caitlin would be that chuffed about it either!' Rupe laughs.

'Caitlin?' I ask. 'Who's Caitlin?'

'My girlfriend,' Rupert says simply as, parked in a tiny car on the side of the road in the pouring rain, my entire world comes crashing down around me.

'You've – you've got a girlfriend?' I can hardly speak with the shock. 'I . . . I . . .' I can barely breathe.

'Well, that's the conventional way of putting it,' he says. 'But you know how much I hate labels.'

His beautiful face is almost touching mine as his hand strokes the back of my neck.

And much as I love him, right now I hate him so much, it scares me.

'She got chucked out of the lower sixth last year and is doing some business studies course there,' he says, as if explaining about her makes this nuclear bombshell somehow less explosive. 'I thought I'd stay with her, save on rent and all that.'

His touch suddenly disgusts me.

'You're cheating on me with her and her with me!' I gasp, pulling away from him as hot tears start to bounce off my cheeks. 'How could you?'

'It's not like that,' Rupert says. He tries to put his arm around me but I push him away. 'She knows all about you.'

Can this be for real? Am I about to wake up and see pink walls and piles of dirty underwear and realize it's just some dodgy dream brought on by eating too much cheese late at night?

I bite the inside of my cheek and, when it hurts like hell, realize it's not a dreadful dream but a living nightmare.

'And she doesn't mind?' I'm so shocked I can barely hear my own voice. 'Doesn't she care you've been seeing someone else?'

Rupert shrugs. 'We have a fluid relationship. The agreement is, when we're apart we can fool around with others as long as there's no removing of underwear.' He starts to laugh but then thinks better of it and purses his lips. 'We both know how far to go.'

So *that's* why he never made a move under my school shirt! It was nothing to do with respecting me. He's been fooling around with me but only under the conditions set by his posh girlfriend.

'So when I've been waiting for you to call or text, you've been in Oxford with her?' I say. 'I've been looking for you here and you've been there?' I think of my weekends, wandering around the streets hoping to bump into him, staring at my moby willing it to ring, thinking of him constantly.

Rupert nods. 'Sometimes. Mostly.'

'You were with her last weekend, weren't you?' I say accusingly, though I already know the answer.

He nods again.

'And that's where you'll be this weekend, with her, isn't it? That's why you won't make plans with me! You won't make plans with me because you've already got plans with her!' I feel as if at any moment I could become *totally* hysterical, the sort of hysterical that can only be stopped by a slap in the face or a shot of sleep-inducing tranquillizer in the arm.

'Yes,' he admits. 'I'll be in Oxford, with Caitlin.'

I look out of the car's windscreen. It's steamed up so there's nothing to see except water running down it. I used to sit in this car next to Rupert and feel unbelievably happy, the sort of happy that makes you smile inside and out. The sort of happy that lights up your face and makes everything seem possible. The sort of happy you can't believe will ever end.

I'm in the same car with the same lad but I don't think I've ever felt as desperately unhappy or alone as I do right now.

There's something I need to know, even if it sends me into hysterical orbit and requires an ambulance and medication. I wipe away the tears, which won't stop falling, try to gather myself together, take a deep breath and steel myself.

'Do you sleep with her?' I ask. There's a massive lump in my throat and my chest feels so tight I can hardly breathe. 'Do you?'

Rupert looks straight out of the steamed-up front window, bites his lip and nods again. 'Yeah,' he barely whispers. 'Yeah, I do.'

Oh. My. God. I feel violently sick and clamp my hand over my mouth.

I try to get out of the car, but through my tears and panic I can't work out how to get my seat belt undone. I pull it sharply but it doesn't move.

I've got to get out.

I've got to get away.

I need to get home but I can't because the bloody belt is trapping me.

'Electra, don't,' Rupert pleads, trying to stop me from scrambling free. 'Don't be upset.'

'Don't be upset? Don't be upset?' I scream, practically spitting at him. 'I've found out I was just some comprehensive-school chav to fool around with during the week until you got back to your posh girlfriend, and you tell me not to be upset?'

'NO!' Rupert shouts. It's the first time I've heard him raise his voice and I'm surprised at how deep and strong it sounds. 'You've got it all wrong.' He leans his body over me, and holds on to the door handle. 'At least let me explain!'

'Get off me!' I snarl, hitting him in the shoulder and finally freeing the seat belt from its catch. I push his hand off the door handle, grab my school bag, scramble out of the car and start running along the side of the road in the pouring rain. I *so* want to retch on to the grass verge, but I'm not giving the cheating lying scroat the satisfaction of seeing me do it, so I just choke back the taste of acidy vomit that keeps lurching into my mouth.

Rupert catches up with me and tries to take my arm.

'Get away from me!' I scream, shaking him free. 'Leave me alone!'

'NO!' Rupert jumps in front of me, holds both my arms and shakes me. 'Electra, I told you I was bad news. I warned you what I was like.'

'You didn't warn me you had a girlfriend!' I yell. Cars are whizzing past, spraying us with mucky water. 'You didn't tell me that part. I gave up my kind, gentle, reliable boyfriend for you, but you still kept your snotty girlfriend to sleep with!'

'Get real, Electra.' Rupert sounds angry. 'You didn't give up Limpet Boy for me! You gave him up because he smothered you and he bored you and you wanted some uncomplicated fun. We both did. I thought you knew the rules.'

I didn't know there were rules. I just know one thing.

'I loved you!' I scream in his face. 'I loved you and all the time you were doing everything with her, I'd have done *anything* for you.'

'Oh, Electra,' Rupert sighs, pulling me to his chest where

255

I sob and sob and sob. 'I'm so sorry. I never meant to hurt you. You've got to believe me. You're cool and cute and I've loved every second of being with you.'

'But you don't love me, do you?' I say, looking up at him. Water is dripping from his hair and off his bumpy nose but, unlike me, it's only rain, not tears, falling. 'You've never felt the same way about me as I have about you, have you?'

Rupert doesn't say anything.

He doesn't have to.

He just strokes and kisses the top of my head as in the pouring rain on the side of the dual carriageway, my heart shatters into a trillion tiny pieces.

I didn't want to get back in the car.

I don't know whether I love Rupert or I hate him, but I do know that I don't want to be anywhere near him.

But he wouldn't leave me on the side of the road and I was too shattered, too soaked and too lost to start walking home, so he bundled me into the car and we drove back in soggy sob-punctuated silence.

When we pulled up outside Mortimer Road he was saying stuff, trying to tell me he was sorry over and over again, but I didn't want to listen. I just wanted to get out, get away and get into the Rupert-free safety of my house and my bedroom, which is where I am now, lying on my bed in my wet school uniform, still wearing my shoes, looking up at the skylight as I watch the rain lash on the glass and the sky grow even darker. It's a toss-up as to whether my face or the window is wetter I'm crying so much.

There's two knocks on the door and Mum pokes her head around it.

'Electra! I thought you were going to Sorrel's after school and having tea there,' she says.

'Shouldn't you be lying down?' I say, trying to sound normal.

'I was, but I heard noises,' she says. 'Why are you lying in the dark?' She switches a light on and sees my face, which feels so swollen from crying it probably looks as if I've been attacked by a swarm of killer bees.

'Oh, love, what's happened this time?' She comes over to the bed. 'What's gone on now?'

I look up at her, huge and worried.

'Oh, Mum!' I cry. 'I've been such an idiot!'

She sits on the bed and just holds me as I weep. She doesn't press me as to what's happened or tell me that it's all going to be all right in the morning because we both know it isn't. She just lets me cry and hands me tissues.

Eventually, when I run out of tears and she runs out of tissues she says, 'Is this about Rupert?'

'Rupert?' I pull back from her. I'd like to have pretended

it wasn't so as not to worry her and get me into mega trouble, but the mere mention of his name sends me sobbing and snotting again. 'How did you know?'

Mum puts her arm around me again. 'Oh, a lethal combination of being young once *and* being your mother,' she laughs. 'I might be confined to barracks but the fact that you didn't mention this Love God even once after we had that row made me pretty sure you were seeing him behind my back.'

'And you didn't say anything?' I can't believe Mum has managed to keep quiet for so long.

'I figured it would burn itself out,' Mum says.

'And if it didn't?'

'Then I'd have gone mental and locked you in your room until you were at least twenty-one.' She smiles. 'Do you want to talk about it?'

I shake my head. 'It's over,' I say. 'There's nothing left to talk about.'

I flop back on the bed and look up at the window.

'Once,' I say, 'I was lying here and a helicopter flew in.'

'Really?' Mum feels my forehead, clearly thinking I'm delirious.

'It was FB's. He wanted to explain about things, say he was sorry. I wouldn't listen to him so it was the only way he could contact me.'

'He was a nice boy,' Mum says. 'Serious, but nice.'

'I was so mean, Mum,' I choke. 'I swapped burgundy patent for fringed suede and didn't realize at the time just how badly I hurt him.' I can feel myself getting hysterical again.

'And now you do?' she asks.

I think of how I felt on the side of the road in the rain as what little relationship I had with Rupert crashed and burnt. When I thought FB had finished with me that night in The Curry Cottage I felt mad rather than sad, mega-miffed rather than heartbroken. I was upset but it didn't feel like the end of the world. My heart didn't feel so broken it physically aches.

It does now.

'Yes,' I gulp, 'and I'm so sorry.'

'Then tell him,' Mum urges. 'Go and tell him you're sorry.'

I shake my head and start to sob again. 'I can't. It's too late.'

'Oh, Electra.' Mum takes my hand. 'It's never too late to say sorry. Frazer might not accept your apology, but that's the risk you'll have to take.'

'And Luce and Sorrel. I've mucked them around, put *him* before them,' I say. 'I've been shallow and selfish to so many people.'

'You've just been human,' Mum assures me. 'You've been in love.'

There's something else I need to apologize for. Something really important.

'I'm sorry I've been such a cow about Ermintrude or Zebedee, Mum,' I say, wiping my nose on the back of my blazer. 'I'm sorry I've been so horrid about the baby, about you, about Phil . . .'

'It's OK, love,' Mum says soothingly, holding me as my tear ducts go into overdrive again. 'It might take a while but everything will be OK, I promise you.'

Chapter Twenty

I didn't go in today. I felt so wiped out Mum agreed to ring the school with some story about me having a brain-crushing migraine, but only on the condition that I went back on Monday morning as usual.

I didn't text the girls to tell them what had happened. I want to tell them myself, face-to-face, and also to say soz for letting them down when I was hoping Rupe was around, especially Sorrel. I just texted to say I was sorry I'd left them stranded under a pink brolly in a downpour, I'd explain fully later, and I was staying off because I felt grotty. And when I was adding Lucy's name to the text I saw *Lust* listed under hers, and in floods of tears deleted Rupert's number for good, even though it hurt me to do it.

I wanted to lie in bed all day and shut the world out, but I didn't. After a few hours more of sobbing and wallowing and listening to suicidal-type music on my iPod, I got up and cleaned the house from top to bottom whilst Mum watched and issued instructions. And although housework isn't ever going to mend a broken heart, it felt good to have Mum to myself whilst I worked out how to change the Hoover bag for the first time in my life, talking to each other about nothing in particular but collapsing in fits of giggles when I dug a fossilized banana out from under the sideboard.

But as soon as the giggling stops, the tears start.

I know Rupert's not going to knock on the door and tell me he's dumped Caitlin and it's me he wants, but, oh, how I wish he would.

Mum's lying down, Phil and Jack are eating the (shop-bought) chicken pie and veg Phil's cooked, and I'm pushing peas around my plate as I'm not hungry, when above us the letterbox rattles.

Jack jumps up from the table and races upstairs before stomping back down clutching a white envelope.

'It's for Poo-Head,' he grumbles, throwing it in my general direction where it lands on a lump of buttery mash.

I tear open the carb-smeared envelope on which someone has written *Electra* in strong looping black letters.

Inside is a red elastic band.

Printed in tiny letters in black biro around the inside are the words, *Sorry – Sorry – Sorry – Rxx*

With a hammering heart and shaking hands, I ring the doorbell to 7 Compton Avenue, FB's house.

I can hear Archie racing towards the door, his nails clattering on the wood floor in the hall before he starts bouncing at the half-glass like some mental muppet dog.

And then through the glass I see the outline of FB approaching.

What a relief! I'd been dreading seeing Doc Burns and her slamming the door in my face.

Frazer opens it, and stands with Archie wriggling in his arms.

'Electra!' he smiles, his face lighting up. Standing on his doorstep, the hall light in the background framing him, Archie trying to break free and lick his face, I remember why I fancied FB in the first place and get an overwhelming feeling of relief and safety and love for him. It's not the sort of racy love I had for Rupert, but something more comforting. Frazer doesn't have a car or smoke dope or have a girlfriend on the side. He might not be as exciting as Rupert, but I didn't know that being safe and reliable and straightforward doesn't have to mean boring.

I do now.

'Can I come in?' I ask. 'There's something I need to say.'

'Umm . . .' FB looks round. 'Well . . .'

'It's OK,' I assure him. I don't really want to face the family Burns yet. 'Frazer, look, I'm so sorry that I treated you so badly. I was a right bitch and a total idiot.' At the thought of hurting him, tears begin to prick my eyes. After all the sobbing I've done in the last twenty-four hours I'm surprised there's any more tears left to sob.

'It's OK,' FB says, smiling. 'I don't blame you. Not any more.'

My heart leaps. FB doesn't hate me! He doesn't blame me! He's smiling that lovely smile. He's always been there for me. He's *still* there for me. I don't deserve him, but I'm getting a second chance to make things right.

'So will you start your watch again?' I say. 'Can we start over?'

'I take it it's all over with Rupert?' FB asks.

'Hi, Electra.'

Angela Panteli appears behind FB in the hall. Angela Panteli, the original dark-haired Greek Goddess with long eyelashes, whose father runs The Galloping Greek restaurant. Angela Panteli, who's at FB's house on a Friday night. And from the way Archie is wagging his tail when he sees her, she's been here before.

She's clearly as surprised to see me as I am to see her.

I look at FB standing with Archie, Angela stroking Archie's head, realize what's been going on, and turn and run.

Mum and Dad always told me never to go to Victoria Park alone as the place is full of winos and weirdos. Sorrel tried sleeping on a bench here when she ran away before Christmas, but it was too weird and too cold even for her. FB and I used to sit here and spend what seemed like hours, snogging in between him telling me fascinating facts such as duck quacks don't echo or butterflies taste with their feet.

But it's no longer me and FB. It's FB and Angela, Lucy and Josh, Sorrel and Joz (if only she'd admit it), Rupert and Caitlin, and me and no one.

A man approaches. He could be a flasher or a weirdo about to drag me into the bushes but I'm too upset to make a run for it.

'Electra?'

It's FB.

'I thought I'd find you here,' he says, sitting next to me. 'You shouldn't be alone. It'll be getting dark soon.'

'Shouldn't you be back with Angela?' I say bitterly. 'Your new girlfriend.'

'She suggested I follow you,' FB says, and I notice he

doesn't deny she's his girlfriend. 'She was worried about you. We both were.'

'So you *are* going out together,' I say.

'It's early days, but yes,' he agrees. 'We are.'

'I didn't know you knew her.' I've never seen them so much as speak, let alone snog. 'It seems very sudden.' So much for him yelling that he'd never get over me and find anyone else.

'She cleared away my lamb souvlaki when I went to her dad's place for my birthday and it just went from there,' he says, smiling at the memory.

I didn't realize that FB had still gone to The Galloping Greek without me. How could I have been so shallow and selfish as to really believe that his life stopped when I told him to stop his watch? Of *course* life carried on without me, and now FB is carrying on without me but with someone else.

'Do you remember when I saw you sitting on this bench and Archie tried to hump your leg?' FB laughs.

'He covered me in goose poo,' I groan. 'I looked minging.'

'Even with bird poo you looked lovely,' FB says.

'But not as lovely as your new Greek Goddess,' I say slightly more sourly than I intended. 'It's her not me now, isn't it?'

'I always said you were out of my league,' FB says, ignoring my jibe at Angela. 'You're bright, you're beautiful and you're funny, but if we went out together you'd soon find me boring and break my heart again. I can't risk it.'

'I *so* wouldn't!' I say, taking FB's hand. 'I promise I wouldn't. I know what I want now.'

'What did you do with Rupert?' FB asks, putting his other hand on top of mine. 'What did you get up to?'

'I didn't sleep with him, if that's what you're implying,' I say indignantly, pulling my hand away.

'I'm not,' FB says. 'You and I sat on benches and walked round the shops. What did you and he do?'

I think back to these last few weeks: the drive to London at midnight; bunking off school and kissing on Copse Hill; listening to rock music; looking at the stars whilst he whispered poetry in my ear; leaving the car door open and the stereo on and smooching to music whilst parked in a field, him nuzzling my neck, me worried that the cows grazing nearby might start stampeding.

'There's no going back, is there?' I say, realizing FB is right. Things have moved on, for both of us. I put my hand in my pocket, pull out the red rubber band and slip it on my wrist. I still love Rupert even if I can't have him, and I love FB, but not in the same way. And even though my heart feels so shattered it hurts, I wouldn't have missed these last few weeks with Rupert Lennox-Hill for the world.

FB puts his arm around me. It feels lovely, warm, comforting, familiar, but it's the touch of a friend, not a boyfriend.

'We'll never go out again but I'll always be there for you, Electra,' FB says. 'I promise you. And remember, a boyfriend is for snogging, but a friend is for life.'

Chapter Twenty-one

At first I wanted to find out all about Caitlin: what she looks like, where she lives, why she'd been expelled from school, how long has Rupert been seeing her, does she have naturally perky boobs, etc. I wanted to hunt down Tamara and force her to give me the gory details of her brother's love life, even if it meant strapping her to a desk in an empty classroom with my tie and torturing her by tickling her with my fluffy-tipped gel pen.

But I didn't, firstly because I don't want her to tell her bro that two weeks after the side-of-the-road split I'm still gutted. I want him to remember me as cute and cool, even if the last he saw of me was stumbling out of his car in a sea of snot and tears. And secondly, what would be the point? Rupert's with Caitlin and I'm with no one and no amount of juicy info can change that. And what if I found out Caitlin's a zit-free stunning minx with legs up to her armpits? It would only make me feel worse, and if I feel any worse than I do now, I might as well be measured up for a coffin and something loose in white cotton.

I've taken Rupe's red band off my wrist, not because I wanted to but because my wrist got sweaty under the rubber and all the *Sorrys* started smearing into one long inky mess. So I printed off the quote by Shelley that Rupert used to recite, Soul meets soul on lovers' lips, wrapped the band in it, put it in a little pink heart-shaped box Lucy gave me years ago for my birthday, and in floods of tears buried it in my knicker drawer, before trying to get on with life and GCSEs.

But living life with a shattered heart is hard. *So* hard.

It's the Easter hols at the mo, and instead of having fun and gorging my gob on chocolate, I can't stop thinking about Rupe moving in with Caitlin in Oxford and I wish I could, because when I do, it tears me apart and I can't face cracking open even the poshest candy-filled egg. In fact, I've been off my food since we broke up so whereas Mum thinks I'm looking gaunt, I'm thrilled that I've finally got cheekbones.

The girls have been great, taking me shopping, organizing a pamper session in my bedroom where they painted my nails and did my hair, always being there for me, trying to cheer me up, but I'm not sure that Sorrel forcing me to go on one of her Saturday afternoon eco-crusades in Sainsbury's car park will do much to mend my broken heart, which is where I am now.

She finally decided what she wanted to do with the extra Bling Bag money, and it wasn't planting a flowering cherry tree in Victoria Park, which is what Bella suggested. It was getting a whole load of yellow balloons printed with *Gas Guzzler* in black ink, balloons that match the stickers Yolanda has been slapping on Beast Cars for years.

'I don't really think I'm cut out for this eco-warrior stuff,' I say as Yolanda hands me a huge bouquet of balloons. 'It's not really my thing.'

'Electra,' Yolanda says, putting her arm around my shoulder. 'Sorrel tells me that you are still pining for some young man. Believe me, the best way to get over a broken heart is to keep busy and do something useful.'

If only repairing a shattered heart were that simple I'd have a perfect pumper by now. With Mum being in bed I've been cooking and cleaning non-stop, not to mention catching up on all the schoolwork I've let slide. And without FB to help, things have been really slow on the science and maths front. Even though he said he'd always be there for me, I'm not sure it would be fair on Ange to bust their dates just to grill her boyfriend about some equation I can't solve.

Whilst Yolanda heads off in another direction, Sorrel and I amble along a row of cars, nattering about whether we can get out of going to Josh's Dogs of Doom concert at the Methodist Church hall on Chapel Street tonight. Sorrel says we have to go as Josh will be performing a song he's written for Lucy and she'll never forgive us if we don't hear it. I want to support Luce but I don't want to go, because in my still-fragile post-Rupe state I'm not sure I'm up to hearing declarations of undying love set to twanging electric guitars without crying the sort of tears not even the toughest waterproof mascara can stand.

'Look at that!' Sorrel growls, pointing at a huge blue car, its backside jutting out of the parking bay. 'A classic example of a planet-wrecking Beast Car.'

She slaps a sticker on the windscreen, I stand on my tiptoes and tie a balloon to the aerial and we carry on ambling and gossiping.

'What the hell do you think you're doing?' It's the voice of a nuclear-angry man.

We turn round. A bloke with a red face, bulbous nose and no hair is marching towards us holding a long golden baguette.

'What did you do that for?' he demands, brandishing his baguette in a very threatening manner.

'Your car is polluting the environment and killing the

272

planet for the next generation,' Sorrel says primly. 'We're pointing it out to you in the hope you may consider a different model in the future.'

Baguette Man's face goes from red to purple. 'You stupid, misguided, yoghurt-knitting kids,' he spits, waving the bread stick around. 'That car is a hybrid. It runs on petrol *and* electricity. It has very low emissions!'

'Oh,' Sorrel says, looking about as embarrassed as an eco-warrior who's got her environmental facts wrong can look. 'I didn't realize.'

The man goes back to his car and tries to rip the sticker off, but leaves half of it plastered across the windscreen. He then tries to untie the balloon from the aerial but just manages to bend the slender black stick.

'You vandals,' he yells. 'I'll have you for criminal damage.'

He shakes his baguette, but there is clearly only a limited amount of time in which cooked bread can be used as a potentially lethal weapon without disintegrating as half of it snaps off and falls on to the ground.

Sorrel and I giggle at this display of dough droop as the man swears and boots the broken bread into the road.

'What's going on?' Yolanda shouts, heading towards us. 'Who's upset?'

'We got a hybrid,' Sorrel shouts back.

'Hang on, girls!' Yolanda calls, waving. 'I'll sort this out.'

She's so busy jogging towards us, braids and boobs bouncing as she weaves between the parked cars, she doesn't notice a man trundling an enormous snake of empty trolleys down the middle of the road until the last minute. After a body swerve worthy of a Premiership footballer, she successfully dodges the trolley train, jumps over the broken baguette, but then stumbles and starts staggering forward until she finally loses her footing and lands in a crumpled heap by the back bumper of the pretend Beast Car.

I'm so shocked I let go of the balloons and they head up and away over the car park, their cords dangling, looking like giant yellow sperm.

'Mum!' Sorrel cries. Yolanda's lying on the pavement surrounding by fluttering yellow and black stickers. 'Are you all right?'

Yolanda sits up. She looks dazed and a bit confused, and there's a slight graze on her forehead, just above her eye.

'I'm fine,' she says, touching her face and wincing slightly. 'It's just a scratch. I should have looked where I was going.'

Strangers start asking if they should call an ambulance or a first-aid person, but Yolanda won't have any of it. She even turns down a lift from Half Baguette Man when he offers to run her home.

'It's my pride, not my body, that's hurt,' she smiles as she gets up, Sorrel and me either side of her. 'A cup of chamomile tea and some arnica ointment on my bruises and I'll be fine.'

'So your mum just tripped?' Luce asks Sorrel as we wait for The Dogs of Doom to finish plugging things in and start twanging.

The gig last Christmas was a great success and the place is packed already.

'She tried to avoid a bit of broken bread and just fell,' Sorrel says. 'She was fine when I left. Her and Ray were rinsing out the sprout jars and refilling them.'

'Who's here?' I say, looking around. 'Anyone I know?'

'*Everyone*,' Luce says. 'I don't know how we'll fit any more in, and James and his lot aren't here yet.'

'James does know Naz is in the band?' I say, thinking of the whole Naz–Fritha–James triangle and wondering if a punch-up between James and The Dogs' drummer would be seen as a disaster or *totally* rock and roll.

'Oh, James is so over Fritha,' Luce says, scanning the crowd. 'He's seeing some girl called Clemmie. Fritha's now going out with Jags even though he's shorter than her, and Naz is concentrating on his A levels.'

'Jags!' I screech. 'You never said!' I'm amazed that Luce

hasn't filled me in on this dating merry-go-round, particularly the Jags bit. 'Why didn't you tell me?'

'I thought you might be upset about Jags and Fritha,' she says. 'You've had a lot of upset recently.'

There was a time when the thought of Jags the Spanish Lurve God going out with anyone but me would have left me sobbing into my pillow broken-hearted, but not now, not when I know what it's like to be *really* broken-hearted.

Claudia, Tam, Shenice and Shaz are here and I'm surprised to see Butterface entwined with a good-looking lad with dark skin and inky-coloured hair. I'm also amazed that Nat seems to be less butterfaced and more bare-faced than I've ever seen her. Without her make-up she's quite pretty. She sees me looking over at her and instead of blanking me, she smiles, waves and then starts eating the face off her date. Clearly she's found an advantage to changing schools, like a whole new gene pool of talent to snog.

I'm pleased for her, I really am. I'm pleased that things have worked out for her after she was expelled, and for James, who was dumped.

FB and Angela look good together even though it's odd seeing them walking out of school together hand-in-hand.

Lucy's mega happy with Josh, and Sorrel has Joz to dream about and his picture to stare at on her screensaver.

Mum isn't happy that she has to stay in bed all the time but she and Phil are thrilled about the baby and can't wait for it to arrive.

Even Dad seems really happy and is looking fit and less mooby, though he hasn't told me about the woman in white and I haven't let on I've seen him with his hands down her pants.

So it's just me who doesn't have anyone or anything except memories and a red rubber band in a box.

'You OK?' a velvety voice with a soft Irish accent enquires.

I'd slipped out of the church hall halfway through Josh's song for Lucy to avoid a major public sobbing sesh. The combination of acoustic guitar, Josh's beautiful voice and the heart-melting lyrics he'd written for Luce was too painful for me to listen to, especially on a Saturday night when I know Rupert will be with Caitlin.

I'm obviously not as over Absurdly Beautiful as I'd hoped.

'I'm fine,' I say, trying to wipe away tears that won't stop falling. 'Honestly. It's nothing.'

'I'm Irish, not stupid,' Velvet Voice says. 'Those tear ducts aren't working overtime for nothing.'

'Guilty as charged,' I say, putting my hand up. 'It is something.'

'You want to talk about it or tell me to get lost?' Velvet

Voice asks. 'I'm good at listening and I won't be offended if you tell me to walk the plank.'

'There's a lot of stuff going on,' I say. 'Boy stuff and parent stuff, but mostly boy stuff – well, one boy. A song set me off.' The tears start again. 'I'm pathetic, aren't I?' I laugh.

'Then I'm pathetic too,' Velvet Voice says. 'I had to leave to stop myself blubbing.'

'Really?' I say. 'You've been crying as well?'

'Well, no,' Velvet Voice admits. 'I can't let myself start or I'd never stop. I'd be like some sort of human fountain, spouting tears here, there and everywhere. And I can't let myself get too upset or I'll fail my GCSEs, which will make me cry even more!'

I giggle and under the street lamp look at who I'm talking to. It's a lad probably a couple of years older than me with a mop of sandy-brown curly hair and a warm cheeky smile.

'Girls and parents stuff?' I ask.

'One girl who went on a school skiing trip before Easter, spent too much time on the old après-ski with some French idiot she met, and now isn't interested in anyone who isn't called Claude Pelletier, which is a bit of a problem seeing as I'm called Séan Brown.'

'No way!' I say. 'We share the same surname. I'm Electra Brown.'

'Well, there's a thing,' Séan laughs. 'With a name like Electra I'm suspecting you're more of a Greek girl than an Irish lass though.'

'I am *so* not a Greek girl,' I laugh. 'I'm just a bog-standard Brit.'

'Oh, I wouldn't say that,' Séan teases.

'Electra?' Sorrel dashes through the doors and into the street. 'I've got to go home. Ray's just rung.'

'This is my friend Sorrel,' I say to Séan, who smiles and nods. 'Everything OK?'

'I couldn't really hear in there, but it was something about me needing to look after the kids so I'd better get back.'

'You want me to come with you?' I say.

'Nah, you stay here,' she smiles. As she hugs me she whispers in my ear, 'He's cute,' before heading off.

'I think I'll go too,' I say. 'I'll just say goodbye to my friend Lucy.'

'Do you want me to walk you home?' Séan asks. 'No strings and I'll keep my hands in my pockets, I promise.'

I'd love to spend more time laughing with Séan. It's weeks since I've been doubled up with laughter, but for some reason I find myself saying no to his offer.

'Two heartbreaks in as many weeks,' he says. 'You women are killing me!' He pretends to plunge a dagger into his heart and I collapse in fits of giggles.

'Well, if I ever need walking home in Ireland I'll know who to ask for,' I say.

Séan smiles his lovely cheeky smile. 'Oh, I left Ireland behind a couple of years ago. I'm in Year 11 at King William's.'

'What is it?' I say sleepily, looking at my bedside clock. It's only nine but Phil has woken me up on Sunday morning by knocking on my door, which is mega annoying as I was having a totally delicious revenge dream where Rupert is in tears *begging* to go back out with me and I'm telling him to get lost whilst pointing at a queue of lush lads waiting to take me out.

'Electra, can you come downstairs for a moment?'

I groan. There'll be something I've done wrong, some incident The Little Runt will be blaming on me.

Yawning, I get up, slip my trotters into my piggy slippers and stomp downstairs.

Standing in the hall is a granite-faced Doc Burns, whilst next to her FB is shifting from one foot to the other, wringing his hands.

'What's happened?' I ask, looking from one serious-faced Burns to the other. 'What's going on? What are you doing here?'

'We came round to see if you'd heard,' FB says. 'Phil said you haven't.'

'Heard what?' I ask as panic rises within me. 'Is someone going to tell me what's going on? Is it Dad? Is it Mum?'

Doc Burns steps forwards. 'I was working in A&E last night when they brought Yolanda Callender in.' Her face is kind but grave. 'We did everything we could but . . .' Her voice trails away and she shakes her head. 'I'm so sorry.'

'Mum came back and told me what had happened and asked if I knew Sorrel's mum,' FB says. 'I wanted to tell you.'

I'm confused. It's early in the morning and I've just woken up. What's Doc Burns getting at? Yolanda had a slight bang on the bonce and was fine. It was nothing. She was potting up sprouts last night. Sorrel was at the gig until she was called back home . . .

My blood turns to ice and for a moment the world stands still. Then my legs go to jelly and I hear someone scream, 'NO! NO! NO!' and realize the person screaming is me.

FB's beside me, holding me up, then letting me sink on to the bottom step.

'There'll need to be a post-mortem but it looks as if the blow Yolanda had on the head yesterday afternoon caused swelling in the brain. By the time it became apparent, it was too late,' Doc Burns explains.

281

'I've got to see Sorrel,' I gasp, breaking free from FB and getting up. 'I have to see her.'

'Electra.' Phil grabs my arm as I dive towards the front door. 'You're in your pyjamas and Sorrel and her family will still be in shock. Try ringing her first.'

'What's going on?' Mum appears at the top of the stairs. Pregnant, pale and in a billowing white nightie she looks like a ghost. 'Why is Electra screaming?'

'Go back to bed, Ellie,' Phil calls up. 'I'll be up in a moment.'

'I heard my daughter screaming,' Mum says, ignoring Phil and starting to waddle down the stairs. 'I'm pregnant, not stupid. I want to know what's going on.'

We've been so careful to keep Mum calm and her blood pressure low. Not only have I been cooking and cleaning I haven't even argued with The Little Runt, even though I'm desperate to and the moment the baby pops out I will let rip. But how can we keep this devastating news from her?

Doctor Burns steps forward and helps Mum down the last few stairs.

'Ellie, I'm afraid that the accident Yolanda Callender had yesterday was more serious than everyone first thought. She died peacefully in the early hours of the morning. Other than the two youngest, all her family was with her.'

Mum lets out a terrible moan. 'Oh, those poor children!' she wails. 'What are they going to do without her?'

'Mum,' I say, crying. 'Don't cry. You're supposed to be keeping calm, remember?'

'I'll put the kettle on,' Phil says. 'Make us all a cup of tea. Electra, can you help your mum back to bed?'

I try to take Mum's arm but she's pressing her right hand over her eye.

'Are you feeling OK, Ellie?' Doc Burns asks, taking Mum's other arm.

'I'm just dizzy,' Mum mutters. 'I think I might have a migraine coming on. The light's hurting my eyes.'

I notice Phil and Doc Burns exchange glances.

'She's had blood pressure problems?' Doc Burns asks Phil as she feels Mum's pulse.

He nods. 'She's been on bed rest for about five or six weeks. Just an hour up and about a day.'

'How many weeks to go, Ellie?' she asks Mum.

'I dunno,' Mum mumbles, sounding confused. 'Seven, eight . . .'

'I think we might just take you in,' Doc Burns says. She's swung into full medic mode and is talking to Mum as if she's a patient, not a fellow mother. 'Probably just a precaution, but always better to be safe than sorry.'

'I need to lie down,' Mum groans, her eyes screwed

up, her hand shielding her forehead. 'Just let me get into the dark.'

'Should I call an ambulance?' FB asks.

'No, let's get her in the car,' his mum replies. 'On a Sunday morning it'll be quicker than waiting. Phil, if you drive I'll stay in the back with Ellie. I'll ring to let the hospital know we're coming in. Electra, if your mum's got a birth bag packed, can you get it?'

I run upstairs and grab the little blue suitcase from behind the door in the nursery and hurtle back downstairs by which time Mum's already in the car, sitting in the back seat with her head in her hands.

'I'll call you!' Phil shouts as I put the bag in the boot. 'Tell Mrs Skinner, and look after Jack!'

They race down Mortimer Road, turn left at the end on to Talbot Road and disappear from view.

FB puts his arm around me. 'Let's go in,' he says softly. 'Everything will be fine.'

'You don't know that,' I sob as Mrs Skinner hurries down her front steps, no doubt having been watching the drama unfold from behind her net curtains. 'They did all they could and they still couldn't save Yolanda. It's never ever going to be fine for Sorrel and the others.'

Chapter Twenty-two

I rang Sorrel but she didn't answer, so I sent a text saying I'd heard the news and I'd be there for her whenever she needed me. I didn't know what else to do.

I didn't ring or text Luce because I knew if I did, she'd ring me straight back and I wanted to keep the line clear in case Phil phones, plus, to be honest, I'm not sure I can cope with Luce in floods of tears at the mo.

There was no point in ringing Dad or Aunty Vicky or Grandma and Granddad Stafford because there's no news to tell other than Mum's been taken in and I didn't want to worry them.

FB insisted on staying, and spent the morning playing bowling with Jack on the Wii, while Mrs Skinner insisted on talking, telling us about how she was in labour for seventy-two hours when she gave birth to Frank Junior forty-two years ago and how her insides have never recovered. About an hour after Mum left, I went upstairs to get out of the pig PJs, came back down in my jeans and a black sweatshirt, and Mrs S was *still* rabbiting on about peeing her pants when she laughs, which explains why she hardly ever cracks a smile.

At just gone one in the afternoon, the house phone rings on the dresser.

We all look at it. In fact we look at it for so long, FB says, 'Is anyone going to answer it?'

With shaking hands and feeling as if my bowels are going to spill on to the terracotta tiles, I pick it up.

'Hello?' I croak.

'Electra, it's Phil.' I can hear a smile in his voice. 'You've got a baby sister. She's tiny and she'll have to stay in the Special Baby Unit for a few weeks, but she's going to be fine. They both are.'

Phil's waiting for us at the entrance, looking pale and worn out but happier than I've ever seen him.

'Congratulations, mate.' Dad holds out his hand to a surprised-looking Phil. As well as ringing all the rellies to tell them the news, including Maddy to tell her she'd got a new cousin, I'd rung Dad and he'd offered to run us to the hospital on Sunday evening. 'Well done.'

'Thanks,' Phil says, pumping Dad's hand up and down.

'It happened so quickly once they decided Ellie needed a Caesarean. We were so lucky there was literally a doctor in the house or we might have lost both of them. Ellie thinks there was a guardian angel watching over them.'

I instinctively look up at the sky and, even though I'm sad, smile at the thought that Yolanda might have been looking out for Mum and the new arrival.

'Give me a ring if you need anything,' Dad says, hugging me and Jack. 'I'll be there. And when you speak to Sorrel, tell her I'm sorry.'

'I will,' I say. 'And Dad? Thanks for *everything*.'

We exchange a look that says we know our lives are never going to be the same again.

'Now, she's all hooked up to tubes and things, and she's an odd colour, being so early, but don't be alarmed, she's fine.'

'Mum or the baby?' I say as we walk briskly through the corridors.

'The baby,' Phil laughs. 'Your mum's on the ward, resting, but the neonatal unit is on the way. We'll look in there first.'

Jack grabs my hand, and I look down at him and squeeze it. He's used to me avoiding any form of physical contact with him unless it's a fight, but I can tell that, for once, we're united in our fear of how our lives are going to change now baby sis is here. Jack and I have had Mum to ourselves for our entire lives, until now, but unlike Sorrel and her sibs, at least we've still got Mum.

When we get to a long glass window on the right-hand side of the corridor we stop and peer in. The room is full of tubes and machines and people wearing aprons fussing around clear-sided incubators. I can just about make out tiny scraps of life in some of them, but I've no idea which one holds my new sister.

Jack can't see in, so Phil lifts him up. He presses his face against the glass and looks all around the room before turning to us, wide-eyed. 'I didn't know you could choose,' he says, beaming from ear to ear. 'Can we have a boy, please, one who'll support Arsenal?'

Phil puts him down. 'It doesn't quite work like that,' he laughs. 'Come on, let's go in.'

Phil talks to someone on reception outside the unit, signs a form and once we're wrapped in our white plastic aprons and I've turned my moby off, a male nurse leads us through two sets of double doors into the room, which feels warm, smells of disinfectant and is filled with machines gently whirring and humming and occasionally bleeping.

'Here she is,' says the nurse, lowering the incubator. 'Small but beautifully formed.'

Lying peacefully on her tummy on a pink blanket in the glass cot, her nappy-covered butt in the air and a little white hat on her head, is the tiniest baby I've ever seen. She looks like a doll. A minute bright-red doll with tubes taped to her nose and wires circling her little mottled bod.

'These are for you,' the nurse says, handing me and Jack a badge.

'Cool!' Jack gushes. 'Thanks.' He pins the *I'm A Big Brother* badge on his apron. 'That's me!' he says to the baby, and points proudly at his badge.

I slip my badge into my pocket. I'm relieved Mum and the baby are OK, but I still don't feel ready to be a big sister.

'Hello, love.' I turn round and see Mum sitting in a wheelchair as one of the nurses pushes her towards us. 'Gave you all a fright, didn't I?' She looks just like Mum but in a wheelchair and wearing a totally gross nightie.

At the sight of her, I burst into tears and go to hug her at the same time Jack decides to throw himself on her.

Mum winces and gently pushes us both away. 'Sorry, love, still a bit sore from the stitches,' she says, taking my hand. 'So what do you both think?'

'Can she play for Arsenal ladies'?' Jack asks.

Mum and Phil laugh.

'Perhaps when she's older,' Mum says. 'Electra? You OK? What do you think?'

I don't know what to say. I thought that when I saw the baby I'd feel either nothing or rampant jealousy that I'm no longer Mum's only daughter. Instead I looked at this tiny creature and the first thought that popped into my shallow brain was, *You lucky girl. You're never going to have meaty thighs like me.*

'That's probably enough for now,' the nurse says, moving the cot back up. 'Now, any thoughts on names?'

Mum needs some rest and Phil's exhausted, so we've left the hospital to go home. We've only been driving for a few minutes when I realize where we are.

'Phil, can you just pull over for a moment, please?' I say. 'There's something I need to do.'

Phil stops the car, I get out and cross to the other side of the road. Wedged between a building with grey metal shutters and a grotty pub is the bright-yellow-and-green shop front of The Bay Tree Organic Café.

There are lights on inside and as I get closer I can see the Callender family sitting at one of the pine tables. They're not crying, they're smiling and laughing.

Jas looks up, sees me, nudges Sorrel and nods towards the window.

'Hi,' I say as Sorrel meets me at the door with a hug. She's puffy-eyed from crying. 'I'm so sorry.' I start crying too. 'FB told me.'

Sorrel puts her arm around me as from inside comes the

sound of laughter. 'We're remembering The Queen of the Mung Beans,' she smiles. 'The twins aren't yet four, so we're recording stories so that they'll have something to remember Mum by.' She bites her lip and her eyes fill with tears. 'We wanted to do it before the memories fade.'

'We'll all make sure they know how special Yolanda was,' I say. 'She'll always be their mum. They'll never forget her.'

'Thanks,' Sorrel says, wiping her eyes. 'It's not really sunk in yet. It all seems so unreal.'

'You'll let me know what's happening, won't you?' I say. 'With arrangements and stuff.' I can't bring myself to say the word *funeral* out loud. 'Luce will want to come too.'

Sorrel nods. 'Yeah, when we have a date. We'd like a woodland ceremony if poss. I rang Dad this afternoon. He and Daphne said they'd come over, and Joz too.' A brief smile crosses her face when she says his name. 'I'd like you to meet him.'

'I'd like that too,' I say.

Sorrel glances over her shoulder. 'I'd better go,' she says, hugging me again. 'Thanks for coming. By the way, did anything happen with that cute lad you were with last night?'

Last night.

Only twenty-four hours between the nineteenth of April and today, the twentieth, and yet it feels a lifetime ago. In a matter of hours there's been a death and a birth and everything feels different, not better or worse, just different.

I think of Séan and his velvet voice. 'No, but I have a feeling that after his GCSEs it might,' I say. 'Watch this space.'

'I will.' Sorrel smiles, and as I watch her go back inside to her family I realize that I haven't had a chance to tell her about my new baby sister or the decision we've made.

But perhaps now isn't the time.

In the dark I pass through a gate and, accompanied by the glare of security lights coming on, crunch up the gravel drive, past a couple of cars and to the front door of 7 Compton Avenue. When I get there, another light floods the entrance.

I ring the bell.

Archie jumps up and down at the frosted half-glass, barking, before the outline of FB approaches. I can see him picking the dog up before he opens the door.

'Electra.' He looks surprised but pleased to see me. 'Everything OK?'

'Yes, fine.' I smile. 'I've seen Sorrel. They're doing the best they can. Her dad's coming back from Barbados for the funeral.'

'And your mum and the baby?' FB says as Archie

wriggles in his arms. He puts the dog down, shoos it into the hall and closes the front door behind him. 'Have you seen them too?'

'Yes,' I nod. 'They're fine. That's why I wanted to come round. To thank your mum for acting so quickly. Phil says if she hadn't been there it could have been curtains for both of them.'

'Mum's back on shift,' FB says. 'If I hadn't come round to tell you about Yolanda your mum's blood pressure wouldn't have hit the roof. I feel so guilty.'

'Don't,' I reassure him. 'It was probably already high. They said it could have happened at any time, even just getting up too quickly. And I'm glad you were the one to tell me.'

'I'll walk you home,' FB says. 'I'll just go and tell Dad.'

'Thanks, but I'm fine,' I say. 'I could do with a walk and a think.'

'OK.' He kisses me on the cheek. 'See you at school tomorrow?'

'You will,' I say, kissing him back. 'Another term, the last one in Year 10.'

'Oh, by the way,' FB says. 'Any more thoughts on what to call your little sis? Did you come up with any names?'

'I suggested Tequila-Becks but they weren't having it,' I giggle. 'Nor Tia Maria.'

'Spoilsports,' FB laughs.

'Actually, they've decided on Saffron,' I say. 'Yolanda mentioned ages ago that if she'd had another little girl she'd have chosen Saffron, and when I told Mum and Phil they thought it lovely. The nursery's bright yellow too.'

'It's perfect,' FB agrees. 'And a lovely tribute to Yolanda.'

'You liked Fleur,' I say, 'as in Oliver and Fleur.'

'Oh, not that again,' FB groans, pulling a face. 'Don't remind me. I won't be mentioning any baby names to girls ever again, I can tell you. I so wish I'd kept my mouth shut over that one.'

'I'm glad you didn't,' I smile, putting my hand in my pocket and fishing out my Big Sister badge. I pin it on my jacket. 'Because I've chosen her middle name. My little sis is going to be called Saffron Fleur.'

About the Author

Helen Bailey was born and brought up in Ponteland, Newcastle-upon-Tyne. Barely into her teens, Helen invested her pocket money in a copy of *The Writers' and Artists' Yearbook* and spent the next few years sending short stories and poems to anyone she could think of. Much to her surprise, she sometimes found herself in print. After a degree in science, Helen worked in the media and now runs a successful London-based character licensing agency which has worked on internationally renowned properties such as Snoopy, Dirty Dancing, Dilbert and Felicity Wishes. With her dachshund, Boris, and her husband, John, she divides her time between Highgate, north London and the north-east. She is the author of a number of short stories, young novels and picture books.

www.helenbaileybooks.com

Life as I know it is going pear-shaped.

**Dad's having a mid-life crisis.
Mum's given in to her daytime TV addiction.
My little bro (aka The Little Runt) has just been
caught shoplifting. Even the guinea-pig's gone mental.**

**And all I can think about is whether green eyeliner
complements or clashes with blue eyes.**

I can be **very** shallow.

**These are the zits-and-all,
no-holds-barred rants of me,
Electra Brown. Welcome to my crazy world.**

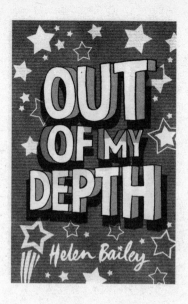

I am *totally* out of my depth.

Everyone's giving me the third degree!
Freak Boy's dad wants to know whether he's being bullied.
Sorrel's interrogating me about Lucy's stroppy moods.

Even Dad is cross-examining me about Mum's
love-life, over garlic bread and pepperoni pizza.

And all I can think is, *How far can you get a piece*
of melted cheese to stretch without it breaking?

I can be **very** shallow.

These are the real-life,
messed-up rants of me,
Electra Brown. Welcome to my crazy world.

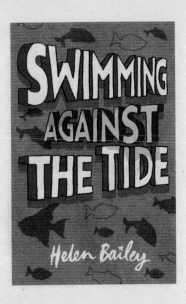

Everyone's got major lurve-action except me.

Lucy's had a holiday fling with a bog-brush-headed Frog.

Sorrel's in lust with a lad who reeks of chip fat.

Even the Wundacousin is dating a model, whereas I'm not even getting any befriend-the-ugly-friend attention!

I hate swimming against the tide. I'd rather go with the flow. I should be planning how to hook a hunk, but all I can think is, *What's for lunch?*

I can be **very** shallow.

These are the up-close-and-sometimes-too-personal rants of me, Electra Brown. Welcome to my crazy world.